Kill
With
Kindness

Kill
With
Kindness

by

DELL SHANNON

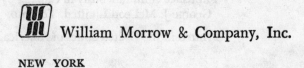

William Morrow & Company, Inc.

NEW YORK

The hypocrite had left his mask, and stood
In naked ugliness. He was a man
Who stole the livery of the court of heaven
To serve the devil in.

—Pollok: *Course of Time*

Kill
With
Kindness

Chapter 1

WHEN he thought about it later, Mendoza realized that it was soon after they'd acquired Mairí MacTaggart that they'd first heard about the Weavers. He never expected to have anything to do with the Weavers himself; and, very likely, if it hadn't been for Sally Mawson and a certain chain of circumstances, he never would have.

Every Thursday and Sunday Mrs. MacTaggart left the house on Rayo Grande Avenue, and in her ancient but sturdy Chevy sedan drove down to a more mundane part of Hollywood to visit her sister, Janet Cox. Mrs. MacTaggart had emigrated from Scotland only five years before, but Mrs. Cox had lived here for forty-five, and for twenty of them in the modest little frame house on Edgemont Avenue below Fountain. It was the kind of block where most of the residents had been settled there for long years: Alison had driven Mairí down on a couple of occasions when the Chevy was in the garage. Old houses, mostly older people. But the Weavers were the oldest, had lived there the longest, in the little house next to the corner across from Mrs. Cox—and everyone admired the Weavers, and did little errands for them when allowed, and wondered how they managed so well.

"Eighty and eighty-one years they are," said Mrs. MacTaggart, "and you do have to admire them indeed. How they manage, on just the state pension. And Mrs. Weaver with the arthritis, she can't get about just so well—but the both of them always so cheerful and a pleasant word for everybody. On the pension, mind you, they've even saved and put money in the bank. And they like to do for themselves—proud, like."

And again, "It does make me feel that ashamed, catch myself complaining about this or that, when I think of old Mr. and Mrs. Weaver. So old and managing so well like they do. No chick nor child nor any folk of their own, and married sixty years this Christmas."

"Wonderful!" said Alison automatically.

"You know, 'tis a thing I never thought about, *achara,* but the old gentleman likes you to call him by his first name— Clyde it is. He says he never began to feel old at all until there was nobody left to call him by name, just mister. And when you stop to think, 'twould be a lonesome thing, that."

Off and on, they heard about the Weavers. How Mr. Weaver had confided to Janet that they had a thousand dollars in their savings account—"Just think, all saved from the pension, such thrifty folk they are—" and the little house had been paid for years back, of course. It was old Mr. Weaver who walked to the market a block away, did their little errands, though the neighbors were good—Mrs. Tuckerby, who had a little dress shop up on Fountain, brought them ice cream in summer, a treat, and Mrs. Oliver next door was always looking in to see if they needed something. Nice old people, good people, proud and liking to feel responsible for themselves.

Mendoza saw a lot of the other kind of people, of all ages; and when Mairí chatted on about the Weavers, it was vaguely reassuring to him to know there were such people still extant, outside the violence, irresponsibility, idiocy and malice that he coped with day by day down at Homicide headquarters, LAPD. And beyond that, old Mr. and Mrs. Weaver, down on a shabby block of Edgemont Avenue, did not enter his ken.

When the chain of circumstances got under way, as it were, he was mainly concerned with the rape-murder of a twelve-year-old girl over on Ducommun, which was keeping them all busy.

Janet Cox had broken her hip in October, Mairí had left them temporarily to look after her, promising faithfully to be back as soon as possible, and Alison had found the little English girl to fill in until then. Homicide had had a busy time through November, and then in the first week of December they got this rape-murder, a really nasty one, and as Hackett said resignedly they were shorthanded with two of the boys in love, and what Homicide was coming to—Higgins, he said, going around in a daze half the time; Higgins hadn't quite assimilated his good fortune in getting Mary Dwyer to marry him. And all Piggott could talk about was this nice girl in the church choir.

As well as the rape-murder, they had the usual unidentified corpses, suicides, and accidental homicides to sort out, when Sally Mawson suddenly and gratuitously thrust an interfering hand into Mendoza's life.

The Mawsons, over in West Los Angeles, had just acquired some new neighbors. "Such nice people," said Sally to Alison. "You'll like her, she's sweet. And they've got twins too—a year older than Johnny and Terry, terribly sweet twins. In fact, their birthday's next week, Alison, and I thought it'd be cute if we had a little party—here—and you can bring your two, and—"

With misgivings, Alison finally agreed. Generally, people you were assured you'd like you detested on sight. But Mrs.

Darling was not detestable, if a rather silly woman, and Johnny and Terry were slightly better behaved than the Darling twins, which was gratifying.

And that was on a Wednesday of the first week in December.

Homicide got the rape-murder the next day, and Mendoza put in some overtime on that. They hadn't got a smell of a lead up to Saturday; and he was not at home that day when Sally called.

Sounding rather subdued, she asked Alison if the twins had had shots for measles.

"Yes, why?" said Alison. "Sally, you don't mean to tell me—"

"Well, I'm terribly afraid," said Sally with a gulp, "the Darling twins have got it. Them. Measles, I mean. The doctor's just been, and Mrs. Darling said—because the incubation period—"

"Heavens!" said Alison crossly. "Of *all* things—the shots don't always take—"

"Well, you should know fairly soon, anyway," said Sally. "I *am* sorry, Alison, but I couldn't *know*—"

Alison admitted it grudgingly. And just as she put down the phone, their English girl, Dorothy Swanson, came to tell her that she thought Johnny was running a little temperature, and Terry seemed awfully fretful.

"Damnation!" said Alison. "They've got it—them. Sally and her new neighbors! Why I ever—"

The pediatrician, Dr. Morgan, was of the old-fashioned breed, and promised to come when he could. "It might be this evening," said the nurse. "He's awfully busy, but he'll be there. Of course they have had immunization shots, Mrs. Mendoza, and that should make it a much lighter case. But the doctor will want to see them, naturally."

It was evening when he came; and Alison had been sounding off about the whole thing to an abstracted Mendoza who was brooding over a couple of reports on the rape-murder. He nodded at the doctor when he came, and was still studying the reports when Alison and the doctor came down the hall again.

"Measles all right," said Morgan cheerfully. Alison was looking resigned.

Mendoza said absently, "Too bad. But I understand, with the shots, it shouldn't be—"

"No," said the doctor. "Have *you* ever had 'em, Lieutenant?" He grinned. "Your wife says she did, when she was eight or nine, and your nursemaid's had 'em too. You?"

"Never," said Mendoza inattentively but rather proudly. Not that he boasted about it, but he never remembered being ill a day in his life.

"Aha," said the doctor. "So you'd better have an immunization shot. And let's hope you haven't already got the bug. Measles can be rough on an adult. Take off your jacket."

"*¡Disparate!* I never pick up bugs. Never mind, I'll be quite—"

"Luis, I really think," said Alison, "if you haven't—it can be pretty serious for an adult, and—"

"I refuse to think about—"

"Take off your jacket," said Dr. Morgan firmly. "Must preserve our noble law-enforcement officers." He advanced with a swab of cotton and a hypodermic. Mendoza swore and began to take off his jacket.

"I only hope," said the doctor, "it's in time, that's all."

Mairí came visiting on Sunday afternoon. She'd soon be coming back for good; Janet was getting on nicely, a marvel how they could put that steel pin in and the hip near as good as new. And they heard a little about the Weavers too, though Mairí spent most of her visit hovering over the twins, miserably in bed and sprouting spots already.

13

Old Mr. Weaver had had a stroke last month, poor man, and was partly paralyzed, but he just wouldn't hear of the General Hospital and it was Mrs. Oliver had thought of the County Health, and found a practical nurse to come in. "What with Mrs. Weaver's arthritis and all, she couldn't look to him, and the nurse seems to be a good soul, cheerful and all. A motherly sort of body, a Mrs. O'Rourke, and she says she's got a son, a minister, though what business anybody with a name like O'Rourke has got with a son a Protestant minister is beyond me, it is and all— But, *achara,* you're sure this English girl has wit enough to take care of them, and the measles and all? I wouldn't just like—"

They got a new one on Monday morning. It was the manager of the building who called in: an old building over on First Street below the freeway. The kind of building where the manager called on tenants personally to collect the rent: that kind of tenants. And he'd found this particular tenant dead.

Dead behind a door whose grimy glass top bore the legend in chipped black paint, *Dr. William Hodges, M.D.* Dr. William Hodges was slumped quietly in the chair behind his scarred old desk, an elderly man with jowls and a big red-veined nose, and as the Homicide officers looked at him they could all guess that it had been a natural death: coronary, probably. He looked at least seventy-five.

The manager said nervously, "As a matter of fact, saves me the trouble of tellin' him to get out. Unnerstand, I don't *know* anything, but I heard things around—an' maybe when you have a look in here, you'll find this 'n' that to show—you know, he was kind of on the crooked side—"

Hackett glanced at Mendoza; Landers' boyish face wore a slight smile. Experience translated that for all of them. Dr. William Hodges, who had probably lost the right to the

M.D. long ago, had been in the market for the illegal jobs: the abortions, possibly the prescriptions for dope of this and that sort; and the manager had known all about it, but he didn't want the police to know that, naturally.

Mendoza was annoyed at the manager and at Dr. William Hodges. He had got up with a headache that morning, which was unheard of for Mendoza; and the weather was nice and cool, overcast and gray, but this office was stuffy and uncomfortably hot, and he felt sweat on his forehead. "Did he have a nurse?"

"I wouldn't know," said the manager. "I just walked in and found him. And called you guys. An' if that's all I can—" he backed away. The interns arrived and said it looked like a coronary, yesterday or the day before maybe.

Mendoza lit a cigarette. The headache was getting worse. He watched Hackett and Landers rummage through the office. They found, among other things, a medical license from the state of Pennsylvania dated 1915. "So we ask, and find out he got struck off the register thirty years back," said Hackett, yawning and running a hand through his sandy hair. Landers had found a set of ledgers. "I wonder if he had a supply of dope here."

Mendoza couldn't have cared less. He was still worrying at the rape. A twelve-year-old—a rather messy murder, it had been, and one like that running loose— He wiped his forehead; it was like an oven in here, though Art and Tom didn't seem to feel it.

The interns took the body, and they weren't going to get any more out of the manager. See what the autopsy report gave them; but ten to one it was a natural death and just the paperwork to be done on it.

Mendoza went back to the office, leaving the mandatory search of the scene to Hackett and Landers. There had been an overnight report of an attempted assault on a teen-ager coming home from the movies, and Higgins had gone out on that; Mendoza wanted to hear about it. If it was the same one who'd killed the Moreno girl—

"It could be, I suppose," said Higgins doubtfully. "But also it could not be, Luis. She got away from him without much trouble, it seems, and by the looks of the Moreno girl he's big and strong and fast. I don't think— You feel all right?"

"I'm perfectly all right," said Mendoza irritably. It wasn't all that cool that they had to have the thermostat set so high; he was sweating again. "Listen, George—"

"You just don't look so hot," said Higgins.

Piggott wandered in and said they had a new corpse. "No big deal, I would guess. A bum by his clothes—in an alley over on Beverly. Nothing on him but four cents and half a bottle of cheap *vino*. So now we spend some time trying to find out who he was—talk about thankless jobs."

"Lieutenant," said Sergeant Lake, looking in, "a new one. The squad car just called in. Looks like a suicide, they said. Apartment over on Fourth."

"*¡Caray!*" said Mendoza. "So you go and look at it, Matt. All I'm saying, George—*George!*"

"Hmm?" said Higgins, his eyes focusing slowly.

"I swear to God," said Mendoza, exasperated, "ever since you married the girl your concentration's gone all to hell!" Higgins blushed, which was sufficiently unusual for big tough cop Higgins that Mendoza grinned unwillingly.

"By the way the girl describes him," said Higgins hurriedly, "I don't think he's the boy we want for Moreno, Luis. She got away too easy. We know the Moreno girl fought that one hard, but couldn't get away. I think— Look, are you sure you're O.K.?"

Mendoza said unwillingly that he had a little headache, was all.

16

They tossed it back and forth a little; Mendoza came to agree that the attempt on the teen-ager probably didn't connect to the murder of Rita Moreno. Higgins went out to talk to some more of Rita's friends, people around where it had happened down on Teed Street. Palliser was on that, too. Mendoza gave in about eleven o'clock and asked Lake to have First Aid send up some aspirins.

And he was a reasonably intelligent man, Mendoza, not one of those stupid would-be toughs who refused to admit the aches and pains; but the fact was that he'd honestly never had any before and the thing came as a surprise to him. The aspirins didn't seem to do much for the headache, and he kept on sweating. He read the autopsy report on the next-but-latest unidentified corpse—acute alcoholism, and no loss, but if there were any relatives the city would like to locate them to pay burial costs—and when Jason Grace and Palliser looked in at twelve-thirty he was rereading the reports on Rita Moreno.

"You feel like some lunch?" asked Palliser. "I think I might have turned up a lead on Moreno. One of the nuns at the school—you know, the one we couldn't talk to because she was in the hospital—I finally got in to see her and she—"

"*Bueno,*" said Mendoza. He stood up, and had to clutch at the desk for support as dizziness struck him. And what the hell was wrong— He reached unsteadily for his hat. "Let's go—you can tell me on the way."

"You feeling all right?" asked Grace.

"I'm perfectly— So what's the lead, John?"

"You don't look just so hot," said Palliser. "A lot of flu going around. Maybe—"

Possibly it was the flu, thought Mendoza. He'd never had it; he never picked up bugs. But possibly—because now he was standing up his head felt big as a balloon, and he was sweating steadily.

17

Ignore it, he thought firmly, and it would go away. He never—

They took Palliser's car up to Federico's on North Broadway; Mendoza listened to Palliser's concise report on what the ailing nun had told him, but Palliser's voice seemed to come and go in waves, and the sense of it didn't penetrate his mind somehow—"A man who'd followed her, she told the sister, see—a big man, and she'd been scared. Of course as far as any description, well, it's worth damn all, but it could be that—"

"Yes," said Mendoza. "I see." He'd be reading the written report later.

Federico's had a liquor license (maybe a drink would pick him up a little—damn it, he couldn't have the flu, he never picked up things like that) and consequently it was dark, with the kind of lighting called discreet. (Alison said it was a holdover from the speakeasies in Prohibition, and she could be right.) He stumbled on the step down to the dining room, and Palliser caught his arm. "There's Art and Tom. I heard we got handed a new one, anything to work?"

Mendoza opened his mouth to say he didn't think so—Dr. William Hodges, said his mind vaguely, probably the coronary—and somebody had turned a thermostat too damn high in here, too—when suddenly the discreet lights went out and he felt himself falling. Damn thick carpets. *Earthquake,* said his mind belatedly. A big one overdue. Safest place in a doorway—

There was a hiatus, and he was aware of hands busy about him, pulling his collar loose.

"He's burning up with fever," said Grace, sounding businesslike.

"An ambulance—my God, the Lieutenant—what's wrong?" Adam, one of the waiters.

"For God's sake, Luis—he didn't look just so good, but I never thought—"

"—Said he had a headache—"

"Better call Alison. She'll know the doctor to—"

"He hasn't got a doctor, damn it, he's never sick—"

"Well, he is now," said Grace. "Didn't he say something about the twins having measles? I'll just bet you—"

"*Measles*, for God's sake!" said Hackett distractedly. "He couldn't have the—"

"Said the doctor gave him a shot. But it might not have been in time, you know," said Grace. "And that can be mighty serious for an adult. It—"

Measles. *Dios me libre*, thought Mendoza muzzily, I'll never hear the last of it. I'll never— He passed out again.

There was a longer hiatus, when he was vaguely aware of people around him, starched white nurses, people doing things to him, a bed in a strange room. Alison's face bending over him, concerned and serious.

Rita Moreno. Had Palliser really got a lead? One like that—

The poor old slob of a crooked doctor, dying alone in the shabby office. The—

Dying. He was on his deathbed, he'd never felt anything like this before—never hear the *last* of it, the measles, for God's sake, him, Mendoza— He felt very sorry for himself; dying at only forty-four, a damn shame—not fair— And so much unfinished business— A kind of vast outrage rose in him, in what was left of his consciousness; the whole thing so damn silly—*measles*— And he could just hear the boys laughing—

Unfinished business—at the office, the largest part of his life, maybe, the job—the thankless job—he couldn't just give up—

19

He could just *hear* the entire LAPD laughing at Luis Mendoza—for the love of God, the *measles*—

But he didn't, somewhat to his own surprise, die after all; he came back, to an antiseptic hospital room and a nurse with a face to stop a clock, who called him *we*. He was weak as water, and he said faintly to Alison's serious face bending over him, "*All* your fault. You and the twins."

"If you want to know, they're fine. The shots. A very light case. And you're going to be all right, too," said Alison. "*Damn* Sally Mawson."

"I can just hear what—the boys—"

"Oh, Luis, everybody's been so worried, honestly. You were terribly sick for a couple of days there. The office calling practically on the hour every hour, and all the cards, and Art or George or somebody coming every day to see—"

"Most ridiculous thing I ever heard of," said Mendoza.

"And all my fault," said Alison, smiling. "Me and the twins. Hostages to fortune. Blame Sally. You're going to be all right, *amante*. Home tomorrow, and I'll look after you."

Mendoza tried to pull himself up. "And what's *happening*—that Moreno thing—how long have I been—and John said it wasn't really a lead—"

"Mmm," said Alison. "Richard's himself again. Lie down and rest."

He came home ten days before Christmas. Alison told him he could buy presents for her when the doctor let him go out, and it didn't matter.

Mendoza was still feeling somehow outraged. Such things as illness happened to other people, not him. And the *measles*—

The twins were as lively and noisy as if they'd never had

the measles. Well, the twins were two and he was— But all the same—

Never hear the last of it. But Hackett came, and Angel, and the other boys, and (he felt) were careful not to laugh. And he began finding it less and less of an effort to move around; he sat up longer, and got back to shaving once a day, with the damned spots cleared up, and went to the dining room for meals.

He was, by the first week of January, entirely himself again, and wild to get back to the office. They hadn't got another damned thing on the Moreno killer—it would end up in Pending, which annoyed him. God knew what else they were coping with down there by now—they wouldn't tell him *anything,* doctor's orders, they said, by God—

He raged at the doctor. He was impatient to put this shameful and silly interlude behind him, and get back to work. He snapped at Alison, barked at Mairí, now back permanently with her beloved twins, and was rude to the doctor.

"A month," said the doctor firmly. "You don't realize how this has pulled you down. I understand you haven't had a proper vacation in years. You take a month off now, and get thoroughly rested. I mean it. You're not to go back for a month."

"I'm all *right!* God damn it, I feel— I'm perfectly able to—"

"The rest will do you good. Yes, yes, you can drive, go out—but take it easy. Stay off the freeways, don't try to do too much. When you feel tired, lie down and take a nap. You're not a young man, and—"

Mendoza snarled that he wasn't senile. "A month," said the doctor.

It was an eternity of boredom. He was, this last week, tired

21

of reading; they hadn't let him use his eyes until last week, but a week's solid dependence on books, even Kipling, brought him to boredom with the printed page. He felt all right again. He *was* all right. Up and dressed and feeling his old self—

And the doctor had said to Alison, damn it, "Don't you let him get involved with his office, even on the phone. Just stir him up." Practically guarding the damn telephone from him, growled Mendoza. And what was going on down there—

And so that afternoon, out of his vast boredom, he was eager to listen to Mairí when she came to him, sitting there with an unopened book in his lap, and presented him with a little problem.

A little problem was just what Mendoza needed at that moment, to get his brain sharpened up and get back to work.

"Nor I wouldn't want to bother you with it, but it's only, you're a detective, and might maybe see through to what's behind it. A very queer thing it does seem to all of us indeed, for when you come down to it, old Mrs. Weaver's got nothing, you know. And the first queer thing is why in the name of goodness that nurse should—"

Chapter 2

IT was a sufficiently peculiar little tale. He listened to it, distastefully sipping the malted milk she had brought him. He had dropped about ten pounds and every time he drew a breath, it seemed, Alison or Mairí were pushing malted milks and nourishing soups at him. As usual he had a cat on his lap—Bast; the cats at least had been pleased about the measles, having someone home all day to provide a lap when required.

A very funny little tale; and what could it add up to?

Old Mr. Weaver had had his stroke in November. They wouldn't go in for this Medicare, said Mairí, they wanted to be responsible to themselves as long as they could; and the old man just couldn't abide the thought of hospital. "I'd rather die at home," he'd always said. And when he had the stroke, Mrs. Weaver put her foot down, too. The doctor— Mairí pursed her lips— "By what Mrs. Oliver says, I doubt he's that much interested in old folk—" had been angry, but they got one of these visiting nurses for a few days, the county service. But those were regular trained nurses, an awful price they got. It was Mrs. Oliver started looking for a practical nurse, and thought of this other county service that gave you names of such. That was how they found Mrs. O'Rourke. And at first she'd seemed just fine. Taken good care of the old man, and Mrs. Weaver too: cooking and all.

"Only we did wonder how long the Weavers could afford her, you know, for even the practical nurses get *such* wages— and wasn't it the reason I went to look after Janet myself? The only one she could find asking a hundred and twenty-five dollars a week! And the Weavers thrifty and all, but just the pension—a hundred and nine dollars a month each."

Old Mr. Weaver had died on the first of December. Nobody had really thought he would get over it, live long. "Which is the thing I'd impress on you," said Mairí earnestly. "Mrs. Weaver, she'd kept all her faculties as they say—a cheerful old soul, bright as a new penny. Sharp, even. Some there are like that—sharp as you please up to the day they die. And often enough, the three years I lived there with Janet, I've heard the two old folk talkin' of when one would be left alone. They knew 'twould come. Mrs. Weaver always hoping 'twould be her go first, seeing as he was still able to get about without help—left alone, she'd have to go in one of these rest homes. Where they take the old folk for the pension." Mendoza nodded and set the glass down.

"And ye'll finish that and not be leaving it," said Mairí severely. But after the funeral—and the old lady didn't attend it, which everyone thought was very funny because they'd been regular churchgoers and conventional sort of people—Mrs. O'Rourke said the old lady was too broken up to go—after that, the practical nurse stayed on. She'd been there four weeks already, and even if the thrifty Weavers had had a thousand dollars in the bank, at what even practical nurses cost now, it must be dwindling. And there had been the funeral expenses, too. But then, Mrs. Oliver—the week after the funeral that was—quite by chance found out from Mrs. Weaver that the practical nurse only charged twenty-five dollars a week.

"¿Que?" said Mendoza. "But—"

"It's queer indeed," said Mairí. "Naturally, Mrs. Oliver hadn't made the arrangements at first. The old lady did that. Twenty-five dollars the week. And there's only Mrs. Weaver's pension now, for to pay Mrs. O'Rourke and buy the groceries and all. And groceries they'll need to feed the nurse alone—a great fat elephant of a woman. Her and her minister son." She sniffed.

"That's very funny," said Mendoza. "Twenty-five—what's she getting out of it?"

"Which is what we'd all like to know. Nobody can make it out. A hundred and nine dollars a month. There's no making sense of it. But there's another thing. Old Mrs. Weaver. Now, the neighbors there, they'd known the old folks years, they're sorry for the old lady, they'll be coming by to see her a few minutes, maybe with a little bite of cake, some treat. And now there's something else not right." Mairí's round rosy face under the silver curls looked distressed and puzzled. "This Mrs. O'Rourke always making excuses—the old lady's napping, or something—and the few times somebody's been let in, well, she's not herself at all—Mrs. Weaver. Why, she didn't know Mrs. Oliver at all, last week—acted all wandery and senile like."

"Well, you said she was—"

"Eighty. I did. But there are folk and folk," said Mairí, "and if you're the sort as stays bright and sharp however many years on you, you don't change all of a sudden. Not in a week's time, which is how it came, piecing together what Mrs. Oliver and Mrs. Tuckerby and Mrs. Fogarty says. And that great fat cow saying 'twas the shock of the old man dying turned her senile all of a sudden! She knew he was going. She was sorrowful, but she was sensible. A sharp sensible old body. And I'll tell you another thing. Mrs. Oliver's done some nursing herself—had her mother bedridden for ten years—and she says the old lady's being fed dope of some kind. To make her seem—"

"Why?" said Mendoza. "Why should the nurse—"

"And why is what we'd all like to know. Old Mrs. Weaver—what in the name o' goodness could this woman get from her? She's got nothing—only the pension. And I'll admit it, by what they all say, the O'Rourke female's an able nurse—she could be out earning five times as much. It's all very funny," said Mairí.

It was a funny little story all right. No shape to it: there wasn't any imaginable motive for the practical nurse's machinations—if such they were. If she was on the make, what was there for her to get? A frail old woman on the state pension— "No secret treasure in the Weaver house?" he said. "No cache of gold or diamonds under the bed?"

Mairí said, "Tosh! The old man was a clerk in a men's store years ago, and when he retired he used to do little gardening jobs he could pick up. The furniture in the place, it's just cheap sticks. I'd say the most expensive bit there is a little portable television they saved for a couple of years back."

"*Extraño,*" murmured Mendoza. The queer little tale fastened on his mind: Why? Why was the nurse still there? At such a preposterous wage? Drugs? But why?

"There's no sense to it. But if she's harming the old lady some way—Can you see any reason in it at all?"

"No rhyme or reason," said Mendoza. "You're sure about the twenty-five bucks a week?" She nodded. "Then all I can think is that Mrs. O'Rourke is the greatest altruist in Southern California. Labor of love."

Mairí said, "Tosh," again. "It's a puzzle. And there's

none of us likes it. If she's giving the old lady dope of some kind to keep her witless—"

"But why, for God's sake? If there was money—jewelry, securities, and she was coaxing it out of her—but the state pension!"

"I know. I said 'twas queer. I shouldn't have come bothering you with it. Are ye feeling tired—would you like to rest a bit abed—"

"I'm perfectly all right," said Mendoza. She shook her head and went away with the empty glass. And of course she left the peculiar little puzzle teasing at his brain.

Why? So they had a thousand dollars saved from the pension—the thrifty old people. There'd have been a doctor bill; and the trained nurse the first several days, at thirty bucks a day. And the funeral expenses, however low they'd been kept. Mrs. Weaver was lucky if there was four or five hundred of that left: there was probably less. And now only one pension coming in. And it was probably a fulltime job, looking after the old lady with arthritis. Even if the nurse expected somehow to get hold of the four or five hundred dollars, what kind of loot was that for a couple of months' hard work?

Twenty-five dollars a week— The eighty-year-old Mrs. Weaver, said to be sharp, might have been surprised at that; or she might not have realized what wages practical nurses could ask now. At any rate, she'd have been pleased to get Mrs. O'Rourke, in their extremity. Twenty-five— Mendoza shook his head, lighting a cigarette. He shoved Bast gently off his lap and got up to wander around the big living room. It was more than funny. Practical nurses were difficult to find these days, and when you did find one (he remembered Palliser saying something when his mother had been ill) they asked nearly as much as trained nurses. There was something very fishy about the twenty-five-buck-a-week Mrs. O'Rourke.

He stared out the front window to the expanse of lawn. A little mystery to unravel. Only, how would you start?

Mystery a homicide cop didn't often run into. The straightforward violence. Mendoza sighed. He was a fool to feel homesick for the Homicide office down there, all the violence and blood and idiocy and malice. . . . Hackett calling, saying, "I've got orders not even to mention any cases to you. You're supposed to be on vacation. How you feeling?"

He wondered very much if they'd got the X who had murdered the little Moreno girl. And what other cases they were working now—what new cases, of those always and forever turning up.

He put out the cigarette and presently lit another one. . . . Now just why in hell would any female who could add two and two take a job of hard work for a fifth of the wage she could rightfully ask? And why in hell would such a woman— Drugs? It made no sense at all. A poor old lady on the state pension. And with nothing else. What could—

"¡Que demonio!" he said to himself. "Por supuesto que no!" But it was a fact, and just why—

The Facel-Vega came slowly up the drive. Alison home from the market. She probably had some new brand of vitamin-rich soup to shove at him, Mendoza thought gloomily. He was perfectly all right and ought to be back at work now—

He wondered what the boys were doing down there.

The nurse— Just why in the name of seven devils—

The newest one they'd got, that morning, promised to be a little offbeat. The call came in, from the Southern Pacific railroad yards, at three minutes to eight that Tuesday morning, and Hackett and Palliser went out on it. It was Higgins' day off, and nobody else had come in yet but Lake.

What they found was offbeat all right, the interns standing around waiting for them to see it, the squad-car men standing by looking stolid, a little crowd of railroad employees all looking horrified, and—shades of the silent movies—a mutilated body which had been tied to the tracks with heavy rope. The freight coming through—one freight or another—hadn't done the body any good, but had neatly decapitated him: the head was sitting tidily two feet away from the body outside the tracks.

"Ever *see* such a thing?" said the bigger intern. "Very funny. We thought we'd let you have the job of going through his pockets."

"Thanks so much," said Hackett. And that was a job he didn't relish. Palliser started to ask questions of the railroad people.

What emerged was a little funny. His wallet was in his hip pocket, under the body, and had escaped nearly intact. He had been one Alfredo Montez, and there was ample I.D. as well as the little card filled out in the first plastic slot. Union membership card: Market Workers. Social Security. Driver's license, a five-year license which said he had a good record. Credit cards, The Broadway, Sears Roebuck, a Shell gasoline card. A few snapshots—a pretty dark girl in several poses, and Alfredo himself, and an older couple. Under the "Notify in Case of Emergency" line on the I.D. card was filled in, "Mrs. Alfredo Montez, 110 Terrace Court, L.A."

"Well, well," said Hackett. "He seems to have been the respectable citizen, John. Funny for the honest citizen to get taken off in *such* a way. By all the blood, he was alive when the train hit him."

"But I don't think he'd struggled against the rope, do you? Knocked out?"

"Bainbridge can probably say."

"Mmm. One thing that seems obvious," said Palliser thoughtfully. "Whoever did it must have known there'd be a train along this track during the night. Because he'd have been seen there in daylight—and—"

"Um," said Hackett. He raised his head and looked around. The Southern Pacific yards was a wilderness of railroad tracks, doubtless all numbered and known to the men who worked there, the engineers and dispatchers and so on, but just a maze of tracks to anybody else. And it was a busy railroad yard, serving a big city. "Chance—" The track the corpse was on was off to the side of the yards, near the high-wire fence enclosing the whole maze and the big roundhouse.

"I suppose we can't say definitely. But, Art, pending whatever time the autopsy gives us, he must have been tied there after dark. And another thing—the gates in that fence are kept locked, and they've got men patrolling to keep out the bums, you know. There were only two trains along here last night, between six last night and six this morning. By what I get from the dispatcher." The dispatcher, a thin gray man in neat tan workclothes, was staring at Alfredo Montez' head as if mesmerized, swallowing nervously. "One at ten-seventeen, one at two-thirty. How did anybody get Montez in—either walking, or unconscious—and all the way up here? I say it's almost got to be somebody who knows the routine of the yards, and where the watchmen would be, and so on."

"It still could've been just a lucky chance. Unlucky for Montez. What a— But I suppose it is also likelier that it was somebody like that."

"Nobody here claims to recognize him." They were standing apart from the little crowd: the dispatcher, the railroad-dick who'd found the body, assorted workmen white and black.

"Not surprising," said Hackett. "You can take him," he added to the interns, who unfolded a rubber sheet. "So now we go break the news to his wife—and why didn't she miss him last night, by the way?—and ask who didn't like him. And don't tell me it must have been a nut of some kind, to do it *such* a way—the things we run into these days, with all the dope floating around, I'm surprised at nothing."

But it was an offbeat one.

And Hackett had maligned Matthew Piggott when he said Piggott was always talking about that girl. Piggot didn't talk about her much, but he thought about her a good deal. He'd only joined the church choir a few months ago, and rather enjoyed it. Prudence Russell was one of the sopranos: a nice girl, kind of a shy girl—which was all right. Some time soon he'd get round to asking her for a date: she'd know he was all right, too, member of the church and all.

He was thinking of her as he came into the office with Landers at five o'clock, and ran into Jason Grace asking Sergeant Lake how the Lieutenant was. Shame about the Lieutenant, thought Piggott. Made a grown man feel sort of foolish, coming down with the measles; but an adult could be pretty sick with it, as the Lieutenant had been. And he thought about Prudence because she had red hair like the Lieutenant's wife—not as red as all that, though, just a nice reddish-brown.

"He's wild to get back," said Lake, "by what Art says. The doctor wants him to take a little rest, but he's rarin' to go. That's our Luis."

Grace grinned. "Thinks we can't get along without him. Well, at that I could use a hunch on this damn Moreno thing. It'll wind up in Pending eventually."

"Unless X goes and does it again," said Landers.

31

"You do have the nicest ideas," said Grace. "It's been a month. No smell."

"So the full moon sets him off."

"That could be a profound remark," said Grace thoughtfully. "Old wives' tale. Only ask anybody who's had experience of the nuts. It can. It does. And why else do we call 'em lunatics?"

"Did you hear about the one in the S.P. yards?" asked Lake. "What a thing. I can hear what the Lieutenant'd say —and I guess Art and John could use some hunches on that one."

Grace hadn't heard about it. While Lake told him, Piggott went into the big communal sergeants' office and found Henry Glasser there typing up a report. "What is it?" asked Glasser.

"Accident. Simple. Two D.O.A.'s."

Hackett and Palliser came in at five-thirty, looking annoyed, and kicked the offbeat one around with a sympathetic Grace, who had been typing a report on this morning's suicide.

"Just nothing," said Hackett, grinding out his cigarette. He was leaning back in Mendoza's desk chair, and it creaked protestingly. "Respectable, upright citizen, Alfredo Montez. Manager of a chain supermart over on Glendale Avenue. We found a couple of cousins—also upright citizens. Very shocked and surprised. Alfredo had no enemies. He—"

"You said, a wife?"

"So cynical," said Palliser. "Her we haven't seen yet. She's visiting her mother in Fresno. Supposed to be back tomorrow. But if you're jumping to the conclusion that any female tied Alfredo to the railroad tracks—"

"I'm not supposing anything," said Grace. "But it's the

first thing to think of, a husband or wife gets taken off—"

"Oh, granted," said Palliser.

"Nobody missed him because he was off duty at the market last night," said Hackett. "Left at the usual time, six o'clock, and nobody knew where he was going. Except home. The apartment tells us nothing—ordinary apartment, ordinary furniture, no liquor around, everything all neat and clean. I'd like to know what Luis'd say about it. The offbeat ones he's pretty hot on, sometimes."

They all felt, but didn't say out loud, that the office felt oddly empty without Mendoza in it.

Palliser said through a yawn, "I'm going home. Nothing more to do on it until we can talk to the wife."

"Still the eager bridegroom," said Hackett. It was five-forty-five.

"Sergeant. New one," said Lake at the door. "Out on Beverly. You want to take it or leave it for the night crew?"

"Oh, hell," said Hackett. Bob Schenke was just getting over the flu and shouldn't have come back so soon; and on an average night on Central L.A.'s beat, no telling what he and Galeano would be hauled out on. "You mind, Jase? We'll let the bridegroom go home. Go take a preliminary look anyway. Whatever." Grace said amiably he didn't mind. "What is it, Jimmy?" Hackett hoisted his bulk out of the chair.

Lake said dryly, "You ought to take Matt. Place called the Temple of the Holy Inner Light. Out on Beverly Boulevard the other side of the freeway. Man dead, is all the squad-car boy said."

"My Lord," said Grace mildly, taking up his hat. "We do see life."

"And death," said Hackett rather heavily. He wouldn't soon forget the sight of respectable-citizen Alfredo Montez

33

lying mutilated there on the tracks with his head tidily set off to one side. A rather handsome young man, Montez, a neat little moustache like Mendoza's. "We might as well take my car."

And Hackett was not given to having hunches—not at all—but he had a kind of feeling about the Temple of the Holy Inner Light, when they got there. Another offbeat one. Once in awhile you got them, and when you got one, you were apt to get two. Just once in awhile.

The Temple had started life as a church, all right; it was an orthodox-looking church building, if very small, with a little steeple. Maybe some small sect had folded, or couldn't pay off the mortgage. It was a white-painted frame building, with double doors. The uniformed man there said, "Straight through, sir, there's a door behind the pulpit." Hackett and Grace went straight through, past rows of decorous pews also looking orthodox; but on the wall behind the pulpit was a violently surrealistic concept of what was probably intended for the Biblical burning bush, and in scarlet Gothic letters above that the text in three-foot-high letters, THOU GOD SEEST ME.

Behind the pulpit was a door, with another uniformed man beside it. Hackett and Grace went through to a smallish office where a third man in uniform stood looking at a corpse and another man slumped in a straight chair.

"—And really what I should *do* about the evening service —people will be *coming*—I really don't know what to— Who are you?"

Hackett introduced himself and Grace. The uniformed man said, "Yes, sir. I'm Froman, sir. This is Mr. Rodney Terhune, who called in. Seems that's the other—er—minister here, a Mr. David Barron."

Mr. David Barron, if that was his real name—it sounded rather too good to be true—was the corpse. He sprawled over most of the floor surface in the small room. The autopsy surgeon would give them details, but it looked as if he'd taken quite a beating. No likely weapon around, at first glance. He had been, at a casual look, about thirty-five, blond, and possibly before the beating not bad looking. He had on a gray suit, a once-white shirt and dark tie.

"S-some burglar," stammered the other man. "The c-collection from Sunday was still here, I think—really too terrible, poor David—I came to p-prepare for the evening service, and—I couldn't take it *in*—David! And I—"

Hackett and Grace looked at that one. Mr. Rodney Terhune was also a young man, possibly thirty, a plump and very well-dressed young man, very natty in a blue-gray dacron suit and a rather gay tie; he had little dimpled hands clutching each other, and a small damp mouth, and very honest blue eyes which engaged Hackett's limpidly, candidly. "Such a dreadful thing," he said. "Some burglar breaking into the *church*—and finding David here— Such a fine dedicated man, David, and my dearest friend—" Rodney Terhune put his hands to his face. There was a fake diamond set in gold on his left little finger.

And neither Hackett nor Grace wondered what the Lieutenant would have thought about Rodney Terhune. Like Mendoza, they had been cops awhile and had some experience with people.

They'd be asking Rodney Terhune quite a few questions.

The maddening little question kept teasing at Mendoza's mind.

Why?

It made no sense at all. The twenty-five-buck-a-week nurse. The practical nurse.

Why?

Something for nothing. Oh, yes? There was nothing there. Human people ordinarily didn't operate that way. Nothing for something. Why? There must be some answer. Some kind of answer.

But what?

The old lady with nothing, nothing but the state pension—

And real altruism was an item in very short supply. The nurse—the practical nurse—

There had to be some logical answer.

A teaser, Mairí's little puzzle.

He'd like to know the answer.

Chapter 3

"WHEN she first came," said Mrs. Oleta Oliver, "we all thought she was nice. And everybody who knew them was so relieved—knew the Weavers, I mean. You can see. The pair of them so helpless."

Mendoza nodded. He smoothed his moustache absently; he wasn't satisfied with the moustache; it felt untidy. During the weeks he hadn't been able to shave, the moustache had got out of hand and he was still trying to coax it into its former elegance. . . . He had found Mrs. Oliver having morning coffee and a gossip with Janet Cox, and when he introduced himself they had welcomed him with glad cries. Mairí's smart detective, who could doubtless explain the puzzle to them instantly.

"And another thing," said Mrs. Cox. She reminded him of Mairí; her curls were white instead of silver, and her face was thinner, but she had the same calm gray eyes. "At first she was all over you, dearie and sweetie and like that, but soon enough she saw Mrs. Weaver didn't care for such, and stopped it."

"Of course if I'd *known* the ridiculous price she asked,

I'd have known there was something funny," said Mrs. Oliver. "But there's nothing to get *at,* really, is there?" She was a plain middle-aged woman, but her eyes were intelligent on him. "The dope—"

"I'd like to hear about that," said Mendoza. "Even trained nurses can't write prescriptions. What do you think she's giving the old lady—if anything?"

They looked slightly indignant; so the detective thought they were making it up? "Something," said Mrs. Cox. "Something it is, all right. You tell him what you saw, Oleta."

"Well, I know she's giving her something for a fact. I'll tell you how it was, Mr. Mendoza—excuse me, Lieutenant. If you'll follow me. Now it isn't just natural that the old lady should be bright as could be one day, and going senile the next, you'll be bound to agree. And she always *was* bright, the little sly jokes, and sensible as anybody, eighty or no. It was a grief to her when the old man died, but it wasn't a *shock,* if you see what I mean. All right. Now, there isn't anything wrong with *her* but the arthritis, her heart sound and all, and she hadn't been doctoring with Dr. Gordon—just went by what old Dr. McCart had told her, took aspirin. And tried to walk about as she could, exercise and keep the stiffness off." She looked at Mendoza to see if he was following her, and he nodded again. "That's all she took, see, the aspirin. And so after the funeral when some of us dropped by, was the first time we saw her—not herself. All vague and not knowing people. Just as if she was *doped.* We thought that afterward. And the O'Rourke woman saying it was the shock, she'd gone downhill sudden. Suddenly feeling her age, the old man dying."

Mendoza thought, Which could be. Chronological ages— they didn't know everything about people yet, the scientists. He fingered his moustache again and frowned absently at the glint of sage-green beyond the front window: the Facel-

Vega at the curb. . . . When the doctor had said he could drive, he'd found the Ferrari's battery dead, and no wonder; and he had let Alison know how he felt. ("You could have run the engine every day, damn it, no need to take the car out anywhere—" "Well, honestly, Luis, we had other things to think about than your idiotic car, after all!") The Ferrari was at the agency garage for a complete overhaul.

"Well, now listen to this." Mrs. Oliver leaned forward earnestly. "Mrs. O'Rourke tries to keep people from getting in, what it amounts to, always says Mrs. Weaver's napping, or too tired for visitors. But some of us have been concerned, and gone on trying. Janet here, and myself, and Edna Fogarty up the block, we've all seen the nurse giving Mrs. Weaver these white tablets to take. 'Time for your aspirin, dear,' all cheery, and who's to say if it *is* aspirin? But this I *can* tell you. That I saw for myself. It was about a month back—no, a bit more. About the start of the first week in December. I dropped by, and the woman didn't want to let me in, but Mrs. Weaver heard my voice and called to me. I went in, and there she was *just like her old self,*" said Mrs. Oliver significantly. "As sensible and knowing as ever. Asking me about Joe and how Benny was doing in college. The same nice, bright old soul she always was. And *then,* a day or two later when Edna stopped by, the nurse lets her in without any trouble—as if she wanted her to come in and see—and there's Mrs. Weaver acting all senile again."

"Oh, really," said Mendoza slowly. "Really." That did seem to bolster the suspicion—the really absurd suspicion —that the old lady was being doped. With something. That the nurse had run out of whatever it was— But why would she be so careless? And why any of it in the first place? "Did anybody say anything to the nurse about that?"

"I said plenty, when Edna and I'd compared notes. But

it all rolled off the O'Rourke woman like water off a duck's back. You can't *talk* to her. She's like a bulldozer or something. Great big fat thing—dyed black hair—and little eyes like a pig's," said Mrs. Oliver irrelevantly. "She says isn't it terrible to see the poor dear slipping so, all right one day and going down the next, just natural, and she just tried to take good care of the old dear— And it's *not* natural, now I don't care, it's not!"

Janet Cox nodded shortly. "But there's nothing to put your finger on, is there? Legally?"

"She's done nothing illegal at all, that you can prove—by all that," said Mendoza. "It's just—funny. Queer. If she is giving the old lady drugs of some kind, she must be getting them under the counter. Unless a doctor—you're sure the old lady hasn't gone to a doctor, maybe had some new medication prescribed?"

They both said no, definitely. "Besides, she didn't like Dr. Gordon. He took over some of Dr. McCart's patients when the old doctor died, and his office right round on Fountain, nearest, he's the one the neighbors called when the old man had the stroke." Janet Cox sighed. "I expect it'll be old age on me, but I don't find doctors suit me these days. Mrs. Weaver said the same. You can't get them to come to the house for love nor money—Dr. Gordon came just the once that day the old man had the stroke—and they're not sympathetic, the new kind. All business. Take this, don't do that, I'll see you next week, and that'll be seven dollars." She shook her head. "Mrs. Weaver wouldn't go to Dr. Gordon, and anyway she's not been out of the house since the old man died. She did go to a chiropractor a few times, said he helped her, too, but not lately, and they can't write up the prescriptions, can they?"

"For vitamins only," said Mendoza absently. Vitamins

were not made up in white tablets. But where was any motive? For what?

"I've been thinking," said Mrs. Oliver. "I could take you over and say you were—were an old friend of the Weavers —you'd maybe recognize—"

Mendoza suppressed a grin. Both of them thinking Hawkshaw the detective kept a roster of pictures inside his brain, every crook on the books. Or could smell them. On the other hand, he would like a look at the nurse. Something offbeat about the whole thing. But he hesitated. He wasn't sure even why he'd come here. Restless and bored at home. But if there was anything at all to this, it just could be that at some later time he'd have an ace in the hole if the nurse didn't know him. The altruistic practical nurse.

He shook his head at Mrs. Oliver. "Look," he said, "there's nothing here for the police, you know that. It wouldn't be my beat anyway. Wilcox Street. But it's just a funny little thing all up in the air. Mairí told me about it and I was curious, that's all."

"I thought maybe—" Janet Cox looked disappointed. "But I see there's just nothing to it legally. But—"

Mendoza put out his cigarette in the dime-store glass ashtray. "I don't see what the woman's after, damn it. If anything. There's nothing to steal from the old lady. But—if you're suspecting the nurse of some nefarious plot, which you are—and which I could suspect with a little nudging— well, it's never been part of a policeman's job to shut stable doors while the horse is still inside." He said it wryly. "We have to wait for the *corpus delicti*."

"You think she's going to *murder* Mrs. Weaver?" wailed Mrs. Oliver, alarmed.

Mendoza laughed. "No, that just means the fact of the crime. The establishing that a crime has been committed.

41

So we can go look for X. . . . But I understand you got hold of the nurse through a county agency. How—"

"You mean, wouldn't she be licensed or something? I don't think so. I first heard about it when I needed a part-time one for my mother—it got too much for me. It's just a —a service, I guess you'd call it, where practical nurses who want jobs can leave their names. And you can call in and get the number to call. As a matter of fact, I called four altogether before I got *her*. Practical nurses these days—you can hardly find one, a dozen jobs for every one around. And I wish to goodness I'd never thought of it!" said Mrs. Oliver. "Whatever she's doing to poor Mrs. Weaver—such a nice old lady, and we always admired them, everyone knew them— And why? What could she be doing it *for*? Staying on, and—"

Mendoza said he couldn't guess. The shapelessness of it, the utter lack of any motivation in the story irritated him. He had a logical mind. He said he'd think about it; that, he could hardly help. The two women looked at him trustfully, and that annoyed him more.

It just crossed his mind that it would be interesting to see if the woman had any kind of record. He asked for details: Margaret O'Rourke, somewhere in the fifties, they thought, black hair (dyed), about five-six or seven, about two hundred pounds or more, blue eyes, no marks to be seen. He didn't really expect to find her in Records, but—

What had the woman done, that even these suspicious neighbors could honestly tell him? Put in a couple of months' hard work nursing a dying old man, keeping the house, cooking meals, looking after an old arthritic lady, for about a fifth of the wage any other nurse would ask. White tablets. Aspirin, for all anybody knew. And for all he knew, people did go senile overnight. And even had good days of being not senile later on, before slipping downhill again.

A mare's nest.

As he pulled open the front door of Janet Cox's house, he paused, and Mrs. Oliver let out a little exclamation. A car had pulled up with a squeal of brakes before the house across the street—the Weaver house. A gray two-door Ford, middle-aged. A man got out of it—a youngish man by the way he moved—and hurried up the front walk to the porch. He pushed the bell; pushed it again.

"I've never seen *him* before," said Mrs. Oliver excitedly. "Who do you suppose he is?"

The man—nondescript suit, nothing much to be told about him from behind—had a briefcase in one hand. He pushed the bell a third time, and the door opened. At this distance, with a screen door between, Mendoza could see only a large white-clad bulk at the door across the street; it moved back, and the man with the briefcase went in. The door shut.

"Well!" said Janet Cox. "A doctor maybe? If she's getting hold of dope, some kind, there'll be a crooked doctor in it."

Mendoza told her she was being melodramatic. And that he'd think about it.

As he got into the Facel-Vega he reflected irrelevantly that Harrington would be annoyed at the way his jacket hung loose on him. He'd dropped weight; soon pick it up again. Very likely never hear the last of it from the boys— measles—but he was all right again now. . . . No shoptalk with his office, said the doctor; did he think Mendoza was blind? The *Times* this morning, and what a thing—offbeat you could say—tied on the railroad tracks, for God's sake, Alfredo Montez. And what more Homicide had than had been in the *Times*—there was usually something more— he'd like to know. No word on the Moreno case in the papers; it had probably been shoved into Pending. A suicide in a hotel over on Fourth; a couple of traffic deaths, the consequent paperwork. (And what he hadn't yet seen in the papers but would, the murder of the Reverend David Barron of the Temple of the Holy Inner Light on Beverly Boulevard.)

He swore, thrusting the key into the ignition. Bored to death, and except that he got tired a little easier than usual, perfectly all right—and so he had seized on this minor little puzzle Mairí had brought him, something to cure his boredom for awhile. It was nothing. Probably a very ordinary explanation for—

For a practical nurse asking twenty-five bucks a week when she could ask five times as much?

The altruists very rare. Thin on the ground.

But for anything else, no motive. No loot to be had.

So, *ergo,* the nurse was an altruist after all. Sorry for the poor old people.

White tablets.

"*¡Bastante!*" he muttered to himself. Why had he bothered to come down here? It was—his logical mind could not honestly say, Nothing. It was something—a funny something. And that was as far as he could get on it right now.

He looked at the block as he drove up it toward Fountain Avenue. A sedate block of modest old houses, small houses, on a middle-class street in an old, sedate area of Hollywood. An ancient stucco court on one side of the street, otherwise all single houses, rather poor little houses if neatly maintained. The Weaver place next to the corner needed a coat of paint badly, and the front lawn looked neglected. No money for anything like that. A street of ordinary houses—and people. Money of any sizable order just not in evidence.

He drove home, to be pounced on by Alison and offered malted milk.

44

"Oh, dear, I can't bear to think about it," said Mrs. Mabel Wheeler. "Been crying all night I have—couldn't believe it —such a spiritual man, the Reverend Barron! Such a— Oh, dear." She hiccuped plaintively. "And now you coming to— As if *I'd* know anyth—"

"Mr. Terhune said," said Hackett patiently, "that he noticed you going into the church about noon yesterday, as he was leaving. All we'd like you to tell us, if you can, is whether Mr. Barron was there then—and if anyone else was there."

"Oh," she said. "Oh." She sat up and looked at the two big officers, Hackett and Higgins, there in her rather dingy apartment. She was about thirty-five, with a pretty, silly face, a loose mouth and pale blue eyes, tinted blonde hair. She'd been crying, and honestly, too; all her mascara was washed away, and without makeup her eyes were too small, the skin about them puffy and pink. Somebody honestly mourned the Reverend Barron, beaten to death at about (by what the autopsy surgeon gave them provisionally) one to two P.M. yesterday afternoon. "Such a *spiritual* man," said Mrs. Wheeler. "I've been really uplifted in the Temple—I've tried and tried to get Joe to come, but men are so *materialistic*." Hackett wondered if she didn't classify the late Mr. Barron as male. It was possible. "What? Yesterday—I just dropped into the Temple—about noon—to say a little prayer. For Joe. He just won't *see*. What did you say?"

"Did you see Mr. Terhune at that time, Mrs. Wheeler?" asked Higgins.

"Oh, yes. Yes, I did. He was just coming out. And I—"

"And Mr. Barron?"

"Yes, I did. Oh, dear—it doesn't seem possible—I've just cried and cried!" She buried her face in a handkerchief, peering at them around it. "Yes, he was there. The last time I saw him. And what will I do *now?*—not the *same* without —oh, the Reverend Terhune's all right, but not as—as—"

45

"Did Mr. Barron say anything to you then?"

She sobbed into her handkerchief. After a long moment she shook her head. "He w-was w-walking up the aisle toward the pulpit was all. He w-went into the little office there and shut the door, and it was the last time I ever— Oh, no, there wasn't anybody else there at all—"

They asked her more questions, but that was all she had to tell them. They came downstairs in this old apartment house (but middling high rents along here, this older downtown part of Wilshire Boulevard) and Higgins said, "Funny how a certain type of female goes for the religious pitch. You'd think anybody could see through—"

"That precious pair of con men. Yeah," said Hackett, "but we're cops, George. We know the score. Poor damn silly woman—and how many more like her? Some men, too. I suppose they get something out of it. But the whole thing looking so phoney—"

"Terhune," said Higgins ruminatively. They got into Hackett's Barracuda. "Thieves falling out?" They thought about Terhune.

The plump young man, with his small mouth pursed and unease in his pale eyes. The apartment he had shared with David Barron. (Real name?) A nice comfortable apartment over on Sunset, about a hundred and a quarter a month. Terhune uneasily affable, grieving, protesting, weakly indignant in turn. On perfectly good terms with David—both of them mainly concerned with building up the church— quite a faithful congregation now—and really, to imagine that this terrible affair had any *personal* motive— Some robber, these days such a lawless element and no respect for religion—. He had warmed up to it as he went along, his tone more confident, his manner easier; the typical con man.

He had, he said, been in the Temple only a little while yesterday morning—"My usual morning offering," he said

—and left about noon. Passing Mrs. Wheeler coming in. "Quite a faithful attendant." He thought Barron was somewhere around then, but hadn't spoken to him. Barron kept the church accounts. Probably that was what he was there for—the collection from the Sunday service hadn't been taken to the bank yet— And Terhune had gone up the boulevard to a coffee shop to have lunch, and then home. And he hadn't gone back to the church until about five-fifteen—or later—to prepare for the evening service. "We have a service *every* evening, gentlemen—we try to make converts every day—" and found Barron. And—

"Thieves," said Hackett. "Now, George. That little slug beating a man to death?"

"Well, Barron probably wasn't much better. Pair of con men," said Higgins. "The funny cult. What other reasonable conclusion is there?"

Hackett started the engine. "I suppose it just could have been the burglar."

"For God's sake."

"After the Sunday collection. You wouldn't expect to find anybody in a church on Tuesday afternoon. Only," said Hackett, "who would know the collection was still there?"

"Yes, he forgot that when he pushed the burglar at us. Not a very bright con man."

"Oh, I don't know. It looks like a going concern. And why was the collection still there?" wondered Hackett. "On Tuesday? Why didn't we ask?"

"We will. I still say—it is usually the obvious thing," said Higgins.

It usually was, of course.

They went down to the Temple of the Holy Inner Light, where the lab crew was busily at work. Marx, taking time off for a cigarette, greeted them sardonically at the door.

"We had quite a little argument with that Terhune before we could shoo him off. The other so-called reverend here. He—"

"You didn't shoo him. He'd agreed—reluctantly—to meet us at his apartment at ten o'clock," said Hackett. And that was another thing; a search warrant for Barron's living quarters, but they could hardly bar the other man from there, and if there was anything significant around, it wouldn't be by the time the lab men got there.

"Oh. Well, anyway, talk about a cat on hot bricks. He maybe thinks the LAPD has sticky fingers," drawled Marx. "Little temptation all right. Seven hundred and eleven bucks in cash. In a little bag in one of the desk drawers."

"The Sunday collection. You think he's not a bright con man, George?" said Hackett. "What's your take-home pay? My good God. Seven hundred and—even split two ways—"

"Very nice," said Higgins. "Have you come across anything else interesting?"

Marx dropped his cigarette, stepped on it. "Not a thing useful to you. Sorry. A confused mess of prints all over, including the corpse's—that Terhune nearly cried when we asked all polite for his to compare—the blood, but nothing suggestive. Yet."

"Yes, we can always hope," said Hackett. "So, back to type up the report." As they came out to the Barracuda at the curb, they spotted Jason Grace sauntering up the block, and waited for him. Grace had been asking around about any activity casually noticed at the Temple yesterday. The church sat a little apart, on its own ground, but nearby down Beverly was a block of shops—cleaners, stationers, dress shop, drugstore, electric repair shop; and on the corner in the other direction was a Shell station.

"So?" said Hackett. "I needn't ask, I suppose."

"You needn't ask," said Grace. His almost handsome, neat-featured coffee-colored face, moustache neat as Mendoza's, wore a slightly amused expression. "Who notices anything? At a church? To use the loose semantics." He glanced up at the Temple, which had obviously begun life as an orthodox church, steeple and all. "Nobody saw anything. To remember. People were busy. Nobody remembers anything."

"They so seldom do," sighed Hackett. "You needn't look so pleased about it, Jase."

"Well, not to sound—um—callous, he wasn't much of a loss, was he?" said Grace. "The fire-proofer—the con on the oldest game there is. Oh, I had a look at that Terhune." He smoothed his moustache.

"I suppose he wasn't. We have to work it," said Hackett. He slid behind the Barracuda's wheel, and Higgins eased his bulk in on the other side. "See you, Jase. . . . How's Stevie doing, George?"

"Fine," said Higgins, smiling, his voice fond. Stevie Dwyer had—in a sort of way—been the reason Higgins had got Mary Dwyer to marry him: Stevie getting hurt, that hit-and-run. Only Hackett didn't suppose she would have taken him unless she wanted to. He glanced at Higgins, wondering. No beauty, George, but one good man. He hoped— "There'll be a lot more therapy on the leg, he still has to wear a brace, but they say it'll be O.K."

"Good," said Hackett. He looked at his watch. "Like to have some lunch before we go back to the office?" They might run into some of the other boys. Seemed a little odd though, Luis not there—at lunch, at his office. This thing— waste of time. No loss, as Jase said, the con man.

Alfredo Montez had fallen to Palliser and Landers to work. They weren't getting much of anything on it. The offbeat thing, but Montez himself, by all they had, the very ordinary upright citizen.

49

They had seen the wife, this morning; she'd just got back from Fresno on the eight o'clock bus. Carlotta Montez. A demure and pretty dark girl about twenty-five—they'd only been married a couple of years. She wept, and said they'd been so happy, she and Alfredo so happy—never the cross word, and he was doing so well at the market, the promotion, the raise, and never any trouble—Alfredo a quiet man, never had trouble with anybody, a good man, nobody had any reason to hate Alfredo.

Alfredo, decapitated on the S.P. tracks.

Palliser and Landers came into the office after lunch arguing about it. "Nobody," said Palliser, "hasn't got somebody who doesn't like him. I'm telling you, Tom—"

"And pretty ungrammatical, too," said Landers. "All right, all right. But you've got to not like somebody one hell of a lot before you tie him to the railroad tracks when a freight's due. And as far as that goes, I'll say—"

"Somebody who knew the S.P. schedules. All right, I said it first, damn it. But the people at the market say the same thing, sober, quiet, ordinary guy. And I don't—"

"Here he is now," said Sergeant Lake to the phone. "John? It's the Lieutenant. Take it in his office." The outside line had to be kept clear.

Palliser strode into Mendoza's office and took up the phone. "How you feeling, Lieutenant? Art said you weren't supposed to—"

"I have," said Mendoza's deep voice, "put my foot down. I see the papers, don't I? The damn doctor—the hell with him, I'll be back next week. . . . *¡No me repliques!*" The aside, Palliser surmised, was to his redheaded wife. "Don't answer back, I'm as good as I ever—and just whose fault—" The Lieutenant sounded annoyed: with reason, thought Palliser, grinning. The measles. He'd been pretty sick that day he— "Listen, John. Practical nurses. No, for God's sake, I'm not in the market for one. But I remembered your saying something, when your—"

"Yes," said Palliser. The long difficult time when his mother was so ill—he had nearly paid off all the debts acquired then, Roberta a good manager, but it had been a bad time. "What? Oh, that county service—yes—what about it? References? Well—" why the hell was the Lieutenant interested in this? "Well, naturally, when I was looking for a woman, I wanted to know she wouldn't steal the spoons or — I gather if they ever get a complaint of dishonesty or incompetence, they'd refuse to list the name after that, but otherwise I think any woman wanting that kind of work can just put her name down with them. Some of 'em have taken a regular course in it, you know, and others just— Well, at the time the cheapest I was offered was one-fifty a week. What? Some of them specialize, I understand—obstetric cases or post-surgery. Why? I don't think there'd be any *check* on the women, of any sort. It's just a service the Health Bureau provides, where you can call to find a practical nurse. By my experience, a reliable practical nurse is worth her weight in gold—you just can't *get* them. A dozen jobs for every woman wants one. But why are you—"

"Nothing. Or is it?" said Mendoza. "A queer little something, John. Thanks very much. The County Health Bureau? Yes. I'll be seeing you."

Palliser stared at the phone, puzzled.

The County Health office in Hollywood was a block up from the Wilcox Street precinct house, Mendoza remembered. No harm to—

"And just what are you up to?" asked Alison.

"Eavesdropping is bad manners," said Mendoza. "Am I or am I not master of my own house?" Sheba leaped on him from behind, all claws extended, and he swore. "I can't read all the time. Even Kipling. And this is a very peculiar little business. I can't—"

"I heard something about it from Mairí. She shouldn't have—"

"No, but listen, *cara*," said Mendoza. "They do say, two heads better than one. The whole thing is just senseless. Because for any crime, a motive there has to be, and there isn't. And—"

Alison sat down on the couch beside him. "So I'll listen, being a dutiful wife. *¿Que eso?*"

"*Muy extraño*," said Mendoza, remembering suddenly that he hadn't got her any Christmas presents. Now that he was mobile again—

Chapter 4

HACKETT went down to Bunco and Forgery after lunch, to ask if the Temple of the Holy Inner Light rang any bells with those boys. He got hold of a sergeant named Isaacs, who said, "I heard on the grapevine your lieutenant came down with the measles. That's what comes of having to deal with all these juvenile delinquents. We'd all better go and have shots for the whole list—chicken pox, mumps—"

"Very funny," said Hackett. "Think how you'd feel. And Mendoza of all—"

"The great Mendoza with the crystal ball. I've heard. He'll never hear the last of it," said Isaacs. But over the Temple of the Holy Inner Light, he shook his head: and over Barron and Terhune. "Look, Sergeant, it's not a real con game when it gets to looking that legitimate—church building and all. The gent who preaches the sermon on the street corner and takes up a collection for the nonexistent missionary society, him we call the fire-proofer—the con who plays on religion. But one of these cults, like—whatever it preaches —this Temple bit, well, we're broadminded. It says it's a church, so it's a church. The people who go to it aren't dragged in chains. They must get something out of it."

"Barron is dead," said Hackett, "but Terhune we can read."

"All right," said Isaacs. "I was going on to say that in that area, sometimes even the preachers con themselves into thinking they're sincere. Con men one step removed, you could say. So this Terhune isn't—knows what he's up to—using the religious gimmick to take the marks." He shrugged. "The people aren't dragged in. What kind of thing is it, Oriental chanting or transmigration or what?"

Hackett said he didn't know. Yet.

"Well, there you are. People go for the damndest things," said Isaacs. "And so many people looking for something—in the way of religion, all vague, and falling for the exotic stuff. Look, so this pair were in it for the loot—that's just your opinion, and the people must get some kick out of it or they wouldn't have shelled out."

"It's still a going concern, far as I know. One preacher left."

"So." Isaacs shrugged again. "A hundred and one of the offbeat sects around. And we're busy enough with the real open cons. Who are always around, too. Your two boys don't remind me of anybody. If the one left starts playing the old Spanish prisoner game, or the pigeon drop, come and tell us. You'd think people would learn after awhile, wouldn't you? I swear to God. We even had the old gypsy switch the other day—put the money in the handkerchief and let the nice lady bless it. I swear *to*—"

"Yes, well, thanks anyway," said Hackett. "I see what you mean."

He went over to the apartment Terhune and Barron had shared. The lab men were there now. A waste of time, of

54

course. Terhune would have cleared out anything significant there. But they had to go through the motions.

They hadn't found anything suggestive. They were looking at the men's clothes—ordinary clothes; and in dresser drawers—ordinary contents; and in kitchen cupboards—one bottle of Scotch, ordinary supplies. And some for-real preachers took a drink now and then; nothing in that.

Hackett wandered from the kitchen to the bedroom. He wondered where Terhune was: what he was doing.

They would probably get the autopsy report on Barron sometime tomorrow.

The closet door was open. A portable typewriter sat on a table under the window. Nothing beside it, no papers. A Bible on one bedside table. Hackett eyed it, feeling depressed. Isaacs was quite right, of course; he and any other cop could look at Rodney Terhune and say, a con: But there were subtleties to it. The religious gimmick. Sometimes they didn't quite realize they were con men. Maybe Barron had been that kind.

There was a silk marker in the Bible. He opened it; the marker was in the middle of the Song of Songs.

Which, of course, said nothing. Suddenly Hackett sniffed. A very faint odor— He followed his nose, sniffing, and got the strongest whiff of it in the closet. What the hell was it? He sniffed harder. An extraneous odor of some kind, faintly sweet— Among other faint odors, hair-oil, some kind of after-shave lotion, the powder Marx and Horder were using, shoe polish, and all the mingled odors of a lived-in place, even reasonably clean—no, it was gone, he couldn't identify it.

"Coming down with a cold?" asked Marx.

"Come here and smell—do you smell anything? Anything different, unusual, I mean—"

55

Marx sniffed. "Not a thing. Your imagination."

"I guess," said Hackett. There was nothing here. He went back to the office to collect Higgins, who was typing a report. They'd spend the afternoon talking to members of the Temple's congregation; there had been a list of names in the top drawer of the desk in the office where Barron died. What kind of people got something that satisfied them there, he wondered: satisfied them so much that the collection on a Sunday ran to over seven hundred bucks?

Of course, it might not all have been the Sunday collection. But it made you wonder. But what they wanted to hear from those people, of course, was not their motivation for attending the Temple but anything personal they might know about Barron and Terhune. Any possible quarrel or jealousy between them.

As he came into the office he passed Landers and Palliser just going out. "You getting anywhere on Montez?"

"Progress," said Palliser. "Some. Though where it takes us—and where to look now—"

"Simple first principles," said Landers. "You know what the Lieutenant always says. Like the idiot boy looking for the lost horse."

"But the waitress didn't know—"

"But somebody knew who his friends were? Who knew him? People he knew? All I say is—"

"It was a friend tied him on the railroad track?"

"Break it up," said Hackett.

Palliser laughed and they went on out. Hackett went into the sergeants' office. "George, did you get that—*George!*"

Higgins was staring dreamily out the window. He jumped and turned to face Hackett. "Huh? Oh. You get anything from Bunco?"

Hackett grinned at him. He didn't remember—at least he didn't *think* he'd gone to daydreaming and goofing off

56

about Angel—either before or after they were married; but possibly the other men in the office would remember different. "We've still got half a day to work, lover. Did you get that list of names from the church?"

"I've got it," said Higgins, standing up. They did say, the harder the fall. Higgins the long-time bachelor, Higgins who might as well have COP tattooed on his forehead, Higgins the tough, topping Hackett's six-three by half an inch, had fallen hard when he did fall. And if maybe it was funny at first thought, it wasn't really funny to the Homicide office—Higgins humbly taking care of Mary and of Bert's kids, Bert Dwyer that other good cop whose name was on the Honor Roll downstairs.

"Come on," said Hackett.

The little progress Palliser and Landers had made on the Montez thing was through one of the market checkers who had been off yesterday, a weedy young man named Joseph Bean. He was shocked over Montez— "A very nice guy he was, fair and all, always nice to everybody, as nice a guy—" And he did happen to know that Montez had been going out to dinner, when he left the market at six o'clock that night. "His wife was away, see, with her folks. He sure was crazy about that wife of his—he showed me a picture once, a pretty girl— Gee, I'll bet she's all broken up, poor girl—they hadn't been married but a couple of years— Al, he was crazy for the home life, wanted a big family, but they hadn't—" When he left the market, Montez had said good night to Bean, who was on until closing time, eight o'clock. And said he was going up to The Copper Coin restaurant, up on Glendale Avenue, treat himself to dinner out.

So they went and asked there, and found a waitress who remembered him. At least they hoped it was Montez she remembered. She reacted to the description, anyway. She was a part-time waitress and had just come on at six o'clock, and he was one of her first customers; that made it pretty sure it was Montez.

"Mexican looking," she said. "That one. Yeah. He had the roast beef plate and a custard. Yeah, he was alone—when he came in, and when he ate, but another fellow went to sit at his table and they went out together."

They asked eager questions about that. She was vague. "How'd I know there'd be cops asking? I didn't take much notice—why should I? Yeah, yeah, I'm sure of that—he was the one this other guy went up to. Just before the first guy got up to leave. What'd he *look* like? Lord, I couldn't remember—just a guy. Wait a minute. I've sort of got the feeling he was Mex, too. I don't remember he had a moustache, like the first guy, but something about him—and I think he was bigger than the other one, kind of stocky."

They asked the cashier and the other two waitresses, but drew blank. It was two days ago, and who noticed customers?

But it was something. Montez had walked out of the restaurant with another man, and it could have been the man who tied him on the tracks to await the freight.

"And if it was," said Palliser, "they were friendly on the surface at least—evidently Montez didn't suspect the other fellow at all—"

"We don't even know that," said Landers. "Maybe they hated each other's guts, only the other fellow owed Montez a gambling debt and said he was going to pay up, so—"

"You and your fancy imagination," said Palliser.

"Well, you know what the Lieutenant always says—"

At two-forty a new call had come in from a squad car, and Piggott and Glasser went out on it. It was at an apartment house on Coronado Street, and when they got there it turned

58

out to be a very messy thing. The tenant, identified by the manager as a John F. Simmons, had shot his wife, three children, and the family dog, before turning the gun on himself. The kids had evidently tried to run, which said he'd killed the woman first. It was messy and inexplicable. There wasn't any note. Just the blood and the bodies.

The neighbors had heard the shots and called in, but by the time the squad car got there it was all over.

Why? There was no immediate answer.

Simmons had had a regular job. Nothing physically wrong with him or any of them, so far as anyone knew. Just, all of a sudden, bang.

There were routine things to do. Piggott and Glasser did them. Took statements from the neighbors, the manager. Looked through the apartment, which was a very ordinary apartment. Explained to the manager and a couple of other people that they'd probably have to testify at the inquest; and come in to headquarters to sign the formal statements. They'd be notified about times and places. They listened to a lot of confused and shocked and horrified people, who didn't know any more about it than they did, and then they came away and started for the men's clothing shop up in Hollywood where Simmons had worked as a bookkeeper. Anything to be found out, they had to find, and it could be that Simmons' employer could tell them something—that he'd been depressed, the doctor told him he had cancer, he'd found his wife was playing around— At least the employer could tell them whether Simmons had been acting normally. They had to cover all bets, and find out what they could for the report, for the inquest.

They took Glasser's Ford.

"Somebody," said Piggott, "said somewhere that to understand the twentieth century is to come to terms with

59

madness. Near as I can remember. He had something there. Seems to me it gets worse all the while. Blood, violence. The —not caring. About anything or anybody."

"Seems as if you said something, Matt," agreed Glasser. "D'you suppose he was on dope, some kind?"

"Could be, I suppose," said Piggott. There was a lot of that floating around, too.

Glasser left the Hollywood freeway and went down Sunset to Vine, turned up toward the boulevard. They got the red light there. They were in the right lane for the turn, as the address they wanted was east of Vine and Glasser had gone round to be on the right side to park. As the yellow flashed on for the boulevard traffic, and Glasser took his foot off the brake, a screaming wide-open engine drowned all the traffic sounds. "God, what's—"

Brakes were slammed on as the car came careening up from the west, a scarlet T-bird convertible, top down—going at least seventy, thought Piggott—weaving in and out, over the double line—car full of people, people all screaming too—drunks, or—

The new Chrysler in the middle lane of Vine, beside the Ford, had been impatient for the green. It started up on the heels of the yellow light the other way, and when the green went on it was halfway into the intersection. The driver gunned it then, and the Chrysler was in the center of the boulevard, going about twenty-five, when the T-bird hit it like a bomb.

"*Christ!*" said Glasser. He and Piggott ducked instinctively. There was one hideous noise, a scream that soared and abruptly died, and then for five seconds an uncanny utter silence. And then more noise.

Glasser pulled the Ford violently over into the red-painted curb, braked and switched off. They got out and looked.

The Chrysler was just a mass of mangled metal jammed against the side of the bank building across the intersection. By the screams there, it had hit pedestrians. At first Piggott couldn't see the T-bird anywhere. Then he looked farther up, past the drugstore on this near corner, and saw it— what was left of it.

It had smashed on, caromed off the Chrysler, on down Hollywood Boulevard, diagonally across to finish mashed together with the front row of cars in the public parking lot on this side of the street. You couldn't tell which car had been which, now. Screams from that direction, too.

Piggott and Glasser ran. The law would need any help available on this, if just to keep the crowds back.

At first glance, Piggott knew there wouldn't be anybody alive in the wreckage of the T-bird, those other cars. But the driver had, incredibly, been thrown clear. He was lying on the sidewalk forty feet down from the mashed-together cars. Piggott knew he was the driver because he was still clutching the steering wheel and about half the steering column, sheered off neatly. He was streaming with blood. He looked about twenty, and he had a blond beard, sopping with blood, and he was, incredibly, getting up and running.

Piggot ran after him. Somewhere a squad car siren screamed. Help on the way.

The driver had dropped the wheel. He ran into the doorway of a hole-in-the-wall nightclub, banged up against the locked door, and turned. He swayed on his feet, dripping blood.

The drunks, thought Piggott in dumb outrage. The idiotic drunks, they never get hurt themselves—

The driver stood there swaying, and Piggott reached for him. The idiotic drunks still had to be offered first aid—

"Don't you *do* that," said the driver, shying away, "I'm a lamp, an' you'll switch me off—yesserday was 'n 'lectric

61

heater, t'day I'm a lamp an' I don' want t' be switched off—"

Piggott knew then what it was. Not a drunk. Worse. The acid. The LSD. They'd all had a briefing on it at the Academy just a couple of months back. About the only way to know the difference—alcohol, H, anything else—was the offbeat hallucinations the acid always produced. They had wings, they were oranges or graham crackers or machines, they'd drip gasoline if you stuck a pin in them, they were glass and they'd break.

God, thought Piggott, and he was not swearing. The kids on the acid—up on the Strip. Told that it wasn't addictive, wasn't harmful. The researchers finding out more and more about it—the brain damage from one dose, the side effects. *God.*

The driver fell down, bleeding. Piggott didn't touch him. He looked at the mess back there—how many people dead, maimed?—and he turned and went back, to help the squad-car men hold back the crowds, to help with the first aid, until the ambulances came.

And after that, they still had to go and see Simmons' employer. Get a statement from him.

Piggott thought, between one step and the next, that tonight was choir practice. Eight o'clock. He thought of the little church with its cheap but colorful stained-glass windows, the kind, absorbed gaze of Mr. McMasters the choir director, and the rising swell of the chorus on what they were rehearsing now, "Come Thou Almighty King." He saw the russet head of that nice girl Prudence Russell among the sopranos. A long way from here and now.

To terms with madness, he thought.

"It's funny," said Hackett, "how people will go for that kind of thing. That Temple. I suppose the orthodox religion isn't—fancy enough for them. Everybody we talked to said the same thing—such a wonderful man, the Reverend Barron, and how uplifting the services were—so spiritual and rewarding. I gather it's a kind of let's-all-be-uplifted-together sort of thing, if you see what I—"

"Not so funny," said Angel. His household was at peace: Mark and baby Sheila in bed, Angel busy over some sewing opposite him, and Hackett had the cat on his lap, purring steadily. "That kind of thing—mmm—fills a need for some people, Art. And does it do any harm? Even if these—con men—aren't sincere?"

"I don't know," said Hackett. "Fanatics?" He considered it. "Too strong a word. But—"

"I'll bet I could tell you the kind of people," said Angel, brown head bent over her work. "Lonely people. Single people. Old people. Dissatisfied people—unhappy people."

"Um," said Hackett, stretching out his legs. "Mostly." He and George had talked to quite a few of them this afternoon. He thought about them. Divorcees, widows and widowers, unmarried women—Mrs. Wheeler one of the few married ones they'd seen. And he'd lay a bet, more than one like that Mrs. Brainard. They hadn't got all through the list of names by a long shot—some hundred and fifty. Mrs. Brainard, a middling-rich grass widow out on Wilshire. Such a rewarding experience, such real exaltation of the spirit, she looked forward to the services at the Temple just like a child, really, she felt she had really been born again, she couldn't explain it to an outsider but everyone who had been to services at the Temple would understand—"I gather," he said, groping for a cigarette, "that they've mixed in just enough exotic Oriental mysticism or whatever with a little orthodoxy, that it does appeal to a lot of people. Funny. But then people are." He flicked his lighter. "I wish I could think of—"

"What? Was that the baby?" They listened; false alarm. "What?" said Angel.

"What that smell was. In the closet at the apartment. It was *something*—something I ought to— No, it's gone."

"If it's important it'll come to you," said Angel.

"And I also wonder," said Hackett, "what on earth Luis wants with a practical nurse. John said something. No, he said he was just interested in them."

"Why on earth? I was talking to Alison today—he's fine now, the doctor just wants him to take a rest—" Angel giggled, biting off a thread. "I'm sorry, darling, I know he was awfully sick, but—the arrogant Mendoza, with the measles. I don't suppose he'll ever hear the last of it."

"Listen," said Hackett, "an adult can be damned sick with them. He was. You needn't— Office isn't the same without him. I hope they'll let him come back pretty soon. I just wonder what he'd say about this thing— But why in hell practical nurses?"

"I couldn't guess," said Angel. "Have you weighed today?"

"Yes, damn it," said Hackett. "One ninety-seven and a half. Which is under what the doctor—" He thought the doctor was crazy. The insurance statistics said he could go up to two-ten safely.

"I—oh, damn," said Angel, putting her sewing down. This time it was the baby.

"—And don't go on the freeways," said Alison. "And if you start feeling tired, come home right away. And—"

"*¡Demonios!* Am I two years old?" said Mendoza. "Presumably I have some common sense. I am perfectly—and I'm not being ordered around by—"

"A mere wife. Yes, *marido honorable*," said Alison meekly. "But just remember you have been sick, and—"

"I'm hardly likely to forget it." Mendoza got up from

the remains of a larger breakfast than he usually had, checked his pockets, and asked Mairí, "Isn't that cab here yet?"

"It's just coming up the drive."

They both dived for the door: the cats were out. One comprehensive glance showed Bast sunning herself on the front steps, Nefertite squatting decorously over a hole in the rose garden, Sheba stalking a butterfly on the lawn and El Señor nowhere in sight. The yellow cab stopped in the drive.

"Now, Luis, if you feel tired or—"

"I've been an adult some time." Mendoza kissed her hastily and started for the cab; the twins were erupting from the house.

The cab took him to the agency garage where he picked up the long black sports Ferrari. The Ferrari was sweet to handle and it was good to be back under her wheel. She took him up Wilcox Street, past the old tan-brick precinct house there, to the rather insolently new County Health Building, all glass brick and synthetic stone.

The LAPD badge usually produced cooperation from other authorities, but the young blonde woman behind the desk labeled *Service* looked slightly bewildered at his request.

"Anything I can tell you, sir—but what do you want to *know* about practical nurses? I don't— And why're you asking?"

Mendoza gave her his deliberately charming one-sided smile. "We needn't waste time on that. I just want to ask about your records."

And of course it was all a waste of time anyway. A mare's nest. Just that he was bored and restless—and his mind had seized on the shapeless little puzzle.

She was helpful enough once she understood what he

wanted, exactly. "We don't keep records on them now," she said. "The practical nurses. It started as a kind of service— the same as the Visiting Nurses service, but they're all registered nurses, of course. You know about that? But it was just too much of a job to keep the records, and not really necessary, you know? I mean, to keep a check of them all, what patients they'd had and everything. It's really a sort of glorified employment agency, now. The nurses call in, let us know when they're available, and people call in and we give them names and phone numbers. Like that. There are always jobs for practical nurses. But—"

"You used to keep more detailed records? How? And are they still available?"

"Goodness, I'd have to look—maybe with all the back files in the junk room—" she caught herself. "Storage room I mean. Yes, records on the cases, to keep a check on them, the same as we do with the Visiting Nurses, you know. But it got to be too big a job. Now, it's—"

"When did you stop keeping files on the practical nurses?"

"About three years ago, I think. It cost too much, too."

"Well, if you'd have a look, see whether you can locate any records you might have—" Without much expectation, he gave her the name. Margaret O'Rourke.

What the hell was he doing here? On this little nothing of a minor puzzle? Only because he was at loose ends, out of his usual routine, away from his desk down there at Homicide headquarters.

After a long time she came back. As predictable, she had responded to the well-known Mendoza personality, and put herself out for him. He wasn't preening himself on it: a fact of life he used without thinking about it.

"There was a file under that name, sir. I suppose it's all right to let you see it." The badge was always useful, too.

It was quite a little file, on Margaret O'Rourke. Terse

abbreviations, but quite a lot of meat in it. Patients, addresses, dates. The file went back to 1954. There wasn't much information about Margaret O'Rourke personally; apparently she hadn't any formal accreditation as a practical nurse, just offered herself in that capacity. The most recently listed patient she had had, listed here, was a Mrs. Thomas Fuller on Cimarron Place; that had been July-August of 1965. The first patient listed was a Mr. William Kidd, at an address on Berendo Street, in February of 1954. And quite a few between.

He took out his pen and started to copy the list.

Chapter 5

GRACE had got to the office before anyone else on Thursday morning, and the first call came in three minutes later, so he went out on it alone.

A body: the body of a man, at the alley door of a bar and grill on Los Angeles Street. The bar owner, arriving early to supervise a redecorating job, had stumbled across it fifteen minutes ago.

The squad car was standing by, and the ambulance on its way. Grace walked up the alley and looked at the body. At an experienced glance, the man had been mugged, stripped of everything valuable on him, and possibly dragged up the alley so he wouldn't be found at once, or just left where he was. This wasn't the classiest section of town, not very far from Skid Row. The citizens out alone down here were letting themselves in for the mugging, and sometimes a mugger struck a little too hard.

He squatted over the body. One of the uniformed men said, "We haven't touched him, sir." Grace nodded. Pockets pulled inside out: jacket thrown back so the breast pocket could be searched. A man about thirty-five, a thin nondescript man with brown wavy hair and an aquiline nose; he was carefully shaved and the gray suit he had on, dirtied with the muck in the alley now, looked like a fairly good one. White shirt, navy tie. The tie was torn where, presumably, a tie tack or bar had been removed.

Grace picked up the wallet lying beside the body, carelessly dropped after it had been rifled. Originally a good wallet, brown cowhide. No bills in it, of course. But plenty of I.D. He looked at the filled-out identification slip in the first plastic slot, a little surprised. Lester G. Cunningham, 270 Court Street, San Diego. Driver's license, Social Security, credit cards, a few snapshots; tucked in the bill section a business card. The Red Rooster Coffee Shop, Main Street, San Diego, open seven days a week, short orders and food to go, Lester Cunningham, Prop.

Grace stood up and thought for a moment. It looked like and probably was the common-or-garden-variety mugging— Cunningham's head bashed in from behind. He said to the uniformed man, "Let the ambulance take him." He went out to the mouth of the alley. About four doors up there, corner of Los Angeles and Sixth Street, was the Greyhound Bus station. He walked up there and flashed the badge.

"Why, yes, sir, officer, there was a bus in from San Diego last night." The ticket agent looked curious. "Eleven-fifty, right on schedule, why? No, sir, that driver's on another run now, I couldn't say offhand when he'd be back here—should I—"

"I don't think it matters," said Grace. "If so, we'll let you know." He went back to the office; everybody was in then but Hackett, and it was his day off. Grace sent off a teletype to the San Diego police, telling them about Mr. Cunningham, so unfortunately done to death up here; would the San Diego police confirm address, break the news to any family, and have somebody who knew Cunningham come up to make a formal identification?

Then he started to type a report on it. He was interrupted by Higgins, who said he needed somebody to fill in for Hackett on this Barron thing. "Always happy to oblige," said Grace, getting up. "What's the schedule?"

"Have we got a new mystery?" asked Higgins, looking at the half-finished report in Grace's typewriter.

"Routine, routine. A poor innocent from San Diego loose in the big city. A mugger hit him a little too hard."

"Too bad," said Higgins absently. "Look, this Terhune—"

The autopsy report on Barron had just come in. It didn't present any surprises except one. Dr. Bainbridge was of the opinion that no weapon had been used; somebody had just given Barron a thorough beating and in that small room, inevitably, he had been knocked against things—the wall, the floor, the furniture—and had sustained rather extensive damage. The inference was that the somebody was much bigger and stronger than Barron. The actual cause of death was massive concussion. Bruises, a couple of teeth knocked out, one rib cracked. Barron had not been in very good physical shape, added Bainbridge; five-ten, but a sedentary man, too thin for his frame, a touch of dormant T.B. on one lung; and by the state of his liver and a few other symptoms, Bainbridge would guess he had been something of a drinker.

"Ah-hah," said Grace, scanning it. "The reverend minister."

But in any case it was time to lean on Rodney Terhune some. Higgins had fetched him in; they took him into an interrogation room and started to lean on him.

Terhune, who had been all to pieces at the scene of the homicide, was apparently bolstered by the frontal attack.

He was affable, open, honest, the frank and willing witness eager to help the police. And he was smooth.

"Oh, really, now," he said, smiling at them, "*drinking*— It's perfectly true that we do stress, in our creed, that gratification of the physical appetite is a divine law, but in moderation—moderation in all things is the significant thing. Yes, yes, David took a drink occasionally, but not, I assure you, in excess."

They asked him everything they could think of, pertinent and otherwise, in an effort to shake him. He went on being open and frank. He was a native of Denver himself, had come to California in 1954. Well, the different jobs around —selling mostly. He had always had a great interest in religious matters, but not until he met David had he— He'd met David three years ago, through mutual friends. Well, he'd had a part-time job then—selling Bibles. For a firm now out of business. He smiled at them. David had been trying to build his little congregation then, had just taken over the Temple—it had been the property of some small fundamentalist sect which defaulted on the mortgage, and the realty company wanted to get rid— It was uphill work, of course, but a labor of love, and David had welcomed any help. He—

"Was he a real ordained minister?" asked Higgins bluntly. "Are you, Mr. Terhune?"

Terhune looked faintly indignant. "Why, certainly, sir. It was then, at David's urging, I—er—took up my studies. I can show you my ordination papers—" Higgins was aware of that. He'd seen them, and Barron's, at the apartment. Fancy diplomas from a mail-order place in the east somewhere; you saw the ads in magazines, Study for the Ministry by mail. And Higgins could also have a shrewd guess what the job selling Bibles had actually been. The old come-on,

71

the little piddling con game, watch the obituaries and show up with the two-dollar Bible, dear departed ordered this, five bucks due. Terhune had graduated to a more legitimate con game.

"I could only think, a burglar," said Terhune earnestly. "When I found David—such a terrible—but thank God the collection wasn't taken. We need every penny to keep our little church going. And I really do feel that we have made some splendid converts—poor lonely people with no purpose in life. David was so proud—" He shook his head. His deliberate projected charm outweighed his physical smallness and vaguely weak features and light tenor voice. "Now I don't know *what* to think—about this terrible, terrible thing. And you know your own business, but it *has* occurred to me—maybe some belligerent drunk from Skid Row wandered in and—"

"Maybe, Mr. Terhune," said Grace pleasantly. "Are you going to carry on at the church in Mr. Barron's place?"

"I shall certainly try," said Terhune, looking brave. "Poor David—such an inspiration to us all. Yes, I shall certainly try to keep the Temple alive, as a memorial to him. His faithful service."

They went on prodding, at random. They got this and that about Barron—he was a native New Yorker, a sadly misspent youth, Terhune feared, until he experienced his great conversion and turned to God. No details of misspent life.

They leaned on him for two hours and he never turned a hair; kept his end up smoothly. They gave up finally and let him go.

"So what do you think?" asked Grace, lighting a cigarette.

"I'll tell you one thing," said Higgins regretfully. "Say what you will about Rodney, he's a typical con man—shy of

72

violence. Any sort. And anyway, can you see him beating a man to death?"

"Not very easily," said Grace. "And I understand you and Art didn't turn up any hint of anything wrong between them."

"No. Everything lovey-dovey. Two fine upright dedicated ministers. They seem to have shared out the services. Sort of a main bit on Sundays, something called the Rite of the Opening of the Chamber, and evening gatherings, too."

"Mmm. Expectable mumbo-jumbo. Why did they join up?" asked Grace suddenly. "By what Rodney says, there's Barron getting his Temple under way—must have had a little investment capital to put a down payment on the property and so on, his private game—and when they met, Rodney's on the old Bible-peddling circuit, very small-time. How come Barron let him in on the deal?"

Higgins thought. "Could be Barron was new on the game, Rodney more experienced, suggesting all the gimmicks?"

"I suppose it could be. I've got just one suggestion," said Grace. "Rodney said he was—"

"For once I'm ahead of you," said Higgins, grinning. "Yeah. Rodney at least had garnered some experience by the time he took to selling Bibles in California. It won't do any harm to ask Denver if they know him. We've got his prints. And, of course, he might never have set foot in Denver in his life—we'll also ask Washington. And ask New York about Barron, if they know him by that name or whatever."

"Yes indeed," said Grace. "Just for fun. But even if they do—if both of 'em have records from here to there—it doesn't say anything about who took off Barron."

"So it doesn't. Damn it," said Higgins, "everybody loved him—dedicated minister—and I can't see—"

73

"He wasn't," said Grace, stroking his moustache, "at the Temple twenty-four hours a day. And if he liked his little nip now and then—or a lot more—it could be he also indulged in other forms of the—mmm—physical gratification."

"You do put things so pretty," said Higgins dryly. "It's something to think about, Jase."

Belatedly, yesterday afternoon, Palliser and Landers had suddenly thought about Montez' car. They had gone back to the market and asked. Yes, Montez had a car: a four-year-old Volkswagen, light green; yes, he had driven away in it when he left that night. They had sent an urgent request to the D.M.V. in Sacramento overnight, and this morning they had the plate number on the VW. Not that it was doing them much good.

There was a parking lot adjacent to The Copper Coin, but no attendant at such a small place; the VW certainly wasn't there now. They put out a general call for it, county wide, which was all they could do.

Today they were back at the Southern Pacific yards, going exhaustively into the matter of gates, shifts, and track patrols. It had seemed at first that it would be difficult if not impossible for any unauthorized person to get inside that high steel fence surrounding the vast complex of the yards: The few gates in the far side from the shops were kept locked, and there were watchmen about, especially at night, on the lookout for bums.

But when they talked to the dispatchers and railroad police, it started to look a bit different. The main gate was the loophole: the gate nearest the shops. The roundhouse was quite a way from the shops, but all the men left their cars in the one dusty parking lot just outside the main gate, no private cars allowed inside. (They looked, but Montez' VW wasn't there either. Well, a long chance.) There were patrols out in the yards, sure, watching for vagrants and tres-passers, but not by the main gate. This wasn't like an air-plane factory where employees had to show badges to get in or out. And apparently it would be extremely simple for anybody just to walk in the main gate, between shifts when everybody was busy at regular jobs.

The shifts changed at eight A.M., five P.M., and midnight.

But it would also be possible, said one dispatcher brightly, for any stranger to walk in while the shift was actually chang-ing. Men going and coming. "I never thought, you know, but we've got a lot of people working here. And a lot of the un-skilled help—car-washers, trackmen, like that, there's quite a turnover. A jam when the shift changes. And also, about that, the car-washers especially, always mooching off and new ones hired. I never thought about it, but—me or anybody else sees a couple of strange faces coming in, do we think twice about it? We think, a couple of new guys just taken on."

"Which takes us a lot further," said Palliser to Landers irritably.

"I think we ought to go at it from the other end. Ask around the family, his friends, his wife. Who he'd had any trouble with, who owed him money—"

"We've *asked* once. But I suppose we can talk to his wife again," said Palliser dispiritedly.

"And look, John—about this sauntering in the main gate," said Landers. "How would anybody coax Montez all the way down here? For what? I don't think Montez got here under his own steam. And somebody would have noticed, my God, if somebody dragged a body through that main gate. I think—"

Just before leaving the office for lunch, Grace had a tele-type from the San Diego police. They confirmed Lester

75

Cunningham as a San Diego resident and owner of The Red Rooster Coffee Shop on Main Street. Mrs. Cunningham had been contacted. In a teletype no words were wasted on reporting her emotional reactions, but the terse information appended was of some value: wife states would have had approximately one hundred dollars cash was in L.A to purchase new restaurant equipment. Wife will come L.A. identify and claim body will contact you on arrival.

Well. So the mugger had got quite a little haul, thought Grace.

Piggott finished typing the report on the Simmons mess about noon. The LSD thing in Hollywood had cost them some time, yesterday—and now they'd both have to attend that inquest, too, of course. Piggott had noticed in the paper this morning that the driver of the T-bird had died.

"And, of course, no loss," he said to Glasser. "But what a mess, Henry. The innocent people dead, too. As well as the moronic kids on the acid. And they tell us we're making progress, Henry? Away from the caves and Neanderthal man?"

"Little Neanderthal in everybody, maybe, Matt," said Glasser.

Piggott sighed. "And the rapes, and muggings, and riots, and vandalism. We've progressed away ahead of our witch-hunting Puritan ancestors?" But he wasn't really feeling quite as pessimistic as usual. He'd asked Prudence for a date last night, and they were going to a show on Sunday.

"The jungle as usual," said Glasser somnolently. "Hackett never got any further on that Moreno rape, did he? That was a hell of a thing. Twelve-year-old on her way home from church."

"That's dead," said Piggott. "In Pending. We'll never get him now. . . . Wonder when the Lieutenant'll be back."

Mendoza had started out, rather unhopefully, with Mrs. Thomas Fuller on Cimarron Place. What could former patients tell him about the practical nurse? Well, whether she'd tried to steal the spoons. The address turned out to be an apartment house, once imposing, now much run-down. There was no Fuller listed in the mailbox slots in the lobby; he found a door marked *Manageress* and pressed the bell, bringing out the badge.

The manageress looked at him blankly. "Fuller? Nobody that name here."

"A Mrs. Thomas Fuller lived here in 1965." Waste of time—so he got a more recent address, the woman still couldn't—

"Oh, *her*," said the manageress, enlightened. "Oh, I do recall now. What you asking about her, all this time after?"

"If you have a forwarding address—"

She stared at him, a dowdy little scrawny woman in a faded cotton dress. "Now that I couldn't tell you," and she tittered. "She's dead."

"When did she die, here? She was ill in July and August of 1965."

She nodded. "I guess that'd be about right. Why're the cops interested, all this time after? Seems funny. Mis' Fuller —yes, I remember her good now you remind me, she lived here nearly fifteen years. I guess she had trouble scraping up the rent at the last, when it got raised a couple times— she was payin' ninety at the last, I think—it's up to a hunnerd and ten now, o' course—she didn't have much, poor old soul, what her husband left in insurance I seem to recall she told me once. I guess it was about then she died. She had cancer. She was pretty old, way up in her seventies."

"Do you remember a nurse she had with her then? A Mrs. O'Rourke?"

"Remember she had a nurse—had to have, at the last—

couldn't say I ever heard the woman's name. Not a *trained* nurse, a hospital nurse, one o' these practical ones. Sure. Why?"

Mendoza shrugged mentally. He was woolgathering. "Thanks," and he was about to turn away.

"It was the nurse cleared things away after she died," said the manageress. "I remember. I guess the poor old lady— Mis' Fuller—went out pretty hard, like they do with cancer. And no relatives, no family. It was the nurse arranged to move out her little bits o' furniture, and paid up the last rent, and all. She didn't have much— But why—"

"Thanks very much," said Mendoza. He felt frustrated.

Why the hell was he expending time and energy on this wild-goose chase?

The next patient of Mrs. O'Rourke's listed, going back chronologically, was a Miss Mary Wilkerson. MacBeth Street. That was somewhere down near Echo Park. He walked back up the block for the Ferrari, drove down there, found MacBeth Street.

An old section of town, this was, and the lots narrow, the houses mostly in the neighborhood of fifty or sixty years old, some older. The address given for Miss Wilkerson turned out to be one of the older houses. It had rather obviously had a face-lifting recently, the gingerbread stripped from it and a fresh coat of tan paint, but it was still an old and not very substantial house, about five or six rooms. Mendoza climbed the high-rise wooden steps and found the doorbell.

After a minute the front door jerked open and a girl about twenty faced him. She was pretty and blonde, and she had on dirty blue jeans and a T-shirt, and there was a dripping mop in one hand. "What do *you* want?" she asked abruptly.

"I'm looking for a Miss Wilkerson—"

"Wrong address, sorry." She started to close the door.

"But I had this address—"

"No. Maybe she lived here before. Nobody named Wilkerson here now." The door slammed.

"*¡Carape!*" said Mendoza, annoyed. And just what in hell he thought he was going to get by—

He descended the sagging steps and tried the house next door. It was about the same period but nobody had spent money to lift its face: its General Grant gingerbread was still much in evidence, and it needed painting. The woman who opened the door to him was fat, elderly, and genial looking. She was eating salted peanuts from a paper bag.

"A Miss Wilkerson," said Mendoza. "Miss Mary Wilkerson. I believe she used to live next door. Could you tell me—"

The woman's eyes filled with easy tears. "Ah, the darling she was. But who are you askin' after her, her in her grave these three years and God rest her soul?"

Mendoza produced the badge. "Ah, a policeman it is, and good luck to you, sir, I've a boy on the force in New York and a good word always for the uniform. But it's beyond me why you're askin' about poor Miss Wilkerson, though whatever at all I could do to help—" she popped a handful of peanuts into her mouth—"I'll be bound to do. Come in, come in—"

"If you could just tell me, I believe Miss Wilkerson had a nurse with her when she was ill in May of 1965? A Mrs. O'Rourke—"

"Not that I ever knew the nurse, was that her name indeed, but good care she took I would say, not that she was with her so long, maybe six weeks, it was the dropsy she had, though some long fanciful name for it the doctor gave, the poor dear, a school teacher she'd been and a terrible great help she was to my Dennis—that's my boy on the force—over his arithmetic, though why he wanted to go back east

79

to all the snow and cold I couldn't tell you—" she popped peanuts into her mouth. "A terrible strict lady, and quite the lady, too, she was, and a great help to Dennis. Alone in the world, the poor soul, God rest her, and the money scarce with only the pension, and at the last I took in the broth and stew and such to be neighborly, and at that it was lucky her getting a good nurse to—" in popped more peanuts—"care for her at the end. But it's years back, and why the police should be taking interest I couldn't fathom with the poor woman not having aught to leave behind her—save the house that is, and of course that's sold long since, and that chit in it now no better than she should be if you ask me, Miss Wilkerson turning in her grave I'm sure, but that's water under the bridge after all—" she dived a hand into the bag; it came up empty and she stared at the bag regretfully.

Mendoza seized the chance and said definitely, "Thank you very much," and turned hastily down the steps.

"And why the police should come asking, all this time, and she was near eighty, nobody of her own and neighborly I tried to be, her being such a great help to Dennis over the long division he couldn't get into his head, and 'twas only right I said at the time, no family of her own at all and the woman kind to her, if she was only hired, no relation, all the poor soul had to leave behind her, seventeen hundred dollars she paid for it in 1922, just fancy, and she said she had to scrape to make the payments, too, the times do change on us—"

The amiable voice faded as he started the engine.

Letting himself in for—what? And he admitted to himself that he was tired. Ridiculous. It was only twenty to twelve, he hadn't been away from the house for three hours. Alison and Mairí fussing at him. But he felt—admittedly—a little lackadaisical. A little inclined to go home and settle down with Kipling and a cat on his lap.

Damnation. First picking up the bug—unprecedentedly —and now giving in to weakness. And he was imagining a hare to run where there was nothing, only because he was at loose ends, but he'd beat the bushes a little more before giving up on it.

Because—admit that, too—the Weaver end of the story was a little funny.

He went back to Hollywood and stopped at the London Grill. He had four fingers of straight rye and a rather lavish lunch after it, and felt better. He drove out to the next address, in West Hollywood, a classy area, big expensive new-ish houses. He was looking for a Mrs. Roberto Antonelli.

He found two Antonellis: Mr. and Mrs. Handsome, polite, wealthy and amiable people in their seventies. They were rather bewildered by a visit from police, but they welcomed him in courteously. Mrs. O'Rourke? They looked at each other blankly. Mrs. Antonelli fingered her diamond brooch. A practical nurse? They were enlightened. That one. Yes.

"I'd forogtten her name until you said it." Mrs. Antonelli smiled gently on him. "After my gall bladder operation. Dr. Martini thought I should have someone—it wasn't necessary to have a trained nurse, but someone— And," she chuckled comfortably, "both our daughters-in-law were expecting, and our daughter was in her senior year of college, so—"

"O'Rourke?" said her husband. "I didn't remember the name. That was the first one, wasn't it, Alida?"

"Yes. And why on earth the police are asking— She was only here a few days. She had to leave— I believe there was family illness, her mother needed her— And then we had dear Miss Lovett, such a nice woman, she was with both our daughters-in-law when the babies came, and so good and kind. But really, why the police should be—"

81

And why was he interested? A little puzzle to occupy his mind. Nothing to it. Some ordinary explanation, for the rather queer business of the surprisingly altruistic practical nurse. (Had she asked, and been paid, the going rate by Mrs. Fuller, Miss Wilkerson, the Antonellis?)

So she had to leave Mrs. Antonelli to look after her sick mother. In February of 1965. It could be so. Nothing said it wasn't so. Mrs. O'Rourke in her fifties; her mother could have been alive three years ago.

Why the hell was he bothering about this? Mairí's queer little tale?

For the first time since he'd been feeling like himself again, the old Mendoza, he felt the little cold finger up his spine.

The hunch.

They made jokes about Mendoza's crystal ball, down at Central Headquarters.

Well, he got the hunches.

Only he didn't think much of this one. If it was a real hunch.

He was headed back up Hollywood Boulevard (quite a spectacular crash that had been along here, yesterday, by the paper) and caught the light at Cahuenga. Idly, he scanned the billboard across the intersection—Open a Christmas Club Account With Security-First Today.

He'd never got Alison any Christmas presents at all. What with the measles. She'd said—

He switched on the left-turn signal, went round the block and back to the public parking lot, walked down to the black-marble and glass front of the big jewelry shop and asked to be shown some diamond earrings. For pierced ears.

It was a quiet night for Central Homicide. Nothing came in at all that couldn't be handled by the squad cars—the rou-

82

tine drunks, muggings, brawls, street fights and so on. Until at two-ten there came in a call from a squad car up on Bruno Street above the S.P. yards: Something a bit more serious.

Schenke and Galeano went out on that. By what the squad car called in—

No crowds, too late, but the householder who had heard the screams and called in, the uniformed men, and the ambulance already there.

Identification in her handbag, found on the lawn up from the sidewalk. Juliet Romano. By the light from the squad car, the flashlights, she looked about twenty. She was dead. At a very good guess, by all the torn clothes, the bruises, raped and dead. Blood and all the evidences of a struggle. A very messy thing. She'd been stabbed and cut, and that—

"You know what, Bob?" said Galeano. "This looks very much like that Moreno thing. Assault, rape, murder. And the knife used. Last month, you remember. I kind of think—"

There was a full moon, a silver coin of a great white moon, sailing the heavens. As Grace said, why else call them lunatics? It might say something about X.

Chapter 6

"Why did it have to be my Juliet?" Mrs. Romano looked at Hackett and Higgins with dull, reddened eyes. "Why? A good girl, my Juliet—why did it have to happen to Juliet? Just down the street at Anna's, helping her with some sewing, Juliet was good at sewing. Why did it—"

"Mom, don't," whispered the younger girl. She'd been crying, too.

Young Robert Egan just pressed his fists together and said over the woman's dull voice, "You find the bastard, you just turn me loose on him—just—not enough left of him to—" Egan had just got engaged to Juliet two weeks ago.

They had got all they were going to get here; all the family could tell them. Hackett said meaninglessly, "Thanks very much," and Higgins opened the front door of this old house on Bruno Street, with its very neat ancient parlor furniture, the religious pictures on the walls.

Egan stood up. "You'll let us know—so we can—about the funeral and—"

"We'll let you know," said Hackett. They came out to the

84

street. They started up the block, past Hackett's scarlet Barracuda. "What do you think, George?"

"I think," said Hackett, "the Moreno case is open again. It sounds—"

"It does," said Hackett.

Juliet Romano, half a block up the street at a girl-friend's, not worried about walking the short distance home even late at night, with the full moon—a short half block. But X had caught her. The rest of it looked a lot like Rita Moreno. The assault, the rape, the vicious knifing.

"One thing," said Hackett. "We tabbed X on Moreno as the child rapist. She was only twelve. But I'm thinking now, George, that picture of her the family gave the press, she was pretty well developed for her age. She looked grown—you'd take her for sixteen easy. Maybe we were a little narrow minded on it. Now we've got Romano—nineteen—and it's a carbon copy. What do you want to bet that the autopsy'll say it's the same kind of knife?—and that wasn't a very usual knife either—wide blade, as I recall. Maybe—"

"I'm with you," said Higgins. "So we go back to Records and this time we don't sort out just the ones with the pedigree of assaulting the kids. We look at all of 'em with any record of sex violence. Is this the house?" It was another old frame house, and down from it was another obviously derelict, unoccupied, with long dry brown grass in front and a broken window on the side. If you looked carefully, you could see the trampled area in the grass, the brown stains of much blood shed, and the used flash bulbs where the lab men had taken their stark photographs.

The door of the occupied house opened before they were on the porch. Mr. Joseph Hoffenberger was anxious to cooperate with the authorities. "You're cops? I been expecting you, where you been? That poor girl—I knew her all her *life,* lived here all her—my God, if I'd been a minute sooner —but I—"

"Let's take it in order, sir," said Hackett, notebook out. "You'll be asked to sign a statement to the effect—"

"Yes, yes, anything, whatever I can do—that poor girl —my God, if I'd *known,* but what do you think, you hear screams and—these no-good kids out half the night and the drinking and horseplay—but Juliet was a good girl, nice girl, my God—"

It had been Mr. Hoffenberger who had been wakened by Juliet's screams, and after a few minutes had got up, put on his bathrobe, and opened his front door to see what the screams were about. Had seen a struggle of some sort going on, in the front yard of the empty house next door, and started over there. And had seen a man get up and run, and then found Juliet.

"My God, do I know how long before I got up? Maybe five minutes. Maybe longer. Thinking just the kids horsing around. What else? And I'd been sound asleep, your brain don't start working right, right off, you wake up sudden like that. But I think after awhile, it ain't kids, those screams are for real—and I get up, hunt around for my bathrobe— maybe another three, four minutes before I go out— What? Well, that's what I'm about to tell you, you listen. Acourse I saw the guy! There was this great big full moon, near as light as day it was— He was a big guy." Hoffenberger stared measuringly at the two big Homicide officers, chose Hackett. "About your size. Not quite as big as him," jerking a thumb at Higgins. "Not that there's much to choose between you. He—"

"Could you tell if he was white or Negro?"

"White," said Hoffenberger instantly. "That I could see in the moonlight— I couldn't give you a *description,* my God, it was all too fast, but he was a white man, and young from the way he moved. He had on a white shirt and dark pants. And when I yelled, he just—my God, and when I went over and saw—my God, Juliet, known her since—"

He'd have repeated it all, but that was all they got from him. It was something, but not too much. It led them to a rather tentative conclusion. They sat in the Barracuda and talked about it.

"Roughly the same part of town," said Hackett. "Six blocks, give or take a couple."

"Yeah. Did he do a little stalking, or take what came along?"

Hackett shrugged. Rita Moreno had lived over on Teed Street, six blocks away. She had walked down to the old Mission Church, about four blocks from there, on an early Saturday evening, with a girl friend, to make her Saturday confession. Barely eight o'clock when they started back, and the girl friend left her at the corner of Teed with half a block to walk home. And X had been waiting. That time the victim hadn't had time to scream; she'd been found an hour later by a home-coming couple.

"Well, go see what Records gives us. We can widen the field now. Ninety-nine percent sure, the same boy."

"And put out the word to the pigeons," said Higgins. He felt, illogically, a little better about the Moreno case. Looking at Rita Moreno dead there, like anybody with kids he couldn't help thinking of his own. Well, not his own, but now his responsibility—Bert Dwyer's good kids. Of Laura coming home from her piano lesson, and even the kids warned and careful, it could happen to. Now it appeared that X wasn't quite that evil a monster: not after the kids, just the females. Which was bad enough.

"So we go paw through Records again," said Hackett, starting the engine. "And give priority to any likely X we run across who knows this area—or lives here."

Temporarily, they would forget the Barron thing. This one a lot more important to find. "Full moon," said Higgins. "If Jase is right, Art, we've got a month to locate him before he goes hunting again."

"I hope that's meant as a joke," said Hackett.

A new suicide had turned up, more tiresome paperwork, and Landers had taken it, leaving Palliser to go out on Montez. They hadn't found the wife to talk to yesterday; she hadn't come home up to six o'clock. Landers had gone and looked at the suicide, a rather ordinary suicide by gas, with a nice orthodox note left, and come back to the office and was briskly typing a report, when Sergeant Lake thrust his head in the door of the sergeants' office and said, "You the only one in? That Mrs. Cunningham's here."

"Cunningham?"

"That mugging found yesterday—Grace was on it. Guy from San Diego off the Greyhound bus."

"Oh, that," said Landers, enlightened. "Oh, sure. O.K., I'll take care of her." It was Grace's day off. Landers straightened his tie and went out to the anteroom.

Mrs. Lester Cunningham was in her early thirties and would ordinarily have been a pretty woman, with naturally blonde hair in a conservative coiffure and a nice slim figure; but she'd been crying, her eyes puffy and red, and her lipstick was on crooked. She was wearing a black dress and low-heeled black shoes, and a black gabardine coat was folded on the chair arm.

"Mrs. Cunningham? I'm Detective Landers," said Landers politely. He felt sorry for the woman, having to come up here for this. They had to have formal identification of the body, of course. "Isn't there somebody else could take care of this for you, ma'am?" he asked delicately. "Mr. Cunningham's father, or some rel—"

88

She shook her head. "There isn't anyone," she said in a low voice. "He didn't have any close relatives at all. I—I'm all right." She looked up at him with more attention. "You don't look old enough to be a detective. Are you?"

She didn't know, of course, that his perennially youthful face was the bane of Landers' life; he'd just turned thirty last August, and he was still occasionally asked for proof of majority by the bartenders. He stopped himself from looking indignant and assured her he was. Poor woman, still all shook up by the news. Damn shame she had to do this.

He drove her down to the morgue, not attempting conversation, and she sat beside him in silence, gloved hands folded in her lap. It was a chilly gray day with a nasty little sharp wind; he wondered if that gabardine coat was warm enough. He told her gently there'd have to be an inquest here, and also an autopsy—that was the way the law read.

"Yes, I understand," she said dully. She didn't shrink or look frightened at the cold room; she looked wide-eyed and calmly at the upper half of the naked body when the tray was rolled out, and said, "Yes, that's Lester—my husband. That's him. Do I have to say, I identify—?"

But outside again she turned faint and the attendant went to get a glass of water while Landers sat her down on the bench. "Why did it have to be Lester?" she asked. "He was only thirty-five—and so proud of the restaurant—and he was only coming up for the day, to—"

"It's tough," said Landers. Poor woman. But she was bearing up pretty well, brave and sensible. She said she'd stay until after the inquest when she could take the body home, and he drove her back to her hotel.

And probably the mugger who had struck down Cunningham, the respectable citizen, was a drunk, an addict, a worthless bum. Always too much of that kind of thing. . . .

He had just finished typing the report on the suicide when

Palliser came in, a frown on his long dark serious face, and said, "Damn it, it's a conspiracy against us. Fate or something."

"Now what?"

"I couldn't get a damn thing out of Mrs. Montez. Everybody liked Alfredo, no trouble, no gambling, nobody owed him money. I kind of think, Tom, that he wouldn't tell her much anyway—a dumb sort of girl—maybe he was the type, women to be seen and not heard. So I went down to the office of that chain of markets and saw the personnel man. He says the same thing. Montez a good worker, hard worker, well liked, and so on. But he says, up until recently Montez had been the assistant manager of another market out on Pico, it was just since he'd been promoted he was at the new market, and probably some of the employees at the Pico market would know him better, he'd been there longer. So I went there." Palliser flung himself into his desk chair and lit a cigarette. "And what do I hear? At that market—now the new assistant manager—is one Raul Obregon, who is Montez' dearest pal, old school buddies, and who is likelier to know all about his friends and enemies?"

"So what did he tell you?"

"Nothing!" said Palliser. "He got run into by a drunk two day ago on the Hollywood freeway, and he's still on the critical list at the General. So maybe we never hear anything from him."

"Fate," said Landers. "Let's go have some lunch."

Palliser said, "Oh, hell. All right. It's just frustrating. I—"

Sergeant Lake looked in. "One of you like to talk to the Lieutenant?"

Palliser picked up the outside phone. "Lieutenant? How're you feeling? We miss you. What—"

"Like to do me a little favor, John? I'm fine, fine, all this continual fussing over me— Have a look in Records for me, will you? A Margaret O'Rourke, age early fifties, black hair, about five-six—" Palliser automatically took out his pen, scribbled down the salient points as Mendoza gave them. "Just see if she's there anywhere. I couldn't guess what lay. Just anywhere. And let me know what you find."

"Well, sure," said Palliser. "But what—"

"Thanks very much," said Mendoza. "I'll be seeing you. I'm fine, you'll have me back before you know it." He was gone.

"I'll be damned," said Palliser. "What do you suppose that's all about? First practical nurses and now—"

"What? That Cunningham woman came in. I took her to identify the corpse. How's the Lieutenant?"

"I thought," said Pallliser, "he was supposed to be convalescing from the measles."

The intensive training of an LAPD officer, and twenty-three years at the job, had disciplined the essentially erratic and conclusion-jumping Mendoza to respect for the routine. It was so often the routine that turned up evidence.

And he was plodding ahead with this routine grimly. Still possessed of the funny hunch that was not quite a hunch.

The next patient, working chronologically backward, on Mrs. O'Rourke's list, had been a Mrs. Regina Pearce on Delongpre Avenue. He had landed there at ten o'clock. The address was one side of an old duplex, ancient stucco, a brown lawn, twin strips of cement for a driveway at one side. An old, narrow street in the middle of Hollywood, and today looking cheerless under the gray overcast and the bitter wind. There had been a fall of snow in the mountains; that always brought the icy wind down here.

He pushed the bell and instantly a dog yapped shrilly inside. After a moment the door opened. "Yes?"

He pulled out the badge. He said his little piece. "Is Mrs. Pearce—"

The woman stared at him in surprise. She looked like one of those weighted tops, an overblown bosom and shoulders tapering down to slender legs and narrow feet. "Quiet, Chico, it's a nice man, a policeman, good doggies shouldn't bark at policemen." She scooped up the yapping little Chihuahua in her arms. "Mrs. Pearce? Oh, no, I'm Elsa Briggs. Why're you asking for Mrs. Pearce? She's dead. Poor thing. She died about three, no, nearer four years ago."

Mendoza had the momentary dreamlike feeling of having lived through this little scene before. He opened his mouth to ask a question, but as was so usefully the case with a certain type of female, found he'd already wound her up. The dog yapped again.

"Hush, Chico, mustn't bark at the nice man. Yes, I knew her, she used to own this place, you know. When we first moved here. She was pretty old then, poor thing, and she had asthma something awful, she was a widow and I guess didn't have much except the rent, she lived this side then and we had the other, we moved after the place was sold because this side's got a newer stove and— Then she fell and broke her hip, poor thing, and she was in the hospital awhile and then came back—quiet, Chico, mustn't interrupt Mother— but she never really got over it and it was about two months later she died. There was a real estate company we paid rent to then until the place was sold, I don't know who she left it to, she hadn't any relations, no children or anything, but like I said to Jim— Beg pardon?"

"A nurse," said Mendoza. "A practical nurse. After she came home from the hospital?"

She looked vague. "Yes, I guess there was. She couldn't take care of herself, I guess she had to have—but like I say— Chico, be quiet, Mother's talking—"

Mendoza escaped, and feeling her curious eyes on him drove the Ferrari a block down and stopped at the curb. He lit a cigarette and studied the list he'd copied down from the County Health records. When they still kept records on the practical nurses. Which they did not now do.

Some idea, something about this list, was trying to get through to his conscious mind. He couldn't pin it down . . . the Weaver end so peculiar, no logic to it at all. And this list—

Antonelli, he thought. The Antonellis. When Mrs. O'Rourke's mother had been sick and she'd had to leave the case. Well, and so what? *¿Pues qué?* That said nothing.

He looked at the list. What was he getting? A handful of nothing. She—

Antonelli. Pearce. Then Lord, on Orange Drive. Black, May 1964 and then Tramelhof, also May 1964. Oh, yes? What really decided him was the nearness of the Tramelhof address to where he was. La Cienega Boulevard.

It was an apartment building—almost, not quite, high rise, but new and smart and very expensive, probably. Mr. and Mrs. Tramelhof lived on the top floor. They were surprised to see him, but polite; they were bewildered at his questions, but answered them readily. Yes, they had employed a practical nurse in May of 1964—they smiled at each other—when Scotty was born. The Tramelhofs were young, expensively dressed, handsome people. Two nurses, actually, they said. The first one had only stayed a day or two when she had to leave—they didn't remember why. Then another one—the doctor located her—and she'd stayed for a month.

"Alice wasn't very strong after the baby came," said Tramelhof fondly.

The upright people like all these he'd been coming across were quite happy to cooperate with police, and mostly so engrossed with themselves and their own concerns, asking no questions as to why police were asking. Which would be a good question, because Mendoza didn't quite know himself. *"¡Santa Maria!"* he said, annoyed at himself. It was a quarter to twelve. He started the Ferrari and went back to Sunset Boulevard to go down to Orange Drive.

Palliser called the house on Rayo Grande Avenue at two-thirty. "Oh, Mrs. Mendoza. Sergeant Palliser. Is the Lieutenant there?"

"No, he is not," said Mrs. Mendoza, sounding cross. "And he *ought* to be. He took off from here at nine-thirty and he isn't back yet. He's got some idiotic thing in his head—I *told* him—and when the doctor said he could drive, he didn't mean he could take off and do a full day's work! I don't even know if he had sense enough to get himself a proper lunch—"

"He'll be all right," said Palliser soothingly. Sounded as if Mendoza was back to feeling his old self, and it'd be good to have him back at his desk again. "What's he up to?"

"Some crazy notion—*I* don't know what he thinks he's doing. Honestly, when the doctor *said* to take it easy—and he hasn't gained back any weight at all. He—"

"He'll be O.K.," said Palliser. "What I called about, he asked me to look in Records for this Margaret O'Rourke. I—"

"Oh, he did! He's not supposed to contact the off—"

"Well, anyway, I did and it's no go. No record, at least under that name. So if you'll tell him—"

"Oh, I'll tell him," said Mrs. Mendoza grimly. *"When* he comes home, I'll tell him. And thanks so much, Sergeant."

Palliser had an inkling she'd be telling Mendoza more than that. Mrs. Mendoza had red hair and was half Irish. But on the other hand, he didn't doubt that the Lieutenant

94

could give as good as he got, and if he was feeling well enough to be out chasing some wild goose (practical nurses?), that was good news.

The autopsy report on Montez was delivered that afternoon. Hackett glanced through it. It wasn't very enlightening, and a covering note from Dr. Bainbridge apologized for that. The body had been in such a mutilated state that it was impossible to say whether Montez had been drunk or drugged; all Bainbridge could guess was the approximate time of death, which had been between ten and midnight the night before he was found. However, the head had been intact, and Bainbridge was of the opinion that Montez had been slugged with something like a sandbag; sustained a concussion, and had possibly been unconscious when the freight hit him. Unconscious, but alive: it was the freight had done for him.

"Helpful," said Hackett. He put the report on Palliser's desk and rubbed the back of his neck thoughtfully. "You know, George, on Barron—we're stymied. It's all very well to say, so he wasn't at that damned Temple all the while— maybe he had a girl on the side, maybe he did this or that, made him a mark for what he got. With the dedicated-minister front, nobody'd be likely to know one thing about it but Rodney Terhune, and he's not going to tell us." He ground out his cigarette in the ashtray on Palliser's desk. "I tell you, though, I keep wondering how that pair attracted so many people to that place. Seven hundred—well, I know, the lonely people, but they were all—the ones we saw—a little better type than that kind of thing usually attracts. I just thought—"

"The Brainard female," said Higgins. "The—but people, Art, they do go for what Jase calls the mumbo-jumbo."

"I just think," said Hackett slowly, "just for fun I might drop into the Temple and see what actually goes on. Because—"

"Waste of time," said Higgins. "Are we going to lean on this punk or not?"

"We'll lean on him."

"We only lived here six months," said the slatternly-looking woman. The baby in her arms yelled and she joggled it automatically. "I wouldn't know nothing about anybody lived here before."

Mendoza was feeling (he admitted to himself) tired. Also frustrated and increasingly annoyed by some insistent small something trying to work itself into his conscious mind. Routine be damned—it was all too damned routine, the ridiculous wild-goose chase.

Orange Drive was another drab backwater of the city. To people elsewhere, you said Hollywood and it conjured up an immediate vision of glamour: But Hollywood was just another city. A city within the big city, and it had more of the old, shabby, middle-class streets, and ordinary middle-class people, than it had the celebrities and mansions with swimming pools.

Along here were more old frame single houses, brown lawns, and ordinary people. Workaday people, vaguely willing to answer questions from a cop, but in this case unable to.

He tried all three houses down from the address given for Mrs. William Lord before he found anyone to answer his questions. There he found a very old man in a wheelchair, who told him in a cracked voice about Mrs. Lord.

"Husband was a railroad man—she had his pension and that was all. Didn't know her, to *know* her, see what I mean—just a neighbor—but I knew that. Old lady—not as old as me now, but seventy, seventy-one. All alone in the world. Owned that house, about all she had. Couldn't say what she died of, seem to recall she had a stroke. She was poorly quite awhile before she passed on. What say? Sure, was a nurse—before she died. She finally got where she had to have a nurse. Was the nurse arranged the funeral and all —know that because I offered—I was a lot better then, on my feet, getting around, and bein' a retired railroad man myself I felt it was the least I could do—but the nurse'd already— Hey? Couldn't say about that. There wasn't no family—nobody. But it's a matter o' four years back, why're you askin' around now?"

Mendoza plodded back to the Ferrari. He had, angrily, to admit that his legs felt a little shaky and the cold east wind was penetrating the topcoat Alison had insisted he put on. Damn fool, out on this business of nothing, chasing around asking the questions and getting— On no business of his, Mairí's peculiar little tale, and nothing in it—

Something, some pertinent fact nudging at the door of his consciousness— But hunch be damned, nothing to it.

He climbed gratefully into the Ferrari. All of a sudden he felt a long way from home. All of a sudden, he wanted to forget this silly obsessive hunt for a nonexistent hare in the bushes, and go home, to the nice central heating and Alison's warm voice scolding him and the twins' noisy energy and a cat on his lap. He shivered, the sudden chill shaking him. Ridiculous.

He'd be all right, fine, if he could just get back to his own job. Very likely the only reason he'd taken any interest in the somewhat puzzling but probably perfectly explicable altruistic practical nurse.

Explicable?

97

—Is the root of all evil, he thought. Not money: the love of it. If Luis Mendoza had learned anything in life, that he knew. And there were very few human people who were not interested in money. Even the honest ones, always in the vast majority, were interested in turning a buck where they could.

Hell, it wasn't any of his business. He was Central Homicide LAPD. This wasn't his beat up here: even if there was something—something a little wrong—some way—

¿A que viene eso? The essential choice made when he took the oath. A cop made the conscious choice, white against black, good against evil, creativity against destruction.

He fumbled for his keys, started the engine. A long way home. He would go home and think about it, and maybe the little something would get through to him.

Alison would be there, scolding him, and the warmth of home, his own place, and—

But for the grace of God, said his mind. Where had that come from?

Higgins took off a few minutes early. He stopped at the bookstore on Hyperion, on his way home (and that had still a strange sound to him, home, for he hadn't had a real home in years) to pick up a new book for Stevie. *Ivanhoe,* he seemed to remember it'd been required reading when he was in school, but not now. From what he remembered of it, Steve would like it. Reading a lot more now, Steve was, since the accident. With the brace, he couldn't do much else. But with the therapy twice a week at Children's Hospital, they said he'd be fine eventually.

Higgins never turned into the drive of the house on Silver Lake Boulevard without a feeling of surprise that it was his place. His new place. Home.

When he went in, Mary was standing over the stove. His beautiful Mary. She smiled at him and he kissed her humbly. Laura was practicing on the piano.

"I've got a new book for Steve. I thought—"

"You spoil him," said Mary. "You shouldn't, George."

"But you like him to read more—you said—"

Chapter 7

RESIGNEDLY Hackett watched the ex-con Jay Benson out of the Homicide office. He said, "Damnation." Benson was the fourth possible out of Records they'd fetched in. Unlike the other three, Benson was definitely out of the running; he had an alibi. He'd been picked up for questioning by the Newton Street boys and at the time Juliet Romano was being murdered had been closeted with the night crew there.

"If you ask me," said Jason Grace behind him, "this office has gone all to pot since we've been missing the Lieutenant. Falling to pieces. What we need is some organization around here."

"All right, tell us what more to do," said Hackett. "Any bright ideas on anything?"

"One—not very bright," said Grace. "John talked to that sister from the school—the one was in the hospital. She said Rita Moreno had told her a big man had followed her and scared her. Which should make us wonder if he—mmm—does a little casing first. Picks the victims."

"And so what?" said Hackett. "Well, of course—"

"It's just an idea. I don't say it suggests any new places to look."

"No—and Juliet Romano hadn't said anything about being followed—the family would have come out with that right away. But she might not have noticed him, at that. She worked over at a dress shop on Broadway, and if he'd had a look at her in the crowds over there—"

"It's just an idea," said Grace again. Hackett grinned at him.

"You're always a great one for having ideas, Jase. Look, while George and I continue at the routine on this thing, would you like to do a little poking around on Barron? I mean, we can't just leave that lay—we ought to go through the motions on it."

Grace laughed. "So we do. As a matter of fact, I've had a little idea about that, too. I don't mind."

Higgins looked out the window. "Seems to me we're getting more than our usual share of rain this year. So now we go and look for the next one on the list—that Marty Coffman. And ten to one find he was in the drunk tank or something." He sighed.

It was nine-fifteen on Saturday morning, and a thin steady drizzle of rain had just started. Another body had been found over on Skid Row; probably dope or *vino;* Piggott had gone out on that, and it was Glasser's day off. Palliser came in from somewhere with Landers, and as Grace left the office Hackett hailed them.

"Look, we could use a hand in grilling these punks—when we locate them. If you—"

"I've got this damn Montez thing—"

Grace went downstairs, turned up his collar and pulled down his hat before ducking out into the rain. Virginia had advised him to take a raincoat. At least he had the top up on the Elva. He ducked into her, his sweet little racer, and switched on the wipers with the engine. He had had just a small thought about the Temple of the Holy Inner Light, a rather simple thought the other boys didn't seem to have considered.

Most churches—using the word loosely—had sextons. Caretakers of some kind. And if the Temple had, wasn't it likely he'd be found there on a Saturday, getting the place all shipshape for Sunday? It seemed reasonable to Grace.

When he pulled up in the red-painted curb section in front of the place, he was gratified to find that apparently he'd guessed right. There was a battered ancient pickup truck parked ahead of the Elva, with an equally ancient power mower in it, and a thin elderly man was just stowing aboard a lawn edger.

Grace hopped out and hailed him, showing the badge, and asked questions. The elderly man was one Tyler Peabody. He looked alarmed and surprised. They sat in the front seat of the truck, out of the rain.

"Sure, I take care o' the grass an' bushes here once a week —Saturdays. I'd be doin' more today except it started rainin'. I took care o' the propitty when it was first built, the People of God Church 'twas then—awful strict church people, disapproved of mighty nigh ever'thing there is. I guess they got foreclosed on, anyway they shut the church, 'n' then awhile back when I see it was open, some other minister, I come and asked. Twenty a month they pay me—used t' have ten, twelve jobs a day, all over, out in the valley an' Hollywood, but now I'm on the pension. A cop, askin' about— they ain't nothin' wrong about the *church* people?"

"Well, now, let's just say you could have a little more respectable employers," said Grace. "What I'd like to ask you, while you were inside cleaning and so on, have you ever just happened to overhear these two ministers talking

102

together—or with any of the members, maybe? Just anything—"

"Oh, I ain't allowed in the church," said Peabody. "I don't do no work in there. Just outside. I guess they got their own caretaker, dust and like that."

"Oh," said Grace. "You don't go into the church at all?"

Peabody shook his head. "It's allus locked, I'm here. Unless the minister, one or t'other, 's there. I never been inside the place. This one minister, couldn't say his name, he made that plain when he give me the job. But there ain't anything wrong with the *church*, is there? Cops coming—"

"I don't know, Mr. Peabody," said Grace, "but I think you could have a—mmm—more secure job."

And if he hadn't got what he'd hoped he might get, that was something to think about. What was in the church that the incurious, obviously honest gardener mustn't see?

The interesting thing was, of course, that the lab crew had gone through the church and hadn't found anything suggestive at all.

Or had Barron and Terhune just been secretive on general principles?

And come to think, they still didn't know why the Sunday collection had been there on Tuesday when Barron got murdered.

The General Hospital—when he finally got his identity across and found somebody who knew something—told Palliser that Raul Obregon was now off the critical list and expected to survive, but still in serious condition and in no state for police questioning.

"When can I talk to him? It's an important—"

"I couldn't give you a definite time, Sergeant—sorry. At least two days. Possibly on Monday, if his progress is—"

103

"This is a homicide and he could be an important witness. I'd appreciate it if you could let me see him tomorrow."

"Out of the question," snapped authority. "You can check with us on Monday, not before, Sergeant."

Palliser swore and put the phone down. He supposed he and Tom might as well help out on the rape-killer, they weren't getting anywhere on Montez, and there was just nowhere else to look. He passed that on to Landers.

"And what about the fellow who approached him in the restaurant and went out with him?"

"We don't know that's got anything to do with it at all," said Palliser reasonably. "A fellow he knew—and his wife was away, so they went and had a few beers together somewhere, and—look, for all we know that was this Obregon, and he hasn't come and told us because he's in the hospital."

"Well, whatever, his car ought to turn up somewhere pretty soon," said Landers.

Palliser agreed, yawning. Roberta was out house-hunting these days, and most evenings had a new one to drag him off to look at. So far they hadn't found anything they could possibly afford, that either of them liked, but at least Roberta was having fun looking.

Hackett poked his head in the door. Beyond him, in the corridor outside, Higgins passed behind a hulk of a ragged-looking big fellow, and a whiff of stale wine drifted in. Hackett looked harassed.

"So all right, go do some work for a change," he said. "Here's another one we want to look at on Romano—Leroy Kegel. Suppose you go see if he's still at this address and fetch him in."

Palliser got up. "O.K., what's the address?"

"In fact, here's the list," said Hackett, "of all of 'em we picked out of Records. You can both go looking."

Alison had said she absolutely refused to let him out of the house today. And he knew how tired he'd been last night —gallivanting all over—he was supposed to be resting. Having a vacation. And he hadn't gained back a pound—

"Two pounds," said Mendoza. "I was up to one-fifty-seven this morning."

"Well, a step in the right direction," said Alison. "But you're staying home today."

"I will not be ordered around by a female," said Mendoza. "I think I'll stay home, *cara*."

He didn't have any compulsion to go out in the rain, in the chill damp day. He sat smoking too much over *Actions and Reactions,* half bored and somnolent in the comfortable central heating. The twins came and demanded to be read to, and he fetched the *Just-So Stories* and complied until Mairí came to whisk them away for lunch and their naps. The rain started to sound more in earnest, and he told Alison to be careful when she came to ask if there was anything special he wanted at the market. "Yes, yes," she said, drawing on gloves, tucking a stray strand of red hair under the rain-hood. "I will be. Be good, *marido*."

He thought, after she'd left, that they'd made a mistake not having a fireplace. There was something about a crackling fire, on a gray rainy day—

He brought out the list from his shirt pocket and studied it. He'd smoked and ruminated over it this morning, after breakfast, but whatever small notion had tried to push itself into his consciousness about it, yesterday, was silent now.

Fuller. Wilkerson. The Antonellis. Regina Pearce. The Tramelhofs. Lord. And about fifty other names on the list. Back to 1954. One place she'd been six months—another five. The altruistic practical nurse, Margaret O'Rourke, in this year of grace working cheerfully away for twenty-five bucks a week. Now, for seven—eight weeks, with poor arthritic old Mrs. Weaver on the state pension.

White tablets. Aspirin.

The house was very quiet. Bast and Sheba were tangled together, sound asleep, on his lap; their warm weight was somehow comfortable. Old ladies frequently had cats: Mendoza wondered drowsily whether Mrs. Fuller, Miss Wilkerson, Mrs. Pearce and Mrs. Lord had had cats, and what had happened to them. El Señor was probably with the twins, and Nefertite with Mairí. The Mendoza cats preferred laps and beds for napping.

Fuller. Wilkerson. Antonelli. Pearce. Tramelhof. Lord. Four poor and two rich. Two quick and four dead.

Mendoza slid down a little in the big leather armchair, his feet propped on the ottoman, and presently, insidiously, he was asleep. . . .

He was back in the old Facel-Vega, that wild night, tearing down the beach highway—Alison, Alison—hearing the high screaming noise of the fender jammed against the front tire, ready to blow any minute—he was trying to remember the words, *Dios te salve, Maria, llena eres de gracia*—Alison—the rape-killer they'd been hunting so long, how many women dead, and an innocent man gassed for it, and now they knew him but he had Alison, he had Alison, and Luis Mendoza was fifty minutes behind him—That tire was going to blow, and Art beside him saying over and over, numbly, For God's sake, Luis, for God's sake—and the scream of the siren behind, faithful squad-car driver hanging on, the speedometer touching three figures—Alison, *Santa Maria, madre de Dios—por nosotros*— He was going to kill him, he was going to—never make it in time—*For God's sake, Luis*—

"Luis! Wake up! What on earth—"

Mendoza snarled and roused up half out of the chair in one motion, suddenly awake in one moment. She was bending over him, shaking his shoulder. His heart was pounding and his forehead wet with sweat. He tried to catch his breath.

"You sounded as if you were having a fit. I just got in—"

"*La pesadilla*," he grunted. "I'm all right. God, what a—"

"You can't have a nightmare in the middle of the afternoon," said Alison sensibly.

"Well, I did." Suddenly he pulled her down to him, annoying the cats, who fled. He adjusted her across his lap and kissed her.

"Well!" said Alison. "You *are* feeling better!"

"*Mas vale tarde que nunca*. I was dreaming that—never mind." And quite suddenly then the thing struck him—the little something that had tried to get through. He didn't do any ruminating then on symbolic dreams, or subconscious interpretations; he simply said, "*¡Vaya por Dios!*" and grabbed for his list, crumpled in his lap under Alison's thigh. "*Dios*—why didn't I—yes, but— A fair sampling? What the hell—"

"Now what?" said Alison. "I thought you were feeling amorous."

"I am feeling—" he stared at the list. He adjusted her more comfortably against his shoulder and reached for a cigarette.

"Manners," said Alison, and he gave it to her, lit it and reached for another.

"Here we have six patients of the altruistic Mrs. O'Rourke," he said dreamily. "Six patients taken at random. The latest six chronologically speaking—that we know about, on this list—but you can say at random. Four dead, two alive. The two quick ones rich, the four dead ones poor. And every one of those four women, we can also say, were very much alike—and very much like Mrs. Weaver. They were old, they hadn't much in the way of material goods, and they hadn't any relatives at all."

"And what are you trying to prove?" said Alison. "In a metropolis of seven and a half million people, *querido,* how many people are there like that?"

"Quite a few," said Mendoza. "And I'm wondering how many more on this list. And how many not listed, since they stopped keeping records. I really do."

"What do you mean?"

"Janet Cox said something about doctors." He emitted a thin blue stream of smoke. "Look, *enamorada,* you take an old woman who's had a stroke, or a heart attack, in the seventies, say, no loving family clustered around—nobody is surprised or very much concerned when she dies. Least of all a busy doctor. Nobody thinks much about it. Poor old soul, a happy release. And—as far as that goes—" he drew strongly on the cigarette—"maybe nobody should wonder. I just say that nobody would be surprised. Nobody to be interested. And I'll tell you what gave me the little idea, too. The Antonellis. The Tramelhofs."

"What on earth—"

"She was sent to Mrs. Antonelli, and there's substantial money there, but also a concerned husband and family. Nothing there but the monthly wages—and I'll bet it was more than twenty-five bucks a week. So she made the excuse to leave. And before, when she'd been sent to Mrs. Tramelhof. Same deal. She made the excuse. Why? No pickings. No—"

"Look, you're talking about Mrs. Weaver's nurse? This— Pickings? From somebody on the state pension?" Almost against her will Alison was interested, arguing. "That's been the funny thing, as Mairí said, Luis. She's got nothing, Mrs. Weaver. And I don't know anything about those others you just—but you said—"

"Poor," said Mendoza meditatively. "It's a relative term, isn't it? I just had a few thoughts about that, too. And I think this little list should be checked through very carefully. I really do." He looked at it. "Names—addresses. It's a frightening thought—it came to me awhile ago, too, you remember our dismembered corpse in Echo Park Lake— frightening, how easily a certain kind of person can just drop out of life and not be missed. Missed, or thought about. Fuller—Wilkerson—Pearce—Lord. Old women with nobody at all close, to care a great deal what happens to them. Old, so when they died, a happy release. They had this and that, as old people usually do—asthma, a stroke, a broken hip. And just died. The doctor signs the death certificate, and that's that."

"But, Luis—you aren't thinking—"

"No, not really, on that," said Mendoza. "What I am thinking—" He smoked in silence, and put out his cigarette in the ashtray beside him, and looked down at her. "You haven't got the diamond earrings on."

"Not in the middle of the afternoon."

"Plain jade, and very nice, too. Worth a little something," said Mendoza, "if not as much. But how much is much? Added to another muchness?"

"You are simply being annoying. Making mysteries, because—"

"No, but just think about it, *cara*. It's only just occurred to me. You've driven Mairí down there, to Mrs. Cox's house. That block of houses. What would you say a house down there—Mrs. Weaver's house—cost when it was built?"

"The *house?*" Alison reached for the ashtray to put out her cigarette. "Heavens, I don't know—in the twenties? Everything was cheap, compared to—three thousand?"

"I'd guess between two and three. What's it worth now, to sell?"

She stared at him. "Well—"

"*Pues si*, inflated values. But what? For the land alone? In the middle of Hollywood? I'd also have a guess—well, I know, that court there—that's R-1 zoned. As most of those blocks would be—old places, a little shabby, business areas grown up around them. Orange Drive," said Mendoza thoughtfully. "Delongpre Avenue. Cimarron——"

"What are you talking about?"

"The root of all evil," said Mendoza. "Only how—but yes, I see it—women like that, widows, and nobody close, so they probably wouldn't think about— But on the other hand, if any of them had, how would— Simple enough. *Si*. White tablets. I wonder. Oh, my God, this is so far out— Am I exercising my imagination?"

"Probably," said Alison.

"And maybe not, too. Because—" he looked at the list. "Nobody knew," he said. "The real estate company collecting the rent for awhile. I wonder. I think—it's something to look at. And, of course, nothing for me. Not my beat. And on the other hand—*naturalmente*—what would Wilcox Street say? Locking stable doors—with the horse still inside —is not a job for policemen. We have to wait for the horse to be stolen. But if this is so—maybe there's been a whole stable full of horses stolen."

"I don't see at all what—"

Mendoza brought her upright, kissed her again, shoved her off to her feet, and slapped her behind. "I don't know that I see very clearly either—just that there's something *to* see. Go and tend to your domesticities. I'm going to try to locate somebody intelligent at Wilcox Street."

Scarne wandered into the Homicide office about three o'clock.

"Hi," he said. "I got this and that for you."

"From the *lab?*" said Landers with elaborate surprise. "On a *recent* case?"

"Sarcasm yet. We like to take our time and be careful. But one thing I've got for you, you've only yourselves to blame you didn't get it before. Sloppy police work," said Scarne. "First things first. We haven't finished with Romano's clothes, but I've got a little something for you on the nail scrapings. She'd fought him, all right. Drawn a little blood. It's type O."

"Great," said Landers. That was the commonest type.

"There were some hairs in the scrapings. They're dark blond."

"That's more helpful."

"And that's all on Romano unless we get something more off the clothes. But—" Scarne produced an envelope—"this you really should have got yourselves. Or am I expecting too much of you Hawkshaws? Maybe. You sent us the clothes from that Barron guy. After, naturally, you'd pawed 'em all over for what he had in his pockets."

"Which was not much," said Grace.

"That's your business. There was a tear in the right jacket pocket," said Scarne. "I was just being thorough—thought something might have slipped down it. Something had." He fished it out of the envelope and handed it to Grace. "No prints on it to identify."

"Well, well, well," said Grace. "How interesting."

It was a business card, bent and rather grimy. On the face was the legend, The Jolly Huntsman Inn, an address way out on Sepulveda Boulevard. Cocktails—dancing—entertainment, said the card, 10 A.M. to 2 A.M. seven days a week. And on the back of the card was a scrawled notation in smeared pencil: *Margie, 9 P.M. 17th.*

"I just thought you'd like to see it," said Scarne.

"Thanks so much," said Grace. "We do. We should have noticed that tear."

Scarne waved a hand and went out. Landers studied the card and said, "A girl friend. The dedicated minister."

"Could be. I just think I'll go down there and have a look. You tell Art where I've gone, hah?" Grace reached for his hat.

It was still raining, a dispirited drizzle that had nevertheless got everything very wet, as much as a real storm. The rain slowed Grace in driving, even in his bright blue little racer, out toward the beach on Sepulveda.

The Jolly Huntsman Inn, when he found it, was typical of a thousand and one pseudo-elegant joints in the county. Old English decor, and Grace would have a shrewd bet they got about fifty highballs out of a fifth of Johnny Walker. He was greeted with dismay, alarm, and suspicion—but he generously reckoned that wasn't on account of his complexion, but the LAPD badge. And it had been a long bet that Margie was connected to The Jolly Huntsman—Barron might have used the back of the card to note down a rendezvous with any girl he knew—but it paid off.

Margie Vacciarello was one of the cocktail waitresses here. With reluctance, after some prying, the bartender parted with her address. "What the hell cops want with Margie? This is a clean place, we don't—Margie never done nothing—"

Margie lived on Second Street in Santa Monica. She wasn't due at work until five oclock. Grace went to have a look at her, hoping she was home. He thought Margie sounded fairly rewarding. For the Barron case still on Homicide's hands.

Margie was home. She was about thirty, a plumpish blonde, by request, with pale mauve lipstick and a Brooklyn accent. The apartment was small, untidy, and rather dirty. A man's jacket hung over a chair, a dirty male shirt trailed on the floor in the doorway to the bedroom, and there was a pipe in the ashtray on the coffee table.

Margie was in kelly-green capris and a tight knitted over-blouse.

Grace was polite—he was always polite—but he terrified Margie.

"I don't know anybody named Barron," she said hurriedly. "I don't—"

"Now, Mrs. Vacciarello—is it Mrs.?"

"Yes," she said. She cast a harried glance at the door. "My husband—I don't know anybody by that name you said. I really don't—I don't know why you—"

"Now, Mrs. Vacciarello," said Grace, "please don't try to lie to us. We know you knew Mr. David Barron. We have —mmm—proof. All I'd like to ask you—"

She backed away from him. "No, I didn't—honest—"

"It'll save time if you admit it," said Grace benignly. "We know that you—"

"Look, we gotta be polite to the customers—if maybe he was a customer and I was a little nice and he thought I— But I didn't— Honest, I—"

"All right, so it was like that. He was a customer and you were nice and polite to him." Grace smiled at her. "Shall we take it from there, Mrs. Vacciarello? Where'd you meet him at nine o'clock on the seventeenth? Last month, the month before? We just want to—"

She put a hand to her mouth; her eyes were shocked and frightened. "Bill would *kill* me—"

Aha, thought Grace. Something very interesting. A good hot lead. So Margie had been playing around with dedicated minister Barron, and maybe husband Bill had found out, and—

113

Willy-nilly, she'd be made to talk. Persuaded to talk. Make a statement. And they'd be talking to Bill, too.

About three-thirty, a very large young man ambled into the office and said, "They told me downstairs to come up here, and that guy out there said to come and ask you."

"Yes?" Landers got up.

"I just seen it." He was about twenty-five, a big young man with dark curly hair and an open, friendly, slightly stupid face. He showed the newspaper to Landers: last night's *Herald-Examiner*. "What an awful thing. It didn't say what he died of, a heart attack or what. Awful. And he wasn't old either."

The newspaper story was a couple of lines, on a back page. "The body of a man identified as Lester G. Cunningham of San Diego was found by police yesterday, on Los Angeles Street. Cause of death is undetermined."

"Oh—yes," said Landers. "What—"

"Well, see, I knew him," said the young man. "I oughta say, my name's Roy Hill. It was Mr. Cunningham give me my first job, back I was in high school—at his restaurant. I was a bus boy. He was a nice guy, Mr. Cunningham. I worked for him nearly three years, see. Until I went in the Army. He was nice to me. I been up here a coupla years now, since I got outta the Army, but anyways, I see this, I feel awful about it. Poor Mr. Cunningham. What'd he die of, anyway?"

"Well, he was mugged," said Landers. "Killed."

"Oh, gee, that's awful. His wife must feel just awful. But when I saw it, I thought I'd kind of like to see him. Pay my last respects, like. You know. He was nice to me. I'd like to go see him. That guy out there said somebody'd hafta take me. Could I?"

"Well, I guess so," said Landers. It was a little nuisance,

but they were supposed to be here to serve the citizenry. Landers took him downstairs to his car and drove him to the morgue. . . . Inquests on Barron and Montez on Monday; on Cunningham, probably Tuesday. The courts were busy.

In the cold room, he gave the name to the attendant and stood idly by, waiting until Hill had paid his last respects. The little routine job.

And when Roy Hill said, looking at the naked torso on the tray, "But that ain't Mr. Cunningham! That ain't him atall—what's goin' on here, anyways? You get bodies mixed up or something? I swear to God that ain't Mr. Cunningham—" Landers felt most completely astonished.

He'd felt so sorry for that poor woman.

Chapter 8

A GOOD deal earlier than that, Mendoza sat in a chair beside the desk of Captain Garden at the Wilcox Street precinct, the list on the desk between them. "You're telling me that this woman has swindled all these people out of—" Garden paused. "That's not the right word."

"No," agreed Mendoza. "If it was done the way I think it was done, it's all been legal, *absolutamente*. Which is the difficulty it poses us. And what a— In the first place, nobody was much interested in these people. Old people alone. And in the second place, everybody thought of them as poor. Relative term. But I'll bet you, Captain, I'll just bet you— she got those houses Pearce and Wilkerson and Lord owned, and whatever personal possessions the Fuller woman had— and who's to say what that was? And there are forty, fifty other names still to check. *Vaya por Dios,* what an imagination—to see what a gold mine it could be!" He laughed. "Pearce, for instance, that old duplex over on Delongpre. Shabby, a run-down street. But what'd it sell for? Income property in the middle of Hollywood? These days?"

"I see that," said Garden. "Twenty thousand easy. But if you think she got 'em to make wills—"

"The only way she could do it, isn't it?" Mendoza leaned back, smoking lazily. "She'd fuss over them all motherly, get them under her thumb, grateful to kind nursie. Some of them would respond to that. And maybe a few on her list hadn't—mmm—kept all their faculties, and were easily persuaded—or fooled. And as long as they weren't obviously senile, would the lawyer think twice? Over a little estate hardly worth the will? And it was only where there was property she'd have to bother to get a will. As with Fuller, clear out all the personal possessions. And it could be, Captain, that she ran across a strong-minded elder citizen here and there, too. But that's where we come in. I think. Because it's no crime to inherit property, but if the wills were made under duress—or under drugs—or under false pretenses, it's a felony. I don't recall the number of the statute, but—"

Garden passed a hand over his heavy face. "But talk about far out—what a lay! And you're right, nobody would think twice. Who'd know? Nothing to connect the people except the nurse, and little people—"

"A lot of little loot adds up to a lot," said Mendoza. "What might any old gent or lady like that have? Ten to one, when there's a house, it's paid for, Captain. Houses like those, old, shabby, not too fancy areas—but clear of debt. Woman like Mrs. Fuller, who's to say she didn't have five or ten thousand in stocks and bonds tucked away? Possibly even negotiable bonds. A little family jewelry. If nursie cleared a thousand or two for every patient like that—and there'd be the windfalls, the property. I've given you six random samples, and they say a lot. Maybe Antonelli and Tramelhof say more."

117

"Yes—the times," nodded Garden. Mendoza grinned at him; Garden was a smart cop.

"She didn't stay. Why? Mrs. Antonelli wouldn't have wanted her long—a week or two. Mrs. Tramelhof ditto. But she couldn't be bothered—she was looking for the suitable marks. The old people alone. A lot like that around. When you think about it, Captain, almost any elderly person who has to hire a practical nurse is going to be alone, minus family. Because if they're not already in a rest home —no need for practical nurses there—it's the ones without family to rally around who'd be in the market. And I wouldn't mind betting that we'll come across a few more like Antonelli—people who hired her, younger people, with families around, and when she'd sized them up she made the excuse to leave."

"Yes, I see it, but this is water under the bridge," said Garden. "Very funny lay, the first time I've come across— but we're kind of busy here. After all, Mendoza—well, it's a damn shame for people to be victimized like this—if you're right—and I'm sorry, but it's a very small count, just the possible drugs, and I think the statute of limitations has run out for some of these older cases. I see it, but I can't use the time or men to do all the legwork on this." He sighed and rubbed his jaw.

"There's no statute of limitations on homicide," said Mendoza.

"You think she went that far?"

"I think it's possible. Just. Considering some of the dates. People don't die to order. I'll just say this. I think very possibly—thinking about Mrs. Weaver—she did come across some of the strong-minded, tough old people—still with all the faculties as the saying goes. Who resisted nursie's blandishments. And that she did use the drugs on them, to dull their minds and keep them manageable, confuse them enough that way so they'd sign on the dotted line, and yet look to the lawyer just like a shaky senior citizen. It'd have been a simple matter—letter to the lawyer, outlining terms of the simple will, and then probably the lawyer coming to the house with witnesses. But if that's so—and it's the way I see it—well, the dope can't have done them any good, you know. And after she had the nice will, the lawyer obviously unsuspicious, she might easily have got impatient and used a little bit more of whatever it was."

"I presume," said Garden, "death certificates on all of them nice and legal."

"*Sí*. Just what I said. The busy doctor—most doctors busy these days—he's a lot more concerned about the patients he can cure than somebody old with the chronic trouble he can't do much about. One like that slips off a little sooner than he might have expected, does he think twice about signing the certificate?"

"And so just what can we do about it? Now? Even if you're right? I don't know about Central Division, Mendoza, but we're *busy*. How the hell can I say I'll use time and men following this—exercise in imagination? No, I see what you mean, I think you're probably right about this female's game, but what the hell we can do about it— There's no way to prove she gave a corpse dope, after this time. It—"

"There may be some more recent than 1965."

"So how the hell do we find them? Paw through all the wills on file?"

"I know. But—"

"There's not one damn thing we can do on it. I—"

"There's Mrs. Weaver," said Mendoza. "The current mark. And the devil of that is—" he ground out his cigarette. "*Amigo*, this female ought to be stopped. For good. That is a vicious little new game she's invented. I don't like it."

119

"Neither do I, but—"

"So we make the bold frontal attack, march in with your doctor here and find out whether Mrs. Weaver's been fed drugs. Scare the hell out of O'Rourke. What's the charge and the longest term?"

"I'd have to look it up," said Garden. "Technicalities. Not a very usual—"

"No. And so she serves thirty days or nothing at all, and goes to Denver or Miami or New York and starts all over again. Also, if she's using drugs, whatever, she's getting them some place and we'd like to know where."

"So?" said Garden.

"So, I'm saying—I know it's your beat, I know you're busy, but—I think somebody should go very thoroughly into this list of patients, and I'd lay you we'll get enough circumstantial evidence—after all, it's sufficiently unusual for a practical nurse to inherit from ten or twenty or thirty patients—that—*por Dios,* we might not be able to charge her with a damned thing, I know, but we could get her M.O. privately circulated around the country. Don't tell me, an empty gesture. I'm aware of the laws of libel. The nurses' employment agencies could be warned—privately. Which is not much, *se.* But, damn it, we ought to try to do *something!*"

Garden poked a pen at his blotter. "And—from six samples—maybe you've got quite an imagination."

"Seven. Mrs. Weaver. Tell me why O'Rourke is on that job for twenty-five bucks per week."

"That," said Garden dryly, "is what convinces me."

"That property would bring her another twenty thousand. Maybe more."

"*What* a lay," said Garden. "Nobody thinks of little people like that having— But what you add it up— Hell! I'd like to stop her, too, but it's just too vague a thing—and nothing of a legal charge— to spend all the man-hours on."

"I was afraid you'd say so. In your place I'd probably say the same." Mendoza shrugged and laughed. "So I'll gamble a little. We'll let a good agency work at it. Have you got a reliable one up here?"

Garden said after a moment, "Forsythe and Mason. That could run into money, Lieutenant."

"*Por des gracias de Dios,* I've got some to spend." Mendoza got up. "I'd just like to see that little game stopped for good."

"Look," said Garden. "You could get rid of a small fortune for nothing. And we've got more authority. Sure, that outfit's all right, but—you're convinced, I'm halfway convinced, this female is working this far-out con game, but it's no evidence—six examples. Look, I think we ought to be a little surer about it before you bring in any private eyes. If you're serious about that. Suppose I let you have a man the rest of today and tomorrow, and you look at a few more names on this list. See what turns up. If any more like that show, well, I'd say that's good circumstantial evidence. And if we can turn up the wills, that's better. First thing my man's going to do is go down to the Hall of Records—yes, I know it's closed until Monday but we can twist a few arms, emergency—and check on those possible wills." He picked up the phone on his desk. "Send Collins in, will you? Collins is a good boy," he added to Mendoza. "He's waiting for a witness in the hospital to come to right now, so he'll have a little time. He'll be interested in this rigmarole. Of *all* the—"

"That's fair enough," said Mendoza. "We'll do that."

"But what the hell *could* we get her on?" Garden reached to the little bookcase on the wall behind him and took out a battered edition of *Statutes of the State of California.*

"Dangerous Drugs—unlawful use of—what'd she likely be using, do you think?"

"There you've got me," said Mendoza.

A tall fair-haired young man came in and Garden said, "Lieutenant Mendoza, Detective Collins. Mendoza's from Central, Dan, but he's been poking around on our beat all illegal while he's on leave. He's got the billy-be-damndest tale to tell you ever heard—" Collins looked interested— "and you're going to do some poking around with him to-day and tomorrow."

"Yes, sir," said Collins.

"Because I suppose, damn it, that we ought to try to do *something*," said Garden. "Even if we only got her on some technicality over illegal prescriptions or something, it'd be a charge and we could pass on the story to the Feds—"

Denver, New York, and the F.B.I. finally got around to answering Hackett's queries about David Barron and Rod-ney Terhune. Denver wired a complete denial of any knowledge of Terhune that Saturday morning. New York had never heard of Barron, and his prints were not among their collection. Washington, however, knew Terhune. At three-thirty, as Hackett and Higgins had just called a break in questioning another possible out of Records, the F.B.I. came through.

They had Terhune's prints listed under the name of Rod-ney Yorke. He had been picked up in Philadelphia in 1953, then aged sixteen, for petty theft; again in 1956 for at-tempted swindling; and in 1960 at a real con game, a door-to-door racket selling nonexistent washing machines. That was the first time he'd been printed. He'd done a year in the county jail, and after 1961 Philadelphia hadn't heard of him. Nor had any other law-enforcement agency.

"Well." Hackett ruminated about that. "Not very helpful, except it confirms what we guessed about him. Rodney Yorke. He likes fancy names, evidently— I wonder if either of them is real. And I wonder if confronting him with this would make him talk more? Probably not. George—"

Higgins was staring out the window of Mendoza's office, smoking. "George!" said Hackett.

"Hah?"

"I swear—" Hackett began, when Landers looked in and beckoned to him excitedly.

"Listen, you'd better sit in on this—I swear to God I don't believe it, I felt sorry for the woman—she must be another Sarah Bernhardt—but why would it cross anybody's mind? Of all things—oh, Jase said to tell you he's off on a lead on Barron. Looked pretty good too, Scarne—"

"What's up?"

"Well, just come and hear," said Landers. "They do say, the female of the species—but she put up a damned good act, never crossed my mind but what she—" He crooked a finger and a big, slightly stupid-looking young man came in. He was looking indignant and bewildered. "Roy Hill," said Landers. "You tell 'em, Roy."

"Well, it ain't," said Hill. "It ain't Mr. Cunningham in that morgue down there. *I* know Mr. Cunningham—worked for him for three years, and I——"

"Cunningham?" said Hackett.

"That mugging down by the Greyhound Bus station," Landers reminded him. "His wife came up from San Diego to identify him. I took her, by God—and I never thought but what—just an ordinary thing, ordinary mugging—and she put on such an act—"

"Mis' Cunningham?" said Hill. "But it ain't a thing like him—she'd know right off it wasn't—"

"Well, for God's sake," said Hackett. "It isn't?"

"And just because Roy here happened to see the paper

and came in— But I figure," said Landers, "we'd better talk to her, don't you think?"

Hackett grinned. "I figure. And we might just hear a little more if there's what Luis might call the element of surprise." He followed Landers to the anteroom. "Where is she, Tom? Staying in town, I gather?"

"Yes—she said she'd stay over for the inquest. The Hotel Grant."

"*Bueno*. Jimmy, get hold of Mrs. Cunningham at the Hotel Grant. All nice and polite, tell her there's a little technicality come up about the inquest, and we need her signature. Say we'll send a car for her. Be soothing."

"Sure," said Lake.

"But I don't get any of this," said Roy Hill. "Why'd Mis' Cunningham say—when it *wasn't* him? I don't—"

The element of surprise worked in their favor all right. Twenty minutes later Mrs. Lester Cunningham walked in, and Landers still felt vague outrage; she looked like such a lady. Quiet, conservative dark suit and white blouse, a little black pillbox hat, low-heeled shoes, not much makeup. She looked eminently honest and respectable. She looked from Lake to Hackett to Landers. "Oh," she said, "Detective Landers. What do you want me to sign? The man who called said— I understood I couldn't—couldn't c-claim the—my husband's body until after the—" Her pale lips quivered a little pathetically.

Landers decided he'd never trust another female again.

"Oh, yes, Mrs. Cunningham," said Hackett easily. "I'm Sergeant Hackett. Just a few more routine questions we have to ask you—nothing to worry about. Won't you come in here and sit down?" He gestured toward the door of Mendoza's office and she bowed her head and went in past him. Hackett and Landers followed.

Roy Hill was sitting beside Mendoza's desk and behind

the desk sat George Higgins. From outside, to anybody who didn't know him, George Higgins' soft and sentimental heart was not apparent: he looked like the archetype of the big brutal tough COP.

Mrs. Cunningham stopped, three paces into the office.

And Hackett said conversationally behind her, "Just who was it you identified as your husband? Mr. Hill's just told us it isn't. And where *is* your husband, Mrs. Cunningham?"

For six heartbeats she was absolutely silent and motionless. Then without warning she exploded into sound and action. She spat out one half-screamed obscenity, whirled and raked at Hackett viciously with both hands, fingers spread. Involuntarily he jumped back, but she leapt at him, and when Landers jerked her roughly off, Hackett's face was bleeding copiously where her nails had dug. He groped for a handkerchief.

"Mrs. Cunningham—" Landers panted, twisting away from the nails reaching for his eyes. "You all right, Art?" Higgins came in a hurry to help Landers hold her, but she snarled another obscenity and went limp.

"Get a policewoman up here, Jimmy!" Hackett was mopping his face. "Damn little—"

"Your wife's going to be asking some questions," said Landers.

"Gosh," said Roy Hill. "Gee, I never see Mis' Cunningham act like that before."

The policewoman efficiently produced restoratives and in another twenty minutes, duly and punctiliously informed of her rights and privileges, Lorna Cunningham sat sipping black coffee and staring dully at them.

"Would you like to talk to us, Mrs. Cunningham?" asked Hackett. He was sporting a couple of strips of adhesive tape down both cheeks.

"Not particularly," she said bitterly, "but I guess I've got no choice. That damn stupid Hill kid—had to be here just now—"

"You don't have to tell us anything," said Landers, and wondered all over again how anybody with any common sense could seriously think that all these rules and regulations didn't hamstring the police in trying, for God's sake, to keep law and order and protect the citizenry.

"Oh, what's the use," she said. "It's all spoiled now and you know. What's the use? And I won't tell you where to find Les, it was all his idea, anyway, and you can't say I did anything but tell a couple of lies. And we thought we were so smart!"

"For a start, who's the man in the morgue?" asked Hackett.

She was silent, and then said, "His brother. Les's. Walt. Nobody'd ever miss him. Nobody'd know he was gone. He's one of those rolling stones, always moving around—no family. Hardly anybody knew Les had a brother. And when he showed up this time, it seemed— I was going to take the body back, to make it look all right, but have the coffin closed and say that was how Les wanted it. Nobody would—"

"Why, Mrs. Cunningham?" asked Landers. He was taking notes.

She looked at him in faint surprise. "Why, to get the money—the only way to— It was Les's idea. The restaurant was doing just terrible—he'd have been in bankruptcy in a couple of months. With nothing. And he'd converted his Army insurance—ten thousand. If we could get hold of that — And nobody'd miss Walt at all. He didn't *mean* anything to anybody. Honestly—"

"How'd your husband get him to come up here?"

"I don't know," she said tiredly. "I think he told him he knew a man here who was hiring people for a treasure-div-

126

ing thing somewhere. Walt was a pushover for things like that. He'd been on an expedition like that before. But I don't know."

"And Les came with him. And after they left the bus depot, got him in a quiet spot and slugged him. Took his I.D. and left his own on Walt. Like that?"

"I guess so. I'm not saying any more."

"They arranged to meet somewhere," said Hackett to Landers. "Maybe here, maybe Acapulco. So we give all this to the press, and he runs."

"I'm not telling you where he is!"

"I'd make an educated guess—after all I did major in psychology—" Hackett was smiling gently—"that right now Lester Cunningham is holed up right there in the Hotel Grant." Her eyes went panicky and his smile widened. "To stay put until after the nice funeral down in San Diego. When Mrs. Cunningham would go away to forget all her troubles, and—"

She started to get up. "You'll be staying right here," said Hackett. "Tom, suppose you take Mr. Hill over to the hotel and stake the place out awhile. Have a look at the register for matching initials. I don't suppose he'll be taking much care—may even stroll down to the lobby or the bar. Not thinking there's anybody here who knows him. His bad luck."

"Goddamn and blast you to hell!" said Lorna Cunningham.

As Landers went out with Roy Hill, Jason Grace came in with a slatternly-looking blonde who looked terrified. Grace was looking pleased.

It had taken a lot of Grace's soft-voiced persuasion to fetch Margie back with him. He told her Bill needn't ever know a thing about it—Bill wasn't due home until six and he wouldn't expect to find her there, her stint at The Jolly

127

Huntsman started at five. And they just wanted to ask a few little questions. Nobody was going to do anything to her.

But she didn't like any part of it. She took one look at Higgins and turned pale, and Hackett didn't suit her much better, looking villainous in his adhesive tape. In the end, Grace got Piggott—thin, mild-looking Piggott—to come and take notes, and his voice went softer and more persuasive than ever.

"Now, Mrs. Vacciarello, you did know Mr. Barron, didn't you?"

"I—I—he was a customer. That's how, at first. That's all. And I—well, he was awful smooth and all, a real nice fella—" she stuck. "Well, I—he was nice. He was a salesman some kind, and—"

"Um-hum," said Grace. "You went out with him some? Just the good times together?" His tone made it sound quite ordinary and casual.

"Yeah. Some. Just— But look, it hadn't been for ages. Two months anyways. It was back before Christmas. I haven't *seen* him since then. Honest." She looked down at her capri pants mournfully. "You drag me outta the house like this—I look awful, you must think—when I'm fixed up I— But you think he's done something, and I—honest, I—"

"No, he's dead," said Grace casually. "Murdered."

She looked ready to faint. *"Davy?"* she said. "M— Oh, my God! Oh, my God, you think I—"

"No, Mrs. Vacciarello, we don't think you had anything to do with it," said Grace mendaciously. "You hadn't been seeing him lately?"

"No, honest. I—I'd kinda wondered, he stopped coming around—he knew when Bill was at work, and he'd—but he hadn't come. I—don't get the idea it was anything wrong—" she eyed them nervously.

"No, no," said Grace. Piggott was taking notes impassively.

"He got m—honest to God, *Davy*. He was a nice guy, why'd anybody want to go and m— I hadn't seen him in two months, honest."

"All right," said Grace. "Did Bill find out about it? You going around with Davy?"

"*Bill?* My God, no—my God, I wouldn't be sittin' here if he had." Suddenly she started talking. "You think I'm crazy? Give him any chance to find out—about Davy or anybody else? Maybe I am crazy, taking the chances, but honest to God, a girl's got to have something or what's the use living at all? I ask you. Where I was crazy was when I married him. Honest to God. I musta been. Like a gorilla or something, and nothing but complain, complain, I can't cook, I don't keep the right brand o' beer inna house, I buy too many things, and take me *out* anywheres, well, might as well ask him for the moon—a real drag, and a girl's got to have something, a real nice guy asks me out, treat me like a lady, am I gonna say no? I'd be crazy. I been saving up to go to Vegas, get me a divorce, and I swear I'm goin' tomorrow—I can always get a job there. I'm not taking it no more—and now just because I went with a nice guy a few times, the cops—and if Bill knew he'd *kill* me—"

"Mrs. Vacciarello," said Grace, "are you sure your husband didn't know about Barron? That he didn't—"

"You think *Bill* murdered him?" She started to laugh wildly. "Oh, mister, you're sure on the wrong track there! If Bill ever found out about it, he'd've murdered me first! It wouldn't be Bill that murdered him. But—" she looked at them with sudden devastating frankness—"it could be it was some sort of reason like that, whoever did. Because Davy Barron—he was a real boilermaker. I tell you. A real hot lover man."

129

They sent her home in a squad car. Grace surmised that Hackett and Higgins were busy with the punks again. Routine, the deadly routine. He said, "I don't think it was Bill. If he's one goes up like a rocket like that. And she should know. But it's interesting to know that Davy was a hot lady's man."

Piggott said mournfully, "And pretending to be a minister. Well, we were told there'd be a lot of false prophets around. See the seventh chapter of Daniel. Wolves in sheeps' clothing."

About eight-thirty Detective Dan Collins showed up at the house on Rayo Grande Avenue. Mendoza had got in at six, been fed a nourishing dinner, and was ruminating with his eyes shut in the big armchair, El Señor on his lap. When Alison brought Collins in he squinted up at him and said, "Let's offer the man a drink, *querida*. I'll have one, too. Highball?"

"Fine," said Collins. He sat down on the sectional opposite. "I got kind of interested in this, Lieutenant. A damn funny one. A new kind of con game, you could say. The old people— And as the Captain said, all up in the air and what's the legal charge? And you've only looked at six. But I got interested. I thought you'd like to hear what I turned up."

"*Bueno*. I would."

"The Captain's twisting some arms so we can get into the Hall of Records tomorrow, see the wills on file. But meanwhile I went and took a look at this Julian Black. One neighbor remembered him. Widower. Had a little house over in the Atwater section, Dover Place. No family. He was eighty-four, and nothing especially wrong with him except that he was getting feeble. Old age."

"So finally he hired the nurse."

"Yeah. And the neighbor says he went downhill very fast. Poor old gentleman, she said. Nurse was there seven weeks. And he died, and there was a funeral, and—get this—the nurse comes back with a pickup truck and a long-haired lout of a kid and carts away the furniture. And pretty soon the house was sold. Same people who bought it are in it now —it was a realty company sold it. I tell you, Lieutenant, I'm itching to see those wills at the Hall of Records. Take any bet we'll find 'em."

"Yes. A little confirmation of the deductions. You don't say. So I offer you," said Mendoza, sitting up and taking the shot glass of rye Alison handed him, "—thanks, *cara*—a Mrs. Louisa Potter." Collins took his highball with a nod of thanks. "On Santa Ynez Street. O'Rourke was with her from August to October of 1963. Mrs. Potter a widow with no family. She departs from the norm, however, in that the neighbors thought she had a little money. Dividends, they said. She was in her seventies, and she had palsy. Finally had to hire the practical nurse. I saw the doctor this time—the neighbors knew who he was. He was annoyed at me— *amante,* you forgot El Señor." Their alcoholic cat was making strenuous efforts to get at Mendoza's glass, standing on his hind legs and uttering loud complaints.

"That cat!" muttered Alison, and departed. Collins stared.

"—He hardly remembered the woman," said Mendoza. "Why should he? An old woman, a chronic disease, nothing important. . . . . You know, we're also going to have to track down the lawyers. Which names we will get from the wills— *¡Basta, Señor!* Your share's coming. I would surmise, of course, all different lawyers—as there were all different doctors—"

"This is a *hell* of a thing," said Collins. "So far out— But once you see it, of course it'd be a gold mine. All these people

131

without anybody close, and the little bits of property, the—"

Alison came back with a saucer of rye and put it down. El Señor uttered a raucous phrase of gratitude and jumped down to crouch over it. "Ought to join the A.A.," muttered Mendoza. Collins stared at El Señor.

"Something to be ferreted out, all right. The damned woman's found a whole new con game. Preying on the old people alone—"

"And if we can prove it," said Mendoza, "just think of all the money she's bilked out of the state. The people without relatives—probably a lot of them had never made a will—"

Collins laughed and said he wasn't worrying about Sacramento. "But these poor damned old people—and damn it, what legal charge is there? The Captain said—"

"We'll let the private eyes have a close look and see what turns up."

"Those boys can cost you a fortune. Well, Forsythe's O.K., I know him, he used to be on the Phoenix force, invalided out. But—"

"I will only say one thing," said Alison, standing over Mendoza. "You might as well be back in the office as usual. Gallivanting around— You're supposed to be convalescing, for heaven's sake! Resting. Taking a vacation. And you get all wound up on this thing—really, Luis—"

"No lo niego. I'm all right. I'm—"

"Esta muy pagado de sí," said Alison crossly. Collins stared at her. "I'm only thinking of you—you shouldn't—"

"You just heard me say we're turning it over to the private eyes." Mendoza leaned back and finished his rye. "After all I'll be back at my own desk and it's not my beat. Collins— you'll let me know what you find at the Hall of Records?"

"Yes, sir. Interesting to see what shows. I'd take a bet you're right. And what a thing—"

Mendoza let Alison take him to the door. As she swung

it open, he heard Collins say, "The Lieutenant's been sick? I thought he was on vacation or—the Captain said—"

"He is supposed," said Alison clearly, "to be convalescing from the measles."

Collins was mute. The door closed.

And Mendoza said, "*¡Sin mujeres y sin vientos, tendiamos menos tormentes!*"

They had picked up Lester Cunningham without any trouble at all, as he strolled into the dining room of the Hotel Grant at seven-thirty. Cunningham was astonished and outraged; advised of his rights, he certainly didn't remain silent but most of what he said was about his wife, and none of it was friendly.

They booked him in at the facility on Alameda and applied for a warrant overnight. Mrs. Cunningham was induced to part with the name of a tramp freighter still, they hoped, lying in San Diego Harbor: the *Hobart S. Gray*. Walt Cunningham had just left it, after several trips as an oiler. The captain and the rest of the crew would know him. Hackett wired the San Diego police—a little surprise for them, the twist in the Cunningham thing—would someone alert the captain and ask him or somebody else to come up and formally identify the body? Thanks very much.

He got home about nine o'clock, having called Angel not to expect him and snatching a hasty dinner at a drugstore. Angel was stirring something on the stove as he came in the back door; she took one look at him, and said, "What did you run into? Or should I say who?"

"Who. One very angry female."

Chapter 9

SUNDAY was just another day to policemen; crime doesn't keep regular hours. Hackett, as acting senior officer while Mendoza was off, went over the current reports; it was about an average to low load for Homicide. Doubtless a couple of new ones would show up soon.

"And on Barron—" Hackett yawned, getting out his cigarettes, "I still say, the women be damned, there's something funny about that Temple. What Jase told us the gardener said. You may think it's a waste of time, but I'm taking an hour off to go over there and see what goes on at their damned rites."

"It's a waste of time," said Higgins. "Some rigmarole made up to impress the marks. But it's your time. I suppose I go and look for the next punk." There were still four or five out of Records they wanted to see; they hadn't found all of them, of course.

It was twenty to ten when Hackett got to the Temple; he'd noticed on the board in front that the Sunday service, something called the Rite of the Opening of the Chamber, was at ten o'clock. Already the congregation was starting to gather, and it struck him at once that it looked like any respectable group of church people. A much more conventional-looking crowd than he'd have expected to see; but that was one thing he'd noticed about the individuals they'd interviewed so far, what had aroused his curiosity. There were flowered and veiled hats on the women, a few garish ties on the comparatively few men, but that you might see anywhere now. Hackett straightened his own tie, strolled up the steps behind a woman he recognized as that probably-middling-wealthy Mrs. Brainard, and stepped through the double doors.

"Er—excuse me, sir, I don't seem to recognize—" A little eager-eyed fellow handing out tracts at the door. "A new brother, let me welcome—"

"I'm *so* sorry," said Terhune at Hackett's elbow, "but I'm afraid we don't admit strangers to our main services." His tone was regretful, friendly. "There's a—course of instruction one must take before— *So* flattering of you to want to come to us, and if you're interested I should be happy to— ah—instruct you *personally,* but I'm afraid—"

Gently but firmly Hackett was ushered back outside, but not before he had caught the astonished stare of the little doorkeeper.

What the hell? How else were they going to pick up new marks to contribute to the collection? If they didn't welcome all comers? By the look on the doorkeeper's face, they usually did—the more the merrier. But of course Terhune knew who he was. And not only Hackett's curiosity but his instinct for evidence was alerted and operating at this unexpected bit.

He hurried back to the Barracuda and got back to the office at seven minutes of ten. Piggott, he thought regretfully, would have been ideal: unfortunately Piggott wasn't there. He looked into the communal office: Glasser with his rather rough-hewn face, and Tom Landers. "Tom," said Hackett urgently.

"What's up?"

"You've got about five minutes—chase down to that Temple on Beverly and see what goes on at the service, hah? They wouldn't let me in. But me, Terhune knows— you, he doesn't. Also, you look less like a cop than any man on the force—"

"When you say that smile."

"O.K., O.K., but get with it! There's something funny about it, and I'd like to know what it is."

Landers obeyed orders philosophically; at least it was less boring than typing reports. When he'd parked the car in a public lot and hurried back to the Temple of the Holy Inner Light, the double doors were closed, but unlocked; he shoved one open and tiptoed in. There was a pretty good congregation, he saw; nearly a full house, call it a hundred and fifty people. The man in dark robes in the pulpit must be this con-man, Terhune. He didn't look so impressive, thought Landers.

He slid into a back pew with a dozen other people, mostly women, and looked around. Terhune was delivering a rather pompous eulogy of our departed brother the Reverend Barron—sighs and even a few sobs—and after awhile a rather amateur-sounding organ began to play a monotonous dirge.

"But we must maintain our spiritual dedication as a memorial to our dear friend gone before. We shall make our regular Sunday offering, the Rite of the Opening of the Chamber, in his name," intoned Terhune when the organ stopped. More sighs and rustlings. "For truly, is not our present created body in truth a Chamber, a holy Chamber? Which must be opened in the spirit, that the spiritual inner light may enter in—"

Several men in dark clothes began passing down the aisles with trays. For God's sake, thought Landers, they've got a nerve—taking up the collection before the service! The usual guff, too, Oriental mysticism or whatever. But when the tray came to the people in his pew, he saw that it contained little flat cakes or cookies, and everybody was taking one. Sandwiched between his neighbor and the pew arm, he took one, too.

"Take, and eat, for the greater spiritual unfolding and understanding—the Holy Inner Chamber of the spirit *and* the body— For in the essential pure understanding of the true Holy Spirit—"

Landers thought, the usual guff. He ate the cookie absently; it was vaguely sweet, but otherwise tasteless. Everybody stood up for that, and then sat down again. Terhune intoned, "For I do believe in the Holy Inner Light," and the whole congregation chanted it solemnly after him.

Guff, and also slightly blasphemous, thought Landers. He wondered why Hackett was interested. The congregation chanted a long litany of some kind after the man in the pulpit, and the organ played again, and then everybody fervently stood and sang a hymn, to the tune of "Rock of Ages" but using totally new words Landers couldn't make out.

He thought he'd rather be back at the office typing his report. He wondered what John was getting on the car— Montez' car had just showed up.

Just when his sensations began, he couldn't have said; but rather suddenly he was conscious of the angels in the stained-glass window at his left. They seemed to be moving; and as the solemn organ notes rose and fell, he thought, vaguely, that the fellow preached a pretty good sermon at that—something powerful in the words— The angels *were* moving; quite distinctly one of them bowed to him, then. There seemed a portentous span of several minutes between one significant word from the pulpit and the next, and an un-specified time after he noticed that, Landers felt the power swelling in himself. It was a heady, marvelous sensation: He was capable of anything, this omnipresent inner power within himself—little problems and worries fled away, noth-ing, he could—

He was vaguely aware of more audible noises, sighs, half screams, little cries from people all about him— "Amen, amen, I can feel the power!" "The spirit's on us now, glory—"

Really a wonderful revelation of power—the power of— Landers' mind fumbled for the right word, but went on be-ing gloriously conscious of the thing itself, a great personal knowledge of timelessness and limitless personal abilities—

Then he began to slide down the other side, and by the time the organ began to play again he was blinking at the pair of quite immobile angels in the stained-glass window and wanting to shake his head to clear it. The woman be-side him, ten minutes ago uttering little moans of excite-ment, was sitting up straight and fumbling with her gloves. Sighs and murmurs from the crowd, and they stood up and sang another strange hymn. Landers peered at his watch; his eyes weren't focusing very well. It was eleven-ten.

It was over. People sliding out of pews and—some of them seeming to stagger slightly as they passed up the aisle, or was that imagination? He sat up, feeling shaky. Low voices passed him—"The power was mighty strong today"—"Oh, it's such a heavenly uplifting of the—" "I had a vision, Mar-tha, truly, the first time, I saw—"

Landers felt that he was staggering a little, up to the door; he blinked in the full sun, and drew a long breath. My Lord Almighty, he thought, and just what the hell had *that* been? Just what the hell— And talk about nerve—

He fell into the driving seat, hoping he could get back to

the office without running into anything, but surely to God that damned con man wouldn't risk—

He got there in one piece. He collapsed on the chair in the anteroom under the concerned eye of Sergeant Thoms —it was Lake's day off—and said, "Where's Hackett? Go get him, Bill, I've got news for him." He shut his eyes until he heard Art's voice, and said without opening them, "Oh, it was wonderful—just wonderful. Damndest sensation I ever — Listen, I've had something, I don't know what, hashish or— You better get Bainbridge to look—was wonderful, talk about uplift. Quite a sensation. Quite a—"

"For God's sake!" said Hackett. There was an interval while Landers thirstily drank two glasses of water from the cooler down the hall, and then tubby little Dr. Bainbridge was there, looking at him testily.

"Right in the middle of an autopsy— So what were your symptoms?"

"No symptoms. I felt wonderful. Saw the damned angels in the stained-glass window bowing at me. There wasn't any time anywhere—suspended. Could do anything," said Landers. "Solved all our problems like that, bang. Everything was fine—just fine. I was uplifted all right. What have I had? That Goddamn con—"

Bainbridge sniffed. "Come along, we'll pump you out and see for sure."

"I'm all right now," said Landers in alarm.

"Come on—we've got to be sure."

"Hell and damnation—"

Thirty minutes later Bainbridge reappeared in the Homicide office and plumped himself down beside Hackett's desk. Grace and Glasser were there and looked up.

"Well, that is one for the books," said Bainbridge. "Why didn't anybody think of it before? Jet-age religion. Don't bother to depend on powerful preaching or the well-known effects of ritual music—just give 'em a shot of artificial uplift. Quite an idea." He laughed.

"Give, give," said Hackett. "How's Tom?"

"He was fine before the stomach pump. He'll recover. That small a dose hardly addictive. What he had—for the books all right—was a variety of marijuana. It—"

"But I thought reefers had to be—"

"The entire plant, which is a cousin of *cannibas sativa*— hemp plant to you—is productive of hallucinogens," said Bainbridge. "Easy to grow almost anywhere in a temperate climate. Different parts of it used in different ways by different people. You can dry the leaves and smoke 'em, or make tea of it and drink it, or bake it in cakes and eat it—apparently how it's served to this congregation, like communion wafers— I will be damned. I really will. I had a pretty good idea what it was by his symptoms, so I went for it right away in the analysis, and there it was. Fancy Hindu name, *charas*. Little cakes with the stuff baked in. Not the leaves, as used in reefers. The pollen dust from the top of the plant. Crushed and mixed with the dough. Standard delicacy in some parts of Arabia, I understand."

"I will be *damned*," said Hackett. "I will be—"

"What they won't think of next," said Grace. "Quite an idea. Instant uplift."

"He didn't have much—you wouldn't dare give much of a dose to an unsuspecting victim. He'd have such hallucinations, he'd suspect something right off. That mild a dose, you just get the exhilaration, the little sensation of time meaning nothing, and maybe a few little visual distortions, depending on the individual. The reason your man realized he'd been fed something, he didn't go there for religious motives, and he's a trained man—he wasn't about to put it down to the spiritual preacher, and not being given to having angelic visions in the ordinary way, he guessed what was going on."

"My good God," said Hackett suddenly, "that's what I smelled in that closet—marijuana—I knew it was something I ought to— Instant uplift, for God's sake. No wonder he didn't want a cop there. And if the stuff's still— Come on, Jase! If we can nab him red-handed—" He tore out with Grace at his heels.

Bainbridge took out a cigar and began to unwrap it. "New little twist on the old con game. Infinite possibilities in it, you know. Just imagine—at a political rally—or a national party convention—"

"Doctor, you give me cold chills," said Glasser. "Where's Tom?"

Bainbridge laughed. "Stretched out on the couch in my office. He'd better take the day off and go home. Not the marijuana—the stomach pump. He'll probably want a large lunch in about two hours."

"I'll go see he gets home safe," said Glasser. "What a thing. What people think of—"

They found Terhune, divested of his robes, standing on the steps of the Temple with Mrs. Brainard, looking a little restive at her monologue. His pasted-on smile slipped a bit when he saw Hackett and Grace coming up the steps.

"Dear lady, I'm afraid I'll have to ask you to excuse me—"

"Oh, I know I've taken up too much of your time Reverend, I do apologize, but I simply had to tell you how wonderfully I thought you conducted the service—the dear Reverend Barron always—but it was simply splendid and I—"

Terhune pressed her hand. "So good of you. I do appreciate—but if you'd excuse—"

141

"Mr. Terhune," said Hackett pleasurably. "We want you."

"Why, Sergeant Hackett. Any way I can help you, about this shocking crime."

"Is the church locked, Mr. Terhune?" asked Grace.

"Why—yes, as a matter of fact I was just—"

Hackett held out his hand. "Key, please. I'd have a guess you left some of the pretty little marijuana cookies inside. We can always get a warrant, you know. You see, Mr. Terhune, I did a little wondering when you wouldn't let me in, and there was a cop at your services after all. Who realized he'd been doped with something. And now we know what. Naughty, naughty, Mr. Terhune. Though an imaginative idea, I grant you."

"Instant uplift," murmured Grace.

"Oh, for the love of God," said Terhune. "You God-damned fuzz have to come snooping into everything—just because that damn fool got himself knocked off! I told him he was— And now you—" He looked very tired suddenly. In a childish gesture he took out a bunch of keys and threw them down the steps. "The nicest caper I'd ever been on, and you come snooping around and shoot it all to hell—"

Grace said afterward what he'd really enjoyed about the scene was the expression on Mrs. Brainard's face.

Montez' car had turned up on a side street out in Boyle Heights late that morning. Palliser went to look at it when it was towed in, and it looked clean. The lab would give it the works, of course. He went out to ask around where it had been found, but nobody knew anything about it. Nobody could say when it had been abandoned there, or who had done the abandoning.

He never got back to the office until two o'clock, when he heard about Landers and the instant uplift. "My God," said Palliser, "what these con men *think* of— Tom's left? I'll drop by on my way home, see if he's O.K., and give him the news—a lead on Montez anyway. I hope."

"So O.K., let's talk, Rodney," said Hackett.

"You can talk all you want," said Terhune sullenly.

"We've got your record, such as it is. From the Feds. Are you Terhune or Yorke?"

"Does it matter? Sweetest caper I'd ever been on, and you come— Oh, what the hell!" said Rodney. "It was all his fault you were there, damn it. That damn fool."

"Barron. How was he a damn fool? Over the women? We've talked to Margie, too."

"You expect *me* to know all his damn women? Who could keep track? I told him he was a fool. Even, naturally, keeping it outside the caper—my God. He started fooling around some dame came to the church, I really came down on him that time, and he saw that much sense. He could put on a good front, but he couldn't stay off the dames—inviting trouble. Somebody's husband getting nasty—which is probably what happened, you know. I'd lay a bet. But my God, when I went in and found him—" He shuddered.

Yes, the con men not given to violence. "You didn't give the alarm right away, did you? You had to get all those doped cakes out of the way. You knew we'd look at the premises. And whose idea was that, anyway? Quite an idea."

"Oh, his, his. And I've got no idea," said Rodney earnestly, "where he got the stuff. I—"

"I just bet," said Higgins.

"No, honestly. I really didn't. He'd read a lot about a lot of different things. He'd found a recipe—in some Hindu book or other, I think. He used to make them himself, at the apartment. I didn't know anything about—"

"I think it was the other way around," said Hackett. "It

143

was you who knew, whoever had the original idea. Where did you get it?" My God, almost anywhere around here; the stuff grew wild, and not long ago the maintenance men at the City Hall had been embarrassed to have it pointed out to them by a passing knowledgeable citizen that the pretty green flowering bushes they'd been tending carefully were, in fact, marijuana plants. Any shady citizen in town growing it in his back yard. "There you were, on a very small-time lay, when you met Barron, and all of a sudden he cuts you in on the sweet legit-looking deal. Why? You had something he wanted. I think that's what it was."

"And I'll buy that," said Lieutenant Pat Callaghan. They had called him in on this, as head of Narco—which was the concerned department, of course. "You'd been here longer, I think, and had contacts he didn't. And maybe knowledge."

"You can't prove that," said Rodney with a shrug. "It's not so." And after that he shut up. He was probably regretting his initial outburst. It wouldn't be possible for him to get off the charge, claiming he hadn't any knowledge of the contents of those cakes; the evidence was too strong, the two men sharing an apartment—but it would have made him look better, and possibly even made some of the faithful congregation go on believing him, if he'd kept up the front.

"You know, one thing we never heard," said Grace, "was why that collection money was still there on Tuesday."

"Oh, for God's sake!" said Rodney disgustedly. "I'll tell you *that,* and it'll show you what a damn fool he was. We'd had a little argument over it. He wanted me to give him my half—even offered interest on it—to give the whole bundle to some dame of his to get a divorce with. The *cash.* The last either of us'd ever see of it, and I said——"

"Was her name Margie?" asked Grace.

"How the hell should I—no, it was Sue or Jackie

or someth— Of all the crazy—I tell you, there were times I was sorry I'd hooked up with him, but it was a good lay—"

They'd found a dozen or so of the impregnated cakes at the Temple. Lieutenant Callaghan applied for the warrant and they stashed him in the jail down on Alameda. Unlawful possession of drugs—it wasn't such a stiff charge, and Callaghan, incredibly looming over Hackett on the jail steps there, said, "He'll be arraigned tomorrow, and probably make bail. Why shouldn't he? And I think he was the one who was getting the stuff. I think also I'll have a tail ready to pick him up."

"And I don't think he had one damn thing to do with the murder," said Hackett, "but we could bear to hear where he goes and what he does, Callaghan."

"I'll see you get reports. . . . How's Luis? I like to died laughing when I heard—the measles. Luis."

"It's no joke for an adult. He was pretty—"

"Oh, I know, I know. I sent him a card. How is he?"

"Getting on fine. Be back pretty soon, I hope."

"Good."

By arrangement, Mendoza met Collins for lunch in Hollywood, at one o'clock. He was waiting, looking at an untouched shot glass of rye in front of him, when Collins came in, looking preoccupied, and sat down. Collins had spent the morning at the Hall of Records, where the arm-twisting had unlocked doors for him.

He ordered a highball and said to Mendoza, "We should have figured. I spot checked, by names. The four you had, and about thirty others on that list. There's more to look for, of course. I found thirteen wills." He pulled out his notebook. "Pearce, Lord, Wilkerson, and ten more. Names off the list. But we should have figured. They were all will forms. No lawyers."

"*Dios.* Yes. Yes, I see."

"I did know that California's one of the only two states that recognize a holograph will. But I didn't realize those printed forms were— Very simple wills, Lieutenant. All of which I die possessed."

"And two witnesses to each. All different names."

"Sure. But what's that?" Collins snorted. "She wouldn't ask the neighbors. I shouldn't think. How do we know those signatures are for real? Do they check on witnesses, the probate—? You don't have to be a registered voter, I do know. I witnessed a will once when I'd just moved and wasn't reregistered yet. Hell, yes, if it was an estate of a couple of million—or if anybody contested it—but—" The waiter brought his drink.

"Yes. *Pues si.* Little parcels of humble real estate. And also, in a place this size, how many wills in probate every day?" Mendoza sipped rye.

"Look," said Collins. "*How does she do it?* That's what *gets* me. How? None of these people—the four we've heard a little about—seem to have been senile, what the neighbors told you. Old, frail, with the chronic things—palsy, asthma, arthritis—but still in their right minds. Hell, Lieutenant, some of 'em may have made previous wills! And yet this— this very practical practical nurse has 'em under her thumb in no time, and meekly signing—"

"Signing," said Mendoza meditatively. "Yes. Will forms. When nobody's going to be looking at it very close, a less than perfect forgery—will forms supposed to be made out all in the same hand. How?" He finished his rye. "Mrs. Oliver saying she's giving old Mrs. Weaver drugs of some kind. How does she get them to—? We can imagine, Collins. An old lady, in pain from the arthritis, and the kind nurse giving her something stronger than aspirin—"

"What?"

"How do I know what? I'm not a pharmacist. . . . I'll have the steak sandwich. Coffee."

"Same for me. Well done," said Collins. "But—"

"Something just strong enough to keep her—dopey. Under par mentally. And—it'd be a little different, maybe, for different situations and people. Some of them, for instance, wouldn't know much about legalities—about—" Mendoza gestured vaguely. "I can imagine. A paper to sign, new subscription to the daily paper. As simple as that. Or some form the doctor wants signed. These days—it could be almost any excuse. But some others, a little brighter and knowing more, even under the dope— And what the hell could she be using?—I don't know. Some plausible story. It could be a couple of them or more were induced by kind nursie to do it voluntarily. Nursie so good to them."

"I'd like to know how the *hell*," said Collins. "I've got interested in this thing. I wonder how many more I'd have found with more time, I'll be sorry to leave it. You going to put the private eyes on it?"

"I think so. I really do. Good circumstantial evidence so far, isn't it? The nurse inheriting thirteen times—that we know about. Possibly more. The will forms in every instance. And very likely if we got a handwriting expert on it, the forms would turn out to be forgeries. By God, Collins, yes—some of the signatures might be forged, too. The ones she couldn't— And then we would have her, if that's so."

"That could be," said Collins soberly. "And I tell you, Lieutenant, I wouldn't doubt now, she did put at least some of them out before their time. The four you checked died pretty soon after she was with them, didn't they? We'll see what shows on the others. I hope you'll let me know what turns up. Of all the coldblooded—"

"Not a nice woman, no," said Mendoza.

When he left Collins he went to the Hollywood Boulevard offices of Forsythe and Mason, Private Investigations, and put the case before Forsythe, the only one in. Forsythe looked at Mendoza and the list, unwillingly fascinated: a big ruddy man with a shock of white hair.

"I will be damned," he said. "Offbeat you could say. And shutting stable doors—and what with the statute of limitations and all—I can see the difficulty. But what you've turned up looks— I will be damned. And I can't recall that we've ever done a job for the police, Lieutenant. You're usually kind of snobbish toward us."

Mendoza laughed and said he was really acting in a private capacity. "I'd like to see this—this vampire stopped."

"I'm with you there. If all this is so. We'll get on it."

Mendoza gave him a retaining check and went home, to be pounced on by an excited Alison and Mrs. MacTaggart. "I came right back to tell you, none of us can make it out at all, the queerest thing and whatever it can mean—"

"*I* say she's decided the neighbors are too nosy," said Alison, "and so—"

"*¡Vaya despacio!* What's all this about?"

"Well, just this morning it was, while Janet and I were having an early lunch after church," said Mairí, "what should happen but a man drives up in a car and puts a sign up on Mrs. Weaver's front lawn. For Sale it says, this real estate company. We couldn't believe our eyes—"

"*¿Que es eso?* For—"

"I'm telling you. And of course Mrs. Oliver saw it, too, and like a scalded cat—a resourceful woman she is—she's across the street with half a cake on a plate as an excuse, and the nurse lets her in. And half an hour later she comes across—Edna Fogarty was with us then, having noticed the sign on her way home from church—and what does she have to tell us? You'll not believe it. And what to do— She says

Mrs. Weaver was pretty much herself again, bright enough and understanding what's said and all—and that nurse smiling and preening and dearie-ing all over the place—and she says, the nurse that is, she's taking the old lady to her own home to look after, going to sell the house so as Mrs. Weaver can have the money to be looked to proper—and Mrs. Weaver nodding and saying 'twas the best way, she'd not like to leave but—"

"*¡Porvida!*" said Mendoza.

"Because of the nosy neighbors," said Alison. "Oh, you know what I mean, Mairí. Concerned."

"And the old lady looking halfway her old self, like that other time when Mrs. Oliver—"

Mendoza's mind made a sudden great leap. *He* was feeling like his old self today. "When—what did you say, Mairí? —about five weeks ago? After she'd been looking senile—"

"Yes, the time Mrs. Oliver found her sharp as she ever was, but then—"

"*¡Parece mentira!*" said Mendoza softly. "Now don't rush me—it's coming—" He was back in that grimy office, the day he'd come down with the damn measles—in early December—and Hackett was saying, "Find out he got struck off the register thirty years ago—" The crooked doctor, Dr. William Hodges—dead of a coronary in his dirty little office— And at about the same time, the practical nurse's patient regaining her sharp senses and— Could that have been where she was getting—? Hell, there'd be any amount—well, not that, but other venal doctors around; but as a coincidence—

"Luis, you've thought of something—what?"

Mendoza dived for the telephone and dialed the familiar number. "Jimmy—oh, Bill. Is Art there?"

"He just got in. I'll call him. How are you, Lieutenant?"

"Fine, fine. . . . Art? That crooked doctor—did he turn

out to be crooked? William Hodges, the coronary the day I— We went out on it that morning, you and me and Tom. How'd it turn out? Was he a genuine M.D.?"

"Wait a minute—oh, that one. Yes, I seem to remember it was a coronary. We didn't check back, why should we, but I seem to— Yeah, among the stuff in his office was a newspaper clipping telling he'd been struck off the register back east somewhere. In an old scrapbook—I don't know why he'd kept it. Why the hell are you interested?"

"Isn't that nice. Any records in the office?"

"What d'you mean, records? We didn't do much looking, as I recall. Why? It was a natural death."

"Just the paperwork on it. *Si*. Nothing at all? Ledgers, accounts, receipts, to tell what he'd been up to lately?"

"Well, it was an ordinary little thing awhile back, I'd have to—what the hell's your interest now? Tom did most of the looking around on it, at the office—"

"So let me talk to him. It just could be important. Is he there?"

"Oh, my, what you are missing," said Hackett, sounding amused. "The excitement we've had around here today— and Bainbridge with his ghoulish imagination saying political conventions—my God. No, Tom's home. But wait a minute, I'll ask John if he knows anything—"

Mendoza waited, Alison and Mairí hanging on in silence, too, until Palliser said in his ear, "Lieutenant? That Hodges thing—" he sounded bewildered. "I know Tom brought a ledger from that office, he said maybe it ought to go up to Narco, because if Hodges had been dealing in any kind of—no, we didn't find anything like that at the office except some morphine, but Tom wanted to look at the ledger and see. But we've been busy and I don't recall if he did. Send it to Narco, I—"

"Well, ask and look," said Mendoza. "It could be important, John."

"Art's having a look in his desk. Tom's. If we don't find —I can ask him. I'm going to drop by to see him, he got a little shot of dope himself this morning, what a thing *that* was, and I—"

"Dope? Tom?"

"Oh, you don't know what you're missing," said Palliser. "I—Art's found it. Hodges' ledger. It was in Tom's—"

"*Bueno.* I want it. *Pronto,*" said Mendoza. If the little hunch paid off, maybe some concrete evidence that O'Rourke had bought this or that under the counter. From the crooked doctor. "John?"

Palliser came back on the line. "Art says he'll drop it off on his way home. O.K.?"

"O.K."

"But, Lieutenant, what's so important about—"

"I'm doing a little extracurricular detecting," said Mendoza. "Get back in shape for my own desk, boy."

Chapter 10

THE inquests on both Barron and Montez were scheduled for Monday morning at ten. Hackett attended the first and Palliser the second; Higgins escorted Rodney Terhune to another court for formal arraignment with a motley crew of other prisoners. As expected, both inquests were brief, and the open verdict handed down. Higgins was not so lucky; he spent two hours in court before Terhune was called, and ten minutes later took him back to jail again.

Bail had been set at twenty-five hundred (that particular judge was death on dope) and Terhune would probably make it within the hour. Nobody had ever counted how many bail bondsmen there were within hailing distance of the jail—that or any other jail.

Sometimes it seemed like the hell of a waste of time to catch them, Higgins reflected. What with all the new Court decisions hamstringing the good guys. But they had to keep at it, of course. He wondered what would happen if some day all the good guys got fed up at the same time, said the hell with it and knocked off.

He called Callaghan's office and said if he wanted a tail

on Terhune he'd better have one waiting here. And there were still three or four of the ones with pedigrees of sex violence he and Art hadn't caught up with. He headed back for the office.

As he went, he thought that Laura had a birthday coming up next month. February ninth. She'd be nine. What should he get her? Consult Mary; she'd know. And Mary being a great one for practicality—which was fine, of course—maybe an extra present just for fun, something frivolous.

It was just as nice as he'd always thought it would be, having a family to take care of.

Palliser got away from the Montez inquest at ten-thirty. It was Landers' day off and he was taking it gratefully—"It wasn't the marijuana," he'd said to Palliser last night, "*that* was quite an experience, but the little dose the doc said I got wasn't—it was his damned stomach pump." Which Palliser could well understand.

He was a little sleepy. Roberta had hauled him out to see two houses last night; and very nice houses too, but one at thirty-eight thousand, the other at forty. My God. This inflation.

But he wasn't feeling like wasting time any longer, and instead of calling he drove out to the General Hospital, flashed the badge and demanded to see Raul Obregon.

He got passed around, of course; but he was on occasion a stubborn man, John Palliser. He was finally admitted to a three-bed room, the nurse grudgingly put up screens around the bed nearest the door, and the intern told him severely he could have ten minutes. Obregon was off the critical list but still a sick man.

Palliser wondered about breaking the news to Obregon that his old pal Montez had been murdered—and in such a way. But he needn't have worried; Obregon knew.

153

He was about thirty, if he was Montez' age, but he looked older, unshaven and ill, bandages on head and one arm, the bedclothes pulled up on his chest. But when Palliser introduced himself, he tried to sit up a little higher; his dark eyes brightened.

"About Al," he said. "About Al. I saw it in the paper on Wednesday morning—didn't believe it. Didn't—Al! Such a — But I wanted—see you people—tell you—because it didn't say in the paper—what showed. Who. If you had anything. I wanted to tell you—"

"You take it easy now, Mr. Obregon."

"I'm—all right. They say I'll be O.K. now. Damn fool drunk. I was—on my way—to see you people—ask you what — Al such a good guy—to think he—" The easy tears of weakness filled his eyes; he panted a little.

"All right, take it easy, what was it you wanted—?"

"Look, I don't know. Anything about it. What you've got. On Al. Such a good guy. But you ought to know—and I don't know if it's anything to do with it—not—not accusing anybody, but that—little tramp he married—. Al would've been—great family man, always wanted a family—he grew up in an orphanage—and then that bitch hooks him. Carlotta Valdez. Try to tell him—just try. Crazy about her. We had a fight about it—made it up later but—. He wouldn't hear anything. Well, some sense he had—her family—no-goods from way back. He tried—get her away from that bunch, but— Trash people. On welfare. An uncle of hers —old wino. You know? No good. And she's got a brother—"

"Yes, don't get so excited, sir—I'm listening."

"I don't know if that's anything to do—but they're the only—bums and no-goods Al *knew*—I just thought— I do know, he was mad once when Carlotta gave money to this brother. This Rodolfo Valdez. A bum. Al—wanted cut her off from her family—settle down, see? She— And just last

week it was—" Obregon paused, gathering strength, and
went on, "I ran into Al at the managers' association meeting
—he said Carlotta'd been after him—give the brother
a job at the market—and he wasn't about to. A bum. She
—gave him hell, he said. I thought—maybe he's about to
wake up and see what she—little tramp. I could guess. But
try to tell—"

"All right, I've got that. Thanks very much."

"You looked—at Carlotta? The bums she knew, the—"

"We will, Mr. Obregon," said Palliser.

"Not—accusing. But you ought to—"

"That's right. We'll look. Thanks."

"And whoever *did* such a thing—Al—"

The intern came in and shepherded Palliser out. And that
was, of course, all very interesting and something to follow
up.

Palliser went back to the office and called the lab. He
got Duke. "On that VW you hauled in yesterday. Any prints?
Usable?"

"Oh, yes. I was just about to send up the report. Shall I
read it to you?"

"Is there anything useful in it?"

"I think you might say so."

"Read it."

"There were prints on the wheel. Quite nice clear prints.
Routine, we asked Records to check. Records had them."

"How nice. Whose are they?"

"Rodolfo Valdez, a pedigree of petty theft, common
drunk, purse snatching. He sort of graduated to the big time
in a hurry, didn't he? If it's him. He's on probation from a
charge of common drunk right now. The address listed
is on Magdalena Street."

Well, well, thought Palliser as he took it down. Was this
going to get cleared up as easy as all that? He thanked Duke,

and debated, looking at his watch. It was ten to twelve. An early lunch, or—?

He decided to try the Magdalena Street address first. It was over on the other side of the S.P. yards. (Had this Valdez ever worked there?) It was an old narrow street with old, narrow houses; the one he wanted was two-storey. A rooming house; a sign in the front window, *Room For Rent*. The woman who opened the door to him was also old and thin, her gray hair drawn back in a knob. She was wiping her hands on a dish towel.

"Valdez?" she said. "That low-down bum. You see that sign? That's for his room. He said to me this morning, gonna come back by noon, pay what's owin'. He *better*. Twelve bucks he owes me, and that's a lotta money down here, cop, where I swear these people—you gotta tie down anything you don't want took! Even my brand-new clothesline I just got—whoosh, gone! The milk bottles on the step the *kids* steal. You gotta draw the line somewheres, and I don't want bums in my house. You want that bum for something?"

Palliser decided that he might. Valdez suddenly looked like a very hot lead, and if he'd said he'd be back at noon— He was beginning to feel a little hungry but he'd better stake this place for awhile and see if Valdez showed. He'd parked across the street; there was parking that side only; he went back to the car and slid under the wheel, lit a philosophical cigarette and waited for his quarry.

Hackett had dropped off the ledger from Dr. William Hodges' office on his way home last night, just looking in the door; he was in a hurry, he'd promised to take Angel to a movie, he said. Mendoza was annoyed; he'd like to discuss this thing with Art.

And in the ledger he found something, but for evidential purposes it didn't matter a damn.

The ledger, regarded as a symbol of a life going downhill, was interesting. That was all.

Hodges had apparently been a precise, punctilious man to start with. The ledger started out with the year 1948, and the entries were in a neat small hand, almost copperplate. Records of his take from the illegalities, though he had covered up, no details; you could only guess which were abortions, dope supplied, or whatever. He used initials for his patients. About midway of the year 1952, the records began to appear in a more careless scrawl, and they got progressively worse. It was easy to guess on some that he had been half drunk, or under some drug, when he made the entries. They got scantier, too, and the dates, when they appeared, were at longer intervals. There was no date listed after August of 1960.

The only entry that interested Mendoza was one dated in May of 1957. It read simply, *M. O'R. Prescrip. Empirin No. 3. $25.*

M. O'R. Margaret O'Rourke? And what was Empirin No. 3?

It had taken him some time to pore over the ledger and when he went to bed Alison was sound asleep.

He asked her about it over breakfast. "Empirin Number —oh, it's got codeine in it," said Alison. "No, Sheba—*not* on the table while we're eating! I had some once when I had that abcessed wisdom tooth. The doctor—" Her voice was drowned out by the exuberant yells of both twins, as Johnny erupted into the breakfast room with a toy airplane held at arm's length, emitting a presumable imitation of its jet-engine. Terry behind him echoing that, and Mairí after the pair of them.

"Johnny—Terry! ¡*Basta ya!* For heaven's sake—"

"Now you two—" Mairí panted after them, shooing them toward the kitchen door. "*Out* with you in the yard—my soul, the energy they have, *achara,* it's terrible—" All three departed precipitately out the back door, and Alison said, "Monsters!"

"Don't malign our hostages to fortune. Even if they did give me the measles. Codeine?"

"I seem to remember. Rather a potent pain killer, anyway."

Mendoza brooded, sitting in the big armchair in the living room. He began to add another two and two—what had happened yesterday, the Weaver house up for sale—and he thought suddenly, But how simple. Yes. He'd said, different ways for different people and situations. Those wills—it could be that they wouldn't come across any more of them. Or many. There was an even easier way, with the old people who owned a little house, a little property. As per Mrs. Weaver. It was quite likely that kind nursie had used that gambit before. He just saw it after hearing the bit about taking old Mrs. Weaver to her own place to look after proper, and selling the house so Mrs. Weaver would have enough money—

It was plausible. The old woman on pension. His active imagination supplied details. Whisk the old woman away (where did the nurse live? Address from the County Health was dated 1954—had she moved since?). Put the house up for sale—in the old lady's name. Persuading the old lady to do so. Wait until it was through escrow, the check deposited at the bank to nursie's credit—old lady docilely endorsing it on some tale of nursie. And—what? The trusting old woman—or women, how many, and probably old men, too —believing in nursie, and most of them, maybe, nominally under a doctor's care, or if not shown to a new doctor as an obvious case of near senility (with the help of the Empirin No. 3, or something else) so he'd have no qualms about signing a death certificate—

158

Por Dios, he thought. Could it be? It would be quite easy that way; he could see it. Especially where there were nosy (concerned) neighbors, old friends. Maybe the first inspiration had been caused by a situation like that. The wills used where nobody cared, nobody was taking notice.

He wondered. After what they had turned up, it looked too likely. His imagination working overtime? It all seemed so smooth: the wheels well oiled, the situation with Mrs. Weaver. At first apparently she thought she could do it as with Pearce, Wilkerson, Lord. Then the neighbors began to be too nosy. So she had put the alternate plan in operation. Persuaded the old lady, temporarily taken off the drugs (and her mind confused under the dope, the old lady not realizing she had been doped) and—

"You must be feeling better," said Alison. "Pacing like a lion in a cage."

"I'm fine," said Mendoza absently. Imagination. It occurred to him that he'd never laid eyes on this woman he was fitting into such a monstrous role. He went down the hall for a tie and jacket, checked his pockets, went out to the garage. What was the name of that realty company? Janet Cox had said—Newbury.

He checked the whereabouts of twins and cats and backed the Ferrari out carefully. After the rain on Saturday, the weather had settled down to the usual cool sunny January.

The Newbury company was on Sunset. He told the salesman he was interested in low-income rental property, had passed this house on Edgemont and would like to see it.

"Well, let me call the owner and see if it's convenient, Mr. Mendoza. It'll go into multiple listing tomorrow, ought to be snapped up, good central location and—we're asking twenty-two-five." The shabby little frame house. This inflation.

The salesman drove him there. He could imagine the eyes

159

watching from across the street. The concerned (nosy) neighbors.

She let them in, the monster he had built up in his mind. Was she? He looked at her, as the salesman made hearty introductions. Mrs. Margaret O'Rourke. She was fat, a balloon of a woman, and a little like the Dutch-doll picture on imported chocolates: red cheeks, white skin, the incredibly black hair cut in a straight bob, unbecoming. She bolstered the image of the nice kind motherly nurse with a starched white uniform, white shoes and stockings. Her mouth smiled widely, perpetually; but she had little eyes like raisins pushed into a lump of dough, and the eyes were cold and dead, black dead eyes—the mouth was what you noticed, what you were meant to notice, but Mendoza saw her eyes. She bobbed politely at him.

"How do, sir. Ackshally Mis' Weaver owns the house, I'm her nurse. It's a nice house, well built and kept up. I'll be glad show you through—"

And there, on the shabby old velour couch, was Mrs. Weaver. Who had inadvertently started Mendoza on the wild goose chase that had delivered such a very wild goose into his—imagination. (Tangible, concrete evidence? He suspected the D.A. would laugh at what he had.) Old Mrs. Weaver, the sharp old lady, the responsible and proud old lady—so thrifty, so admirable. She was a thin little old lady, with a halo of curly white hair, and she smiled at him—obviously all her faculties, as Mairí said. She had on a clean blue cotton dress, and one gnarled old hand clasped the head of an old cane. She said how-do-you-do in a clear voice. "I'm not worth much these days, but we always tried to keep the place up, plumbing and all like that. I don't relish the thought of leaving—" the smile quivered a little—"forty-three years we lived in this house—but there come the changes, and we mustn't complain."

It was only her dark eyes reminded Mendoza a little of his grandmother. Eighty, but life hadn't beaten her; she was still all here, and coping with it. He suddenly saw the fat silent nurse as a lurking evil shadow over old Mrs. Weaver. He would bet—he would just bet—when they went and asked, as Forsythe's man would be doing now—they'd hear about the other old people taken away to kind nursie's home to be carefully looked after— And unless she was operating a rest home, which she obviously wasn't, what happened to them? Happened one by one—the decks cleared to make way for the next. Out of sight out of mind.

The little cold finger up his spine that had said, Something to be found out, hadn't been wrong.

The nurse showed them through the house; the salesman did all the talking. It was clean and very shabby. A single garage at one side of the deep lot, now all the grass brown and long. The nurse followed them into the back yard.

"My boy, he's cleanin' out the garage for us, be all ready to leave. Lot of junk piles up in a garage, you know." She didn't introduce them. The young man busy dumping a pile of old newspapers into a trash barrel glanced up briefly at them, saying nothing. He was in the early twenties, dark, good looking, with overlong hair shaggy on his neck; and a whiff of wildness emanated from him to Mendoza, almost tangible. The smell of incipient violence; the kind of feeling Mendoza had experienced before with the psychotics, this and that sort. There was a little too much white showing in his eyes. He didn't speak to them; he went into the garage and came out with a battered old steamer trunk, and began with rather vicious efficiency to break it up with an axe, pieces small enough to go in the barrel. The trunk was empty; the nurse would have been through everything, not to miss anything of value.

"Nice big yard," said the salesman chattily. "You can see—lots of potential—"

The nurse's car in the drive. A '61 two-door Ford, blue. Janet Cox had said she only left the old lady, as far as they knew, to go up to the market on Fountain. But she had a car. She could go farther, at night, nobody noticing. Where?

"Mis' Weaver's kind of anxious to sell, now she's decided. Like to get settled, you know—she puts up a good face, but she isn't really so good, the arthritis and—"

Mendoza thanked her. As he got back in the salesman's car, he felt cold. That woman—he didn't think his imagination was working overtime. The wide smiling mouth and her warm voice would dupe so many unsuspecting people—

He told the salesman he'd think about it.

He sat in the Ferrari and he thought, coldly, that the D.A. would just throw up his hands. The wills—the wills could even be genuine. People easily duped. Perhaps some old people even easier. The death certificates, all nice and aboveboard. Old people with the chronic troubles so apt to slip away—and nobody close to care. Even the concerned neighbors—poor old thing, a happy release. The busy doctors more interested in patients they could cure. Probably hopeless to expect anything from exhumations. They had a list of patients only up to 1965, three years ago—how to find names of any between then and now? The anonymous old people, the unimportant people, with the little unimportant possessions of small value. How many taken kindly to her home to be looked after? How many trusting her, grateful to find the good kind nurse, persuaded into signing the wills? How many—

And no Goddamned evidence at all, that *was* evidence. About evidence he had to know, almost as much as a lawyer. The D.A. would listen, and shake his head. Not enough. Nothing conclusive.

Mendoza remembered the classic quote: *Some circumstantial evidence is very strong, such as when you find a trout in the milk.* And a lot of circumstantial evidence, the best kind. But on this—

Nada absolutamente. And presently nursie would take old Mrs. Weaver—gallant old Mrs. Weaver—away, to await the completion of escrow when the house was sold, and after that—

And where would she be taking her?

He got out of the Ferrari and went up to the corner to a public phone. He dialed the office; nobody was in but Lake. He told Lake to shoot an urgent query up to the DMV in Sacramento: plate-number such-and-such, issued to Margaret O'Rourke, at what address in L.A. County or elsewhere?

It was a hell of a thing. The D.A. would say— Damn what the private eyes turned up, no real evidence—

Piggott and Glasser were placidly heading back to the office in Glasser's Ford. They had been out on a new call, an ordinary sort of thing for Homicide, a brawl in a bar out on Beverly, with a man knifed. They had got the statements and taken names and addresses, and now they were going back to type up the report.

Piggott was thinking pleasantly and sleepily about Prudence, what a nice girl she was and what a pretty girl— and she seemed to think he was a big hero because he was a real detective on the LAPD Homicide crew—

They made the light at Rampart, and Glasser changed to the right lane to be ready for the turn at First, when they heard the siren. Glasser stepped on the brake.

"Ambulance or—" Piggott turned to look. It was behind them. Traffic was obediently halted in all lanes, both ways.

The first car was a beat-up jalopy, but it was making time.

About seventy, Piggott reckoned. It came through the intersection like a bullet, and just past Rampart it veered across the yellow line, driver losing control, and slammed into the first car in the left lane there.

"Christ!" said Glasser. Four cars jammed together, slithering with a great crash half up on the sidewalk—people in the street—

Here came the squad car at high-speed pursuit, siren screaming. "Oh, my God," said Glasser, and Piggott shut his eyes. The damn fool people, running and shouting—people in the street— The squad car, traveling at sixty or sixty-five, tried desperately to avoid the damn fool people. The driver, trained at pursuit, didn't slam on his brakes; he did what he could, which wasn't much, at a crowded intersection. The squad car veered off toward the far curb of Rampart, clear of people then, brakes just beginning to take hold gently, and it bounced off the curb, smashed into the first car in the left lane on Beverly, carried another two cars into the middle of the street, where it stopped upside down half on top of another car.

It was carnage in thirty seconds.

In the short space of silence before the screams began, Piggott said plaintively, "Why does it have to be us, Henry? Like fate. One I can understand, but two in less than a week —all the blood and screaming and— Why us?"

Glasser switched off the engine and they got out of the car. Find out about the squad car driver first.

Palliser was very nearly starved to death by the time Rodolfo Valdez showed. Twice he'd decided to go have lunch, and come back; twice his obstinacy had kept him there, across from the rooming house, waiting. At two-fifteen patience and obstinacy were rewarded.

A stocky short dark man came ambling up the street and

went into the rooming house. Palliser got out of the car and crossed the street. He found the man in the entrance hall arguing with the landlady. "I gonna pay you tomorrow, my sister says you tell her she get the money tomorrow—"

"Today, you bum!"

"Is this man Rodolfo Valdez?" asked Palliser.

They looked at him in surprise. "Oh—you back. Yeah, this is him," said the landlady. Palliser put the arm on Valdez, showing his badge. Just a few questions. He led him across to the car and drove him back to headquarters. Valdez was dumb on the way; but Palliser's stomach was rumbling loudly.

He handed Valdez over to Lake to keep an eye on, and went out for a sandwich and coffee before attempting to question him. When he came back, the only one in was Grace, and Palliser said, "Like to help me heckle a suspect?"

"Need you ask? The original brutal cop, that's me." Grace stood up. "What on?"

"Montez. I think he's a pretty good bet—" Palliser filled him in. "And just because we couldn't hear Obregon any sooner, we went chasing our tails—"

"Open and shut," said Grace. "You'd have got there without Obregon. These prints. I like the prints. Nice concrete evidence."

"Always useful. The kind the D.A. likes all right."

They took Valdez, who was merely looking stupid, into an interrogation room and started to work on him.

"Always pickin' on me," Valdez grumbled. "I try find a job. Carlotta says she make Al gimme a job. But he's mean. Judge says, gotta find a job, tell the officer. The probation guy. But—now you pick on me—"

"Al Montez, Valdez," said Palliser. "He was mean to you, was he?"

Valdez looked at him earnestly. He wasn't very bright to

165

start with, and a steady intake of *vino* and, when he could afford it, the harder stuff, had deteriorated him a good deal. He looked at Palliser and his eyes narrowed and he said with foolish cunning, "You gonna try make me say I did for Al."

"Did you, Rodolfo?" asked Grace.

"He was mean to Carlotta, too. Wouldn't give her money. He made a lotta money, but inna bank, save, save. He's mean. Carlotta say she make him gimme good job at the market—so I can tell the officer—but he don't. Call me a dirty name."

"So you took him off, Rodolfo?"

Valdez looked vague. "I *looked* for a job. Nobody gimme a job. Like the judge say I gotta get or go to jail." Belatedly they both realized that he was a little drunk. With one like Valdez it was sometimes hard to tell. Palliser straightened, consulting Grace mutely. Press him? And have a smart lawyer claim duress afterward? Grace shrugged, and his eyes were cynical. No need to incorporate into the notes the fact that Valdez was under the weather. Likely he wouldn't remember himself.

"That was how it was, wasn't it, Rodolfo?" said Palliser. "You decided to teach Al a lesson—he was mean to you and Carlotta—and you—"

"Carlotta said—Carlotta said, she said, 'Dolf, we getta a lotta money when Al's dead—somethin' he got, ins—ins— for Carlotta when he's dead. He was a drag, alla time save, save, 'n' she says to me— But when he didn't gimme no job —so I could tell the officer—"

"You phoned him and asked him to meet you at the main gate of the S.P. yards," said Palliser deliberately.

"What? What?" Valdez looked confused, focusing on him hazily. "What—yards? I never. I never *thought* about doin' anythin'—I went to that place he works—Al—an' I was gonna ask him, real nice, gimme a job, just awhile so's I

could tell—only when I come up, I see him just drivin' off
—that funny little car—an I think no go, only I seen it go
inna lot just up the block—so I go up there, it's a restaurant,
an' I think, go in an' ask him nice. Only then—I got thinkin',
why do I hafta be nice 'n' polite to *him?* Al? Alla time mean
to Carlotta, she says—an' I go in, an' he's just finished eatin'
—he leaves a seventy-five cent tip for the girl! Seventy-fi'
cents—when he's mean with C—"

So maybe would they have enough to make Carlotta ac-
cessory-after? Probably not. These things rather subtle sometimes. Palliser grimaced at Grace; this one was clearing up
fast, Valdez talking as if he talked to himself.

"He says no, no, about the job, but he's—kinda like lookin' down his nose at me, Al. Him. Like he done a favor,
marry my sister. He says he drive me home—I come onna
bus up to the— An' the parkin' lot's dark, an' I'm feelin'
good 'n' mad at him, I just slug him—an' pretty soon I'm
inna car an' he starts to wake up, I slug him again—"

Gaps there would be.

"An' I think what Carlotta said—lotta money if—she
allus gives me money, I ask an' she's got it— An' I see a movie
once, about a train runnin' over—I guess that was after he
woke up 'n' I hit him again an' went 'n' got the rope out
inna back yard. An' I thought—I'm strong, see, strong as a
bull, me, I find a good place, good an' dark, an' I just push
him up over that fence there, 'n' climb over an' fix him
onna tracks like I seen in that movie—"

The deductive logic all wrong on this one; they hadn't
been thinking simple enough. He hadn't known a thing
about the S.P. yards, the schedule, anything. Just chance. A
vague little motive. They'd never prove that Carlotta egged
him on. For the insurance. And both of them, foolish and
ignorant people, would be surprised that the homicide in-
validated the insurance.

167

But at least it was cleared up. The offbeat one. And what a thing. The upright useful citizen—and one like Valdez. No bets that he wouldn't get off with life—which in California meant he would be eligible for parole in just seven years.

Insurance, thought Mendoza. Insurance? Would any of the old people—the patients—have had any? Conceivably. Widows, widowers—quite possibly insurance, to add to the loot.

Quite absently, after stopping for lunch at the London Grill, he was headed back toward Edgemont Avenue. That long-haired lout the nurse had introduced as— Suddenly the bits connected in his mind: Hadn't someone said, on Fuller, that a long-haired kid had helped her clear out the apartment? Son. She said she had a—

A wild one, that. Something about him—

And why the hell was he on Fountain Avenue, driving back there? Nothing he could do. Nothing. Whatever the private eyes turned up, such vague evidence—no evidence the D.A. would consider.

The wild-goose chase had turned up too wild a goose. . . . Like the female versions of poker, he thought: every other card wild. The D.A.—

He caught the light at Western, and as he sat waiting he noticed the Ford across the intersection facing him. An old blue Ford, '61 two-door; its right-turn signal was blinking. And it was the '61 Ford that belonged to the nurse, by God, the plate-number— The man at the wheel, the youngish man who had given off the almost tangible smell of the jungle, the violence.

Mendoza flicked on his left-turn signal; by the grace of God he was in the far-left lane. The light changed; the Ford swept around onto Western, and Mendoza waited, swearing under his breath, for the amber to stop oncoming traffic, finally made it around. He gunned the Ferrari, spotting the Ford three blocks up.

When it turned left on Hollywood Boulevard he was right behind. And he wasn't sure why. What did he expect?

All the way down Hollywood to Fairfax. Out Fairfax to Sunset, out to Beverly Hills and all the way to Coldwater Canyon Drive. Right turn signal. The Ford gunned up Coldwater Canyon, and Mendoza closed up a little, recklessly—the Ferrari wasn't exactly an anonymous job and anyone might spot it easier than any other car, dogging the Ford all that way across town—

Ahead of him, the Ford suddenly swerved left and vanished. Mendoza stepped on the gas, then the brake. A side road. Royal Drive, said the sign. He turned up it. It curved; he heard the Ford ahead. He passed a parked car on the opposite side of the road, noting it idly—somebody sitting in it—and drove on another quarter mile, and stepped hard on the brake. He had a quick glimpse—around the next gentle curve, a dead end: a big circular space of blacktop, the roof of a large house, and the back end of the stationary Ford.

The Ford, home? Here? Another bit of the unusable vague evidence? Expensive houses up here. The loot she must have taken—

In any case, he wasn't going to show the Ferrari out in the open. He backed down the curving road slowly. He came even with the parked car: an unobtrusive dignified '64 Rambler, dark blue. He glanced at it, head out the window guiding the Ferrari.

The driver leaned out the window and said, "What the hell are you doing here, Luis? I had it on the grapevine you had the measles. That's what you get for finally letting a dame hook you."

169

"*¡Porvida—vaya el diablo!*" said Mendoza. He braked and switched off, got out and walked across to the Rambler. "And what the hell are you doing here?"

Sergeant Stefano Benedettino offered his hand. They didn't often run across each other these days, but they'd been through the Academy together too many years back. Benedettino grinned; a dame had hooked him long before Alison had got Mendoza, and these days Benedettino was a little too fat, getting bald, and settled into middle age. He was up in Narco now.

"I'm on a tail. What are you on?"

"A tail," said Mendoza. "Who's yours?"

"Kind of a funny one," said Benedettino. "A con man, but we think he could be a supplier. It's tied up to your office in a kind of way—"

"For God's sake how?"

"Well, he was involved in a homicide, this Rodney Terhune—but Sergeant Hackett doesn't really think he——"

"Terhune? So tell me the story."

The autopsy report on Juliet Romano had just been sent up, and Hackett was discussing it with Higgins—the same wide-bladed knife as on Moreno, so it looked—when Lake uttered an exclamation and got up. "Well, Lieutenant, good to see you—"

"What are you doing here, Luis?" asked Hackett. "You're supposed to be on leave."

Mendoza looked around the office. "God, it'll be good to be back—the damn doctor—I'm all right." He gripped Hackett and Higgins by the arms, between them. "So tell me things about one Rodney Terhune. I've seen the papers, but I could bear to know more. He seems to link up with my—mmm—extracurricular case."

Chapter 11

MENDOZA sat down in his desk chair and looked around the office affectionately. It seemed years since he'd sat here, his own familiar place. "And what happened to you?" he asked Hackett.

Hackett felt the deep scratches on his face, healing now but still visible. "I ran into some female fingernails. So what are you up to and what's this about Terhune?"

Mendoza lit a cigarette and started to explain, but before he got far Palliser and Grace came in. "Jimmy said the boss is back. How're you doing, Lieutenant? We got that Montez thing cleared up," Palliser added to Hackett.

"Don't tell me. Wrapped up tight? Who was it?"

"Wife's brother. Stupid damn thing beginning to end."

"They so often are."

"Sit down and listen to a little story," said Mendoza. "But first, let's hear what you've got on this Terhune." He listened while Hackett filled him in on that, and laughed over the instant uplift. "*Vaya*, what an idea. You know, I have a strong suspicion it was Rodney's idea. Maybe inventiveness runs in the family—because I have also a strong suspicion that

171

Rodney is the minister son. Mmm, yes, wouldn't that sound reassuring to the victims. So Narco's tailing him. I ran into Steve Benedettino an hour ago up there—"

"Where? What are you—"

"He picked Rodney up at the jail after he made bail and took off. Steve says he went back to this apartment you tell me he shared with Barron, and came out about an hour later with three suitcases. Went straight up to the house in Coldwater Canyon. Is he planning to jump bail? Well, let Narco worry about that. Now, listen—I've got quite a tale to tell you. I got into it by accident, because Mairí MacTaggart—" He put out his cigarette, almost immediately lit another, and started to tell them the saga of the practical nurse who'd found a new game for collecting the loot. They listened, with muttered comments.

"I'd lay any money on it—probably we'd never find out how many of the poor old people she's brought a happy release to." Mendoza looked grim. "Once I suspected—you see what a nice easy M.O. it is. Diabolical. A cold-blooded artist at it she'll be by now. We'll see what the private boys turn up further, and I'll swear—"

"My God, yes," said Higgins, looking horrified. "What a racket—and all those wills are suggestive, but my God, Luis, you think she's actually knocked off all those—"

Mendoza gestured. "I don't say some weren't natural deaths, but it was damn convenient for her, how at least four we know about so far passed quietly out of the picture as soon as those wills were signed—or very shortly afterward. I'm just saying, when we get more history on it, it'll look even more suggestive. But you can see, that's just what it is and no more—suggestive. There's absolutely no concrete evidence. You can see what I—"

They thought about it, and nodded. "Damn it," said Mendoza, "this—vampire ought to be stopped, some way. Have the fear of God put in her. But as I said—so Captain Garden goes and tells her we know all about it, tries to scare her, what happens? She'll know there's no chance of our charging her with anything. My God, we haven't even got a reason to ask for a warrant, search her place and find the prescriptive drugs to make a little charge of unlawful possession!" He put out his cigarette angrily. "So tell me it's not our beat, not our worry. It's a damned devilish murderous business and that cold-blooded bitch ought to be stopped."

"I'm with you there, if that's so," said Hackett. "But—"

"So now it seems this Terhune is linked up with her. I'll take another bet, the minister son. And there's another one, younger—that one's a wild one. He smells of the jungle," said Mendoza seriously, and they all knew what he meant. Most of the people they had to deal with were stupid, foolish, greedy, unthinking people, in trouble—or dead—because of stupidity; but they did also come across the wild ones, the ones with the inherent evil built in, or that was what it looked like. "Terhune, Yorke, O'Rourke. I wonder which is legal, if any of them. Where'd you get Rodney's pedigree, from Philly?"

"No, the Feds. He told us he came from Denver, but Denver'd never heard of him. Which didn't say he hadn't a pedigree somewhere, so we asked J. Edgar, and it turned up there."

"*Bueno*. Let's ask Philly direct for background. You said he'd been tagged first when he was sixteen? All right, the juvenile bureau ought to know something about his family at the time. Ask. Marked urgent."

"O.K., but, Luis—this isn't—"

"Our case. No. I agree with you, Rodney didn't have anything to do with Barron's murder. He's Narco's business. And I know kind nursie isn't our business either. She's *my* business," said Mendoza forcefully, "and by God if it's humanly possible I'll catch up to her with retribution. So let's cheat a little and use our facilities to check back on her. I'd like to know, first of all, whether that is her house up on Royal Drive in Coldwater Canyon. Big, expensive—and isolated—places up there. Well, she'll have taken a lot of loot in the last ten years or so. I asked Jimmy to contact Sacramento on the plate number. We should know that for certain by tomorrow."

"You think that entry in Hodges' ledger refers to her?" asked Palliser.

Mendoza shrugged. "Take your choice. It could, it couldn't. I suppose she'd want to renew the prescription in eleven years—but he wasn't noting down everything the last eight or nine. One thing. Rodney told you he'd come to California in 1954—well, that's the year she first listed herself as a practical nurse with the County Health service. Rodney was tagged back in Philly later—apparently he went back home alone for awhile. And I'd like to know what name the other son is using—I'd also lay money he's got a pedigree. Somewhere. For something. Whole family a bunch of wrong ones."

"That," said Grace, "is a word for it, Lieutenant—diabolical. Not a vampire, a vulture. Preying on the old people, alone and poor. And not one damn bit of good evidence on her. Show she got left all their possessions by the old folk; twelve, thirteen, more of the old folk—she smirks and says it shows what a good kind nurse she is, they appreciated her. Handwriting experts—on those wills—well, it isn't an exact science, you'd have a dozen swearing one way and a dozen the other—"

"I see it, I see it!" said Mendoza.

"A real mass killer," said Higgins, "if you're right—and nobody can touch her. In one way it's so obvious, and in another—no court evidence worth a damn. The D.A.'d laugh in your face."

"So what do I do?" asked Mendoza. "Here's another old lady unwittingly in nursie's power. The house is up for sale. *Such* a simple easy M.O. The old lady eighty years old. Nurse whisks her away to that big isolated place up in Coldwater Canyon, pretty soon the house is sold—and it's all clear, it wouldn't take ten days to go through escrow—the final check paid to the old lady. Who has arthritis, walks with a cane, so what more natural than that she endorses the check over to nursie? Nursie assuring her it'll be deposited in her name in the bank and it's more than enough to enable nursie to keep her comfortable and happy the rest of her life. I don't suppose Mrs. Weaver knows much about banking or allied matters—she wouldn't hesitate about signing. And after that, how long has she got? How long?"

"My God, that's—" Higgins shook his head.

"This particular old lady not under a doctor's care regularly. Nursie's grammar is a little shaky, but I'll bet she knows all the rules and regulations about sudden death. Anybody not under a doctor's care, seen by a doctor within ten days, the autopsy mandatory. So she fills the old lady full of Empirin No. 3 or whatever, and lets a doctor see her. Quite willing to pay the extra fee to have him come to the house. Maybe cannily picking a young doctor recently in practice. Or, what am I saying? That kind sometimes all the keener —a tired old doctor used to the humdrum routine. In any case, he sees an obviously *non compos mentis* senior citizen, he won't be surprised at irregular heart action or pulse. Maybe the nurse lets him see her twice, before *kaput,* old lady slips away in her sleep. Happy release. Does he hesitate about signing the certificate?"

"We've all got imaginations," said Hackett. "You turned up something here, Luis. But not one damned thing to—"

175

"I've had thoughts. Futile thoughts," said Mendoza wearily. "Wilcox Street has jurisdiction—flashes the badge at the realty company and says, hold off on selling the house. What good does it do? Stop the sale while we check all the records, all the patients we can find names for? We'll never get concrete evidence on the homicides. She's been too careful, I think. In the end, we'd have to—

"Send some big tough cop like George here to scare her; we know all about you, sister, cease and desist—" Mendoza laughed, lit another cigarette. "She'd drop Mrs. Weaver, sure, and go somewhere else and start over."

"It's a bastard," said Higgins seriously.

"Say it again. But I may think of something yet—or we may just come across something, looking into her history, where she was a little careless—something we can get her on. Keep the fingers crossed." Mendoza got up. "I suppose I'd better get home or Alison'll have the police out after me. But you'll have me back permanent in another week or so. . . . I'd like to get this—vulture put out of business before I—"

"We'll see what Philly can tell us."

"Mark it urgent." Mendoza picked up his hat reluctantly, looking around the office again.

"You really found something with nursie," said Palliser.

"You see what I mean—older son at least takes after mama," said Mendoza sardonically. "The inventive mind. Brand-new twists on the con games."

Grace got up, too. "I'll go send that query to Philly. Our beat or not, one like that ought to be stopped cold."

When Hackett got to the office on Tuesday morning, he found an overnight report signed by Galeano on his desk. Another rape-assault, at least it could be assumed rape was intended; but the girl had got away. One Jeannette Anderson, in General Hospital, bruised and shaken and sustaining a knife slash, but in good condition. They hadn't questioned her last night; she'd been in shock. The day crew probably could see her. It was at least possible that the attacker had been the X on Moreno and Romano.

Hackett agreed that it could be possible. Not Homicide's business, when nobody had been killed, but she ought to be interviewed anyway. It was Higgins' day off, and everybody but Palliser was out on something new; Palliser was typing his report on Rodolfo Valdez. Homicide in a big city is kept busy. Hackett put on his hat again and went over to the General Hospital to see Jeannette Anderson.

She couldn't, however, tell him much—hadn't caught a glimpse of her attacker. She was cashier at a movie house, and coming home alone late most nights, always carried an open can of pepper— "My mother always says better than a gun," she told him cheerfully. It was the pepper that had confounded the attacker, evidently, but she'd been lucky to get away safe at that. And nothing said it had been the man responsible for Moreno and Romano.

It was Higgins' day off. He got up a little later than usual and after breakfast went out to mow the lawn. Stevie used to do that, earn his allowance, but of course with the brace he couldn't now. Mary drove them both to school and called for them on account of Stevie; ordinarily Higgins wouldn't approve, they could walk just as well—good for them. But the therapy was helping, and the doctor said maybe in another few months the brace could come off.

He'd just finished the front lawn when Mary came back from the market. He followed her into the house. "About Laura's birthday," he said. "I thought—"

"She needs school clothes," said Mary briskly.

"Well, there's a couple of music books she's asked for. I

177

can get those, and you can get the clothes. And a party, for all the kids she wants to ask—"

Mary plucked a can of coffee out of the big market bag and put it on the counter. Her gray eyes smiled at him: his lovely Mary, and he'd never quite believe, his wife. "You spoil them, George. We ought to be saving for college. And all the medical bills—"

"We get along all right. And I never had anybody to spoil before," said Higgins a little wistfully.

Landers, recovered from the stomach pump, and Grace, who was inclined to brood over the offbeat mass killer Mendoza had turned up, were out on one of the new ones. It looked, when they sorted it out, like one of those they'd work into the ground and eventually file away in Pending.

The boy, Juan Garcia, had a cold and wasn't going to school that morning, but when his mother didn't come to see how he felt, bring his breakfast, he got up and went into her room, to find her dead on the bed. He'd gone to the neighbors, who had called the priest and the police, in that order, and by the time Landers and Grace got there at eight-forty the ambulance was there, too. The boy was upset and crying, but he was a good, level-headed, bright boy; they were gentle with him but there were questions they had to ask, and a picture emerged.

It looked as if the woman, Mrs. Stella Garcia, had been strangled. There'd been a little struggle in the bedroom. The house—which Mrs. Garcia had owned—was on the corner of Avila and Vignes, and there was a street light at the corner. One of the bedroom windows was on the Avila Avenue side, and the street light would illuminate it somewhat. After they'd looked around the bedroom—the handbag dropped on the floor, valueless contents spilled, the billfold empty—lamp on the bedside table knocked over—the signs

178

of struggle—they could piece out what had most likely happened.

Somebody maybe by chance glancing in that window (or maybe having cased the job) carefully prying off the screen, raising the window farther, getting in, after the handbag. The boy said she always put it on the table by the window: but the window too high for anyone just to reach in for the bag. And she'd woken, stirred, and maybe even tried to scream, and he'd had to shut her up. He had. Probably no intention of killing her. And the boy so deeply asleep he hadn't heard anything.

There were a few vague footprints in the narrow flower bed under the window; the little house was kept up and Mrs. Garcia had watered her flowers that day, so the earth was damp. There were marks on the windowsill. The lab would be looking at them. Something might show up. There might even be fingerprints in the room.

The lab men showed up as Landers and Grace were ready to leave. They wished the lab men luck.

"Unless there are prints—even if the footprints are clear—" said Landers.

"Damn all," agreed Grace. "Anonymous. And for about fifteen bucks, by what the boy said." Mrs. Garcia had been a widow; her husband had been killed in Vietnam two years ago. She had worked as a window dresser at The Broadway. "Even if the footprints are good enough to make casts— we can't look at every pair of shoes in the county. Or even just on the Central beat."

The anonymous ones came along. And even if there were fingerprints, on the handbag, in the room, they wouldn't necessarily be in Records, all neatly filed under a name and an address.

About ten o'clock a big man impeccably dressed in navy

blue wandered into the Homicide office and asked for Hackett. "Fredericks," he said, offering a hand. "F.B.I."

"So what can we do for the Feds? Sit down," said Hackett.

"Maybe the other way round," said Fredericks. "It just occurred to me. I don't say it's so. I had to come down here, see a fellow up in Narcotics, I just thought I'd pass this on. Been reading about this rape-killer you're after. Any solid lead on him?"

Hackett spread his hands. "Nil. Oh, a few things. He's a dark blond, big, strong, no special accent, white."

"So." The Fed accepted a cigarette and light. "Just reading between the lines in the papers, Sergeant—which gave me your name—it just occurred to me. Suppose you've been combing your records—"

"What else?"

"—But he isn't necessarily there. You taken a look at the current Ten Most Wanted list?"

"Why?"

The Fed pulled a flyer out of his pocket and laid it on the desk. "Patrick Albert Rooney. Just made the list last month. Six-three, a hundred and ninety, age twenty-two, ash blond, white, all these tattoos. Wanted for three rape-murders—knife used—back in St. Louis. It just occurred to me. We don't know where he is. He could be here."

"Oh, *hell*," said Hackett, looking at the photograph. "My God, it could be. It just could. And what use to show this to the Anderson girl? It was dark. We can try. Thanks very much for nothing."

"I just thought I ought to pass it on," said the Fed.

The operative from Forsythe and Mason came to the house on Rayo Grande Avenue at three o'clock on Tuesday afternoon. He was a big burly man about forty, and his card said *Chauncey F. Fitzpatrick*. He said to Mendoza, "A very preliminary report, Lieutenant. We've only been on it thirty-six hours. But I thought you'd want to hear. You given to the hunches?"

"I've been known to have them," said Mendoza. "This one was kosher?"

Fitzpatrick grinned. "We all know the LAPD is sharp. My God, yes. My God, what a thing this is. Forsythe put two of us on it. Garrison spent yesterday at the Hall of Records. On wills and then death certificates." He pulled out a notebook. "I've been backtracking patients off that list. This is —and not one damn bit of court evidence, but—"

"Nothing? Nothing that could be—"

"I'm ahead of myself. I'll give you the circumstantial stuff. Garrison found five more wills. Will forms. I won't clutter your brain with names. He's out now checking the circumstances on those people, looking for neighbors who remember anything and so on. I backtracked nine patients—I checked with Garrison, and no wills for those nine—and they showed as a little different. I don't know what this'll say to you." Fitzpatrick lit a cigarette and shied away involuntarily as Sheba landed on his shoulder from behind.

"Little monster—put her down," said Mendoza. "So give! What showed?"

"Nice cat," said Fitzpatrick, stroking Sheba. "We've got two Siamese. Well, as expectable, elderly people. God, talk about a new con game—! In four cases, the neighbors remembered that the people had relatives back east or somewhere, but not close. The other five were all alone. Nobody. I got a little detail because the neighbors had known all these people fairly well, been—you know—a little concerned about them. The elderly people alone."

"*De veras*. The nosy neighbors," said Mendoza. "So?"

"Nosy? Well— In every one of those cases, Lieutenant," said Fitzpatrick, "the same pattern showed. Six of those nine people owned houses. About all they owned—little old houses. And every time, the house was put up for sale, and it got around that the nurse was taking the patient to her own home to take care of there—the rest of his or her life. All kind and comfortable."

"*De veras*," said Mendoza again. "I didn't think I was imagining things. The simple M.O. Yes. And her address is unlisted in the phone book—under any of those three names, at least. Even if one of the nosy neighbors was persistent—she wouldn't let an address be pried out of her, but even if the patient knew, and passed it on, what could the neighbor do? When the patient seemed satisfied with the deal? Any enquiries later, it'd be, so sorry to tell you that Mrs. or Miss or Mr. Blank passed away peacefully— There were old men, too?"

"Three old men. All on pension. A retired railroad man, a—"

Mendoza waved that information away. "You're synchronized with Mr. Garrison. Ferreting in the Hall of Records. Tell me about the death certificates."

Fitzpatrick sat back. "This is the Goddamndest thing I ever ran across, Lieutenant. . . . I wouldn't doubt you get the hunches. I had lunch with Garrison. He'd checked seven of those nine people—six women, three men—ages between sixty-nine and seventy-eight—for the death certificates. For the dates. And every one of them, Lieutenant, died between one and two months after the nurse had taken them to her own home to take such good care of." Fitzpatrick looked shaken. "One went within three and a half weeks, one lasted as long as seven weeks."

"*¿Ya lo decía yo?*" said Mendoza softly. "I said it. So."

"This—my God, and the certificates all in order—back to 1954, my God, not that we've checked back as far as that yet, but— We have to know something about evidence, and as far as I can see there's not one damn—cardiac failure, say those certificates, acute senility, other things—all in order. And if any of the doctors remember the cases, are they going to admit—"

"No. No evidence at all, that the D.A. would say was valid. *¡Diez millon demonios!*" said Mendoza savagely. "This—vulture—has got to have the fear of God put into her some way— Damn the legal evidence. But—who, for God's sake, is to say some of those weren't natural deaths? Not the damn doctors, always so sure! We can show she profited—the wills —but that's up in the air legally." He was up, pacing. "By God, how to get at her—"

"There's just no handle," said Fitzpatrick. "It's plain as day, but legally—people that age, and as you say the doctors wouldn't back down, and——"

"By God," said Mendoza, "damn the court charge, if she could be stopped—scared cold into quitting— How, for God's sake? If I could think of some—"

"It's a bastard. We'll go on checking—all the backtracking—but it's a bastard. Damndest thing I ever—"

Barron's funeral, Hackett remembered, was scheduled for four o'clock this afternoon. It was a little convention—which sometimes (only very occasionally) paid off: Homicide attended the funeral of a violently dead body. It was a bore, but he supposed somebody had better go, and everybody else was busy. He picked up his hat and went down to the lot for the Barracuda.

Chapter 12

WHO had arranged the funeral, he didn't know; evidently Rodney had bowed out completely, couldn't have been less interested. Possibly some of the faithful attendants at the Temple had made arrangements before the Sunday arrest of Rodney. It could be guessed that Mrs. Brainard had spread that around. But there hadn't been much in the papers: all Homicide had given out was the charge of unlawful possession. Hackett hadn't entirely been joking when he called Bainbridge's notions about the instant uplift ghoulish.

At any rate, there was a fair attendance of the Temple congregation; they could delude themselves that maybe Barron hadn't known about Rodney's little games. In fact, Hackett thought, few con men had enjoyed such a conventional and well-attended funeral.

It was at the Hollywood Cemetery out on Santa Monica, and the parking lot was three-quarters full. A surprisingly orthodox funeral it was, too, all the standard hymns and a chatty preacher who was reading the Ninety-First Psalm rather as if it were a lecture on sociology, when the disturbance occurred.

A man brushed past the door attendants, paused to look around and came striding down the center aisle. One attendant came hurrying after him. "Sir, you mustn't interrupt the—" he began in a loud whisper. The minister paused and went on reading. "Sir—"

"Leave go of me," said the man in an ordinary voice, and reached out to yank one of the mourners up from the pew. "You dirty little bitch, sneakin' out on me! You come out of here!"

"Oh, *Adam*—oh, don't, please—Adam, you shouldn't—"

"*Come* on!" he said roughly. He turned and strode up the aisle, pulling her with him; she struggled and cried all the way, and everything had stopped now, all the mourners on their feet and the minister frankly staring with mouth open.

"*Adam*—"

"You shut up! Sneaky little bitch, try to run out on me—"

Hackett was pushing past the curious, indignant people cluttering the aisle. He was delayed by the crowd, and got out of the place to see the intruder dragging his struggling captive across the parking lot. He pounded after them.

"Stop right there!" he said, catching the man by the shoulder. He had the badge in his other hand. The man was as big as he was, a burly heavy-shouldered man in expensive but untidy sports clothes, and he stared at the badge contemptuously.

"A cop!" he said. "Even the damn cops can't interfere between man and wife. That's the law. I know the law, and this is my wife and I'm takin' her home, see."

"Oooh, you're a policeman?" sobbed the girl. "Oh, don't let him—"

"Law can't come between—"

"Well, it depends on what the husband—or wife—is up

to," said Hackett. "You don't want to go with him, Mrs.—?"

"Johnson," she gasped. "No, I don't! Dragging me out like that—no respect for David's memory—and besides, he didn't even let me know— I don't want *anything* to do with him! I don't—" She was a little thing, in the early twenties, with tumbled short brown hair and a reedy little-girl voice, and she looked at Hackett imploringly with big hazel eyes.

"Then you don't have to go with him," said Hackett. "But I'd like to ask you both some questions. In my office. How about it, Mr. Johnson?"

The man gave him a loud obscenity. "I don't have to answer any questions. And I'm taking my wife home!" He yanked her by the wrist another step and she sobbed.

"You didn't even let me know he was *dead!* Hid all the papers so I wouldn't—and if Mr. Hawkins hadn't called me—"

"Oh, really?" said Hackett. He pulled Johnson around to face him. "Let go of her, Adam. Let go, or I'll put you down—and you know I can do it, too." Just touching the man, he knew. A big man but soft, in no condition. "Come on, let go of her! Now, Mrs. Johnson, you see that Barracuda over there—the little red car," as she looked bewildered. "You go over and get in it. I'll be right along."

"Goddamn fuzz comes—she's my wife, and I—" Johnson blustered at him loudly.

"I'd like to take you along," said Hackett, "but I'd have to knock you out to do it and all these rules and regulations—but I think I'll be talking to you. Get along, Adam." He gave him a shove. Swearing, Johnson staggered and nearly fell over the low curbing around the parking lot. He yelled more obscenities at Hackett, who swung away to the Barracuda.

When he pulled out of the lot, Johnson was standing

there looking after them, an ugly frown on his craggy face. The girl was crying again and Hackett didn't bother her. He got on the Hollywood freeway and headed back downtown. And just what this was all about—but at least something they hadn't heard, about one of the Temple crowd, so they'd better hear.

By the time he parked in the lot at headquarters, she was down to a sniffle and sitting up. "You must think I'm awful," she said. "Oh, thank you for rescuing me like that!" She gave him a starry look, respectful and upward—the white knight who had chased off the dragon. The thought crossed Hackett's mind that this kind of female just naturally wakened the Neanderthal in a man; he had a suspicion that before he finished with Mrs. Johnson he'd have the impulse to mayhem himself. But she had to be talked to.

"Come up to my office," he said.

"Oh, yes, sir." She trotted behind him obediently. Upstairs, she shied away timidly at sight of Jason Grace, but Hackett introduced him and Grace's soft deep voice seemed to reassure her. Hackett beckoned him into Mendoza's office and they gave her a chair.

"Now we'd just like to hear, Mrs. Johnson," said Hackett, "why your husband should want to come and make such a disturbance, because you went to Barron's funeral." Grace's eyebrows rose and he looked interested.

"Oh, he just hated poor David! And the Temple. Because I went there—and, well, got to know David. He was the minister there, you know? And Adam was awfully mad. But David was so good to me—and—and—he was going to give me the money so I could get a divorce from Adam—and then he went and died and I never knew anything about it till Mr. Hawkins called this morning and told me about the funeral!" The last part was a wail. "I never knew! I wondered why the paper didn't come this last week, Adam said it was the boy, or we'd forgot to pay—but I suppose he got hold of them so I shouldn't— I suppose it was in the paper—"

"Yes, it was," said Hackett. "Did your husband know Barron, or—"

"Oh, well, he didn't *know* him." She batted her lashes at him earnestly. "I mean, when David was so nice and let me talk to him after church and like that, I knew Adam'd be awfully mad if he knew—he was mad about my going to church at all, or anywhere really—but then he followed me once and found out what church and he saw David and he was madder. Because he's always been mean and nasty to me and tried to keep me from going anywhere because he doesn't want to lose the money. I don't know anything about it—" she flapped her hands helplessly—"and right after we were married two years ago, he was *nice* to me before, you'd never think he was the same man, right after he says it's better if he takes care of it. And I'd only just got it, you see, when I was twenty-one, and I said that was all right because *then* I thought Adam was awfully nice. And since he's been so mean to me, I've still got to sign the check every month or he'll do something worse, and I didn't know what to do until David said he'd tell me just how to manage, and he was so nice—"

"What money, Mrs. Johnson?"

"Well, Aunt Louise left me a lot. Only not all at once. A thousand dollars a month, it comes from a bank, and Adam made me— Only David said he'd help me get away from him, and get a divorce, and then I could have the money the way Aunt Louise meant—because I don't suppose Aunt Cissy will die for ages, they say you don't when you're crazy, and she is. Really. In a—place, I mean. And David said—"

"Aunt Cissy," said Hackett patiently, wondering why an

188

all-seeing Creator had seen fit to set such females among an already put-upon mankind.

"Oh, she's left me a lot more, I think it's two million dollars. The lawyer said. But anyway——"

Hackett's eyes met Grace's, which were amused and cynical. They saw, suddenly, several things. Rodney had been contemptuous of Barron, wanting to give their hard-earned money to a girl friend, and Barron couldn't explain the deal or Rodney would have demanded a cut. Barron, the canny con man, had seen a very sweet deal fall into his lap out of the sky. He'd been angling for it. Anybody at all could manage this female, and in contrast to Adam, the gentlemanly Barron—all con men were gentlemanly—would probably have had her falling into his arms five minutes after the divorce was final. Twelve grand a year and the prospect of more loot to come was worth a few sacrifices. But maybe he had reckoned a little hastily, not remembering that another man, then in possession, might do this and that to keep it.

"——And I never even knew David was dead—the newspapers—and I don't know *what* to do now! It's so sad—him dying so young, I know he said once he'd had tuberculosis, I suppose it was——" She sniffed into her handkerchief.

This time Hackett's eyebrows rose. "Mrs. Johnson——"

"My name's Joyce," she said pathetically. "Could you tell me what to do? I'm not very good at planning things, and besides Adam doesn't let me have much money. Oh, I can charge things, but not much because he complains I——"

"Joyce," said Hackett gently, "when did you see David last?"

"That sounds so sad. It's awful to think, too—the very last time I saw him, it all had to be spoiled! We had an appointment at the church. It was just a week ago today. At one o'clock. He was going to give me some money and tell me just how to go over to Las Vegas and what to do about starting to get a divorce. And I had an awful time getting out of the apartment—Adam's so suspicious, as if I'd do anything wrong! And he followed me—he'd made me promise not to go to the Temple ever again, but I crossed my fingers when I promised—and he came right in without knocking—" She stopped with a little gulp.

"And then what, Joyce?"

"Oh, I was frightened and I think David was, too, a little —Adam's so big, you know—but he just told me to go home. He said I was to go straight home, and David said I'd better. He sort of winked at me, so I knew he'd still phone me or something and find a way to get round Adam. So I did—I went home, I mean. But David never called me or anything—"

Hackett felt tired. Joyce Johnson must often have that effect on people. It did make you wonder. "And when Adam came home, that day, when did he come home, by the way, and how did he look? What did he say?"

"Well, I was a little scared about what he would say, but he was all quiet. I was looking at TV, and he came in and never said a word—went straight into the bathroom to take a bath, and that was funny because he usually takes showers at night—and so I thought David had sort of talked nice to him and calmed him down. I—"

"Would you mind giving me your address, Joyce?" asked Hackett very gently.

"Why, no. We live on Wilshire, the Hampton Towers. And when David didn't call—"

Grace got up and went out. In a few moments Hackett joined him. "You sent somebody over there after him?"

"Tom was doing nothing but holding down a typewriter. Johnson must be fairly dumb," said Grace, "but he'd surely know that one would open her mouth and go away and leave it. And we'd hear everything."

"He hadn't much choice," said Hackett. "I sort of grabbed her away from him. With no very clear motive but misplaced chivalry at the time."

Grace chuckled. "You should feel chivalrous more often— we seem to have cleared up this case on account of it."

"It looks that way. But I wonder if even an experienced con man—they all have to have the patience of Job, you know—would have thought it was worth it, after awhile. And I think, Jase, we'll have one of our uniformed females up. We'll have to break it to her about David, whether we pick up Johnson or not, and she'll likely have hysterics all over the place."

Grace said he'd have one sent up. With the policewoman standing by, they told Joyce about David; and she had hysterics. About then Landers came back and said he was sorry, they'd missed him. "He evidently realized the jig was up —how'd you drop on him, anyway?—and went home to pack a bag. The maid said I'd missed him by ten minutes."

Hackett swore and told Lake to put out an all-points bulletin. "Adam Johnson, about thirty-five, six-three, two hundred, white, dark hair, wanted for questioning on a homicide." Lake picked up the phone. "Damn it—he's probably got a wad of cash on him. May make for an airport—"

"We'll pick him up," said Grace. "I hope. And anyway, Joyce is loose again. Whether we do or don't. Just ripe for the next sweet-talking male who comes along to see all that money there for the taking."

They were unlucky; the APB just missed Johnson at International Airport. By the description, he was on a flight headed for New York.

They wired New York; would somebody please meet the

plane and pick him up, if it was Johnson? They got confirmation.

It was then nearly seven o'clock. They had sent Joyce home in a squad car. They just hoped the man on the New York flight was Johnson, because it was pretty clear he'd been the X who had beaten Barron to death. At least they knew who, whether they got him for it or not.

They went home.

On Wednesday morning Higgins came back to hear about that. It had been Johnson on the New York flight, he'd been picked up and held, the warrant was applied for, and when all the red tape was wound up he'd be sent back here to be charged.

"And good riddance," said Higgins. "Only some damn fool jury might get the idea that Barron had been interfering with the sacred state of matrimony and acquit him."

Hackett shrugged. "Out of our hands."

"What's been in my mind," said Higgins, "is the wild one Luis turned up. Is there anything on that woman from Philly yet?"

There wasn't. It was fourteen years back, and they had probably had to dig for it—if they had anything at all on her, incidental to the tagging of Rodney. "It's not our case," said Hackett.

And Higgins said surprisingly, "Pass by on the other side? A thing like that is everybody's business, Art."

Sergeant Lake looked up from the phone and said it was Mendoza. "Morning, Luis," said Hackett, taking the phone.

"Is there anything in from Philly yet, on——"

"Nothing. Sorry. They're probably still looking. Anyway we've cleared up a couple more cases."

"Congratulations," said Mendoza irritably. "You call me *pronto* if——"

"We'll let you know."

It was raining again—the winter was turning out to be unusually wet—and that inevitably meant more traffic accidents. They had a call on one, two D.O.A.'s, at nine o'clock, and Piggott went out on it, muttering that he didn't know why it had to be him. All the blood and mess and these moronic drivers trying to beat lights and getting tanked up and doped up and killing other people—

"So look," said Hackett, "can we take it for granted that our X on Moreno and Romano was this Rooney off the Ten Most Wanted?" He wanted to show the photograph to Jeannette Anderson, but he was morally certain she'd say honestly she couldn't be sure.

Higgins looked at the F.B.I. flyer. "Well, of course not," he said. "It might be. But there are at least ten out of our own records who also could be, who couldn't produce any alibis. All it means is we now keep our eyes open for Rooney. Who might be in Florida or New York."

"So we go back to the routine," agreed Hackett. Haul in those possibles again and see if they remembered where they were when Jeannette Anderson was getting attacked. The rest of the possibles: they'd already done some of that, yesterday. They might be able to weed out some who could show alibis. And equally, they might not.

Nothing much happened on Wednesday but the routine. It was Palliser's day off; he was probably out looking at houses with Roberta. Grace and Landers nudged the lab for anything on Stella Garcia. The lab told them the footprints were good—excellent sharp casts, of a pair of size nine shoes with much run-down heels, more on the left than the right. That was going to be just dandy evidence if they ever found the shoes and whoever had worn them. There were also prints on the handbag, but not so good: The lab was trying to bring them up. And, surprisingly, the DMV reported that they had no record of an automobile registered to Margaret O'Rourke.

Mendoza called in again about noon; he was surprised at the DMV report and did some swearing. But Philadelphia was still silent. They got a new one at eleven o'clock; a woman over on Olive had just found her husband dead in bed. Husband worked nights, got home about six A.M., so she hadn't disturbed his sleep; but she went into the bedroom for something—said Landers, coming back at twelve-thirty as they were all leaving for lunch—and thought he looked funny, so— "The interns thought maybe a heart attack. He was a man in his fifties. We'll see."

Mendoza called the office at two o'clock. Nothing had come in. He was annoyed; he said, *"Por dios,* they ought to have something back there! They don't, for God's sake, throw away all their back records every five years or something?" He called at three, and at five. He told Lake to leave a message for the night men to ring him at any hour if anything came in. "We'll let you know, Lieutenant," said Lake patiently.

He was still fulminating about Philadelphia on Thursday morning after breakfast. "They do keep records, for God's sake, I suppose. Three days—"

Alison and Mairí MacTaggart were still regarding him with shocked and incredulous eyes. At Mairí's prodding and in the frustration caused by Philadelphia's silence, he had just told them about nice kind nursie.

"But, Luis, with all this obvious evidence that she—all the patients who made wills in her favor, and the others she took away and after the property was sold— It's diabolical!" said Alison. "Those poor old souls— Do you mean to tell me it's not *enough* to charge her on?"

"I canna just get over it," said Mairí slowly. "We all thought there was something queer and wrong about it, but a thing *this* wrong—it is of the devil indeed, and you saying it canna be brought home to the woman—"

"Nature of evidence," said Mendoza, snapping his lighter with a vicious snick. "It's no good. All that is just presumptive, which judges don't like. So, all the wills. It's not evidence she influenced them. Anybody can inherit a hundred times from a hundred wills—it's perfectly legal. The deaths are nothing in the way of evidence. So the old people died. Old people do. They all had the chronic things—"

"Mrs. Weaver has the arthritis and that's all," said Mairí. "Nobody dies of it."

"We're not talking about Mrs. Weaver—yet," said Mendoza grimly.

"But, *Luis!* There must be something you can do—it's so obvious! That—that bloodsucking creature—"

"Just tell me what. The only reason I've got Forsythe's men working it is in the hope they'll come across something, some little thing, where she wasn't so careful. And—" he stopped, suddenly struck with thought, and lowered his cigarette— "A tail might lead us to whatever crooked doctor gave her a new prescription, for whatever dope she's —but what kind of charge is that?"

"I say," said Mairí, "that if somebody like yourself was to go and tell this evil woman, straight and strong, that her evil is known about and if she tries it ever again——"

"Now, Mairí. You don't cure evil by talking at it. She's been on this lay for quite awhile and she knows the law can't prove it on her. It's worked so damn well for her—" he laughed, and quoted Kipling— " 'Lord, what a handsmooth trade it is!'—she'd laugh in your face. And if you scared her one little bit, which I doubt anybody'd do, what would be the result? She'd be long gone and start over again somewhere else. Old people everywhere. Old people minus close relatives."

"I see that, Luis, but—"

"Well, I am thinking about old Mrs. Weaver," said Mairí stubbornly.

"And look," said Mendoza seriously, "you're not to repeat one word of this to those—concerned neighbors down there. They'd give the whole show away—if by any long chance we can get somewhere on this, don't rock the boat now."

"I see that, too," said Alison, and Mairí nodded unwillingly. "But—"

The phone rang and Mendoza plunged down the hall, both of them after him. But it wasn't the office. It was Janet Cox.

"Oh, Lieutenant—I had to call, I had to tell you—she's taking Mrs. Weaver away today! She came bold as brass and told Edna Fogarty, said if we wanted to come and say goodbye—she's packing everything up, and—"

"*¡Caray!*" But immediately, he thought it didn't necessarily mean the house was sold; other cases where she'd taken the patient away and the house not sold for several weeks. And there'd be the escrow—even if it was sold, show the realtor the badge, tell him to hold up the escrow. For what? his mind asked coldly. Never any evidence—

—"And Edna's just come and told me. She went over, and she says Mrs. Weaver looks just her old self. She's sad at leaving, but she told Edna it was the best way, with the money for the house she'd have enough to pay Mrs. O'Rourke to look after her— And we don't *like* it! There's something not right. An address? Well, that's another thing. Edna asked, and Mrs. Weaver said she'd drop her a note and tell her, it was a nice house up in the hills and no smog, was all she said—

And why the nurse couldn't have told her then and there—"

Coldwater Canyon. Mendoza tried to reassure her, but he wasn't feeling very reassured himself and he didn't think he succeeded. He gave Mairí a stern glance, handed her the phone and went back down the hall.

"Luis, there isn't *any* way to—?"

"It's one of those things, *querida. ¿Cuanto vale?*—all this —this accumulation, it adds up, but not to the letter of the law. As it stands," said Mendoza, "anybody who said publicly that Margaret O'Rourke—or whatever her legal name is— is guilty of deliberate homicide, obtaining money thereby —or even just of fraud and theft—could be had up for libel. The law's a funny thing, and—"

Mairí came back to the kitchen. She said, "And as a rule I would say that prayer can work wonders. But in this case we'll be needing some works as well."

Mendoza laughed. "And you never spoke a truer word."

"It's—devilish," said Alison, troubled. "There must be something—" A squeal of brakes outside; they all dived for the back door. Both twins and cats were out.

Chauncey Fitzpatrick was looking shaken; he had hit the brake so hard he'd slewed the car around into the hedge. "I hope I haven't done any damage," he said. "I didn't know there were so *many,* and I wasn't expecting—" He looked with some astonishment at the four cats. El Señor was crouched on the hood of the Buick loudly talking about Nearly Getting Killed, Nefertite and Sheba nattering back at him, and Bast ambling up to investigate the excitement. The twins were there in nothing flat.

"Do it *again!*" begged Terry gleefully.

"Bang! Crash! *¡Bueno!*" said Johnny.

"And I certainly didn't want to hit a *cat*—"

Mendoza took him in and calmed him. "No harm done.

197

I'm not sure how I came by all this menagerie myself. I forget how it strikes innocent strangers. Would you like a drink?"

"Not at this hour," grinned Fitzpatrick, and then looked serious. "I've come on a little thing that in one way lends a lot of weight to our—basic presumption on this thing, and in another—well, I thought you'd better hear about it. I came across it last night—manageress of the apartment said this and that, and I thought I'd like to see the doctor, so I followed up on it this morning. It's a different kind of case, was the reason. God, this woman—hard to believe, but you do find 'em."

"So? What was different?"

"She was a youngish woman, the patient. A Nancy Putnam. Forty-six. A divorcee, lived alone, had a sister and cousins. And not poor. Not rich, but—substantial. You know? The manageress knew her pretty well. This was in July of 1959, by the way. Apartment over on Sunset, way out. About two hundred a month."

"Mmm?"

"O'Rourke was sent to her after she—Mrs. Putnam—had an emergency appendectomy. She was pretty sick—I'm not telling this in order, some I got from the doctor just now—she had peritonitis and so forth, and she'd had a bad case of 'flu just before, so she wasn't in any state for the operation. Doctor thought she ought to have a nurse with her for a couple of weeks. Just to get meals, do the housework, help her wash and dress and so on. A practical nurse. He sent to the County Health, and got O'Rourke. And she stayed there for six days."

"Oh?"

"She did. And then Mrs. Putnam died," said Fitzpatrick.

"You don't tell me. How?"

"Well, there—I can have a guess, you can have a guess,

Lieutenant. But that's all it is. The doctor—Dr. Isherwood, seemed like a very nice fellow—knew the family, he'd taken care of Mrs. Putnam for years. He was—troubled about it. The woman was weak—not an old woman, but she'd been sick, she was pulled down. The family couldn't abide the idea of an autopsy, and he said there had been a little irregularity of the heart when he last saw her—he put it down to a heart spasm. It does happen all the time, people in the forties and even younger, drop down dead. He—obliged the family. But I don't think," said Fitzpatrick, "he felt very comfortable about it later on. Struck me as an honest man. He'd have liked to be sure. He rambled on about it."

"So what's the rest of the story?" asked Mendoza.

Fitzpatrick smiled. "Trust the LAPD every time. Sure, there's more. I said he knew the family. She left him a little something in her will. So he heard about this. Mrs. Putnam had quite a bit of jewelry. She'd left this one diamond ring to a cousin. And it wasn't there when they came to sort things out. This was a day or so after the funeral, with the nurse long gone. There was a little fuss over it, I gather, but they decided she'd sold it. Doctor seized on that to prove to himself that she was sicker than he'd thought, doing things and forgetting."

"Oh, really?" said Mendoza. "The nurse called the doctor when the patient died? Died bang, just like that."

"Right. He rambled on about it," said Fitzpatrick. "He hadn't a clue about the nurse—he's a chatty type and I egged him on. He thought I was an insurance statistician collecting statistics on middle-aged fatalities."

"How very resourceful," said Mendoza. The other man laughed.

"We have to be sometimes. He said the death was a great surprise to him—he could only put it down to a sudden cardiac failure, by what the nurse told him. He also said that it

199

must have been very sudden and a painful spasm, because there was lipstick on the pillow case. As if she'd turned and almost bit— He was chatty, like I said." Fitzpatrick leaned back.

"*Yo caigo en ello*," said Mendoza very quietly. "Translate it. The nurse thought there might be pickings. She'd pry, to find out. A substantially rich woman, weak and ill—the cash out of the handbag, the— But it was the pretty diamond ring tempted her. Do we say? The patient caught her tucking the diamond ring in her pocket— And of course if Mrs. Putnam reported that to the County Health, no more easy jobs sent her way to choose from. So, all unplanned, Mrs. Putnam has to go. She was very damn lucky, wasn't she, on that one?"

"Over the lack of autopsy? She was indeed. What would it have shown—that it wouldn't show now, nine years later?"

"Fibres from the pillow case in the trachea. How very easy," said Mendoza. "A woman weak from an operation—and big fat Mrs. O'Rourke."

"And," said Fitzpatrick, "we can say it, but not one Goddamn usable piece of legal evidence! This is the Goddamndest thing—"

At one-fifteen the phone rang and Mendoza leaped for it. Alison and Mairí were arguing in the kitchen.

"Lieutenant? We've got a teletype in from Philly, they——"

"I'm on my way!" said Mendoza, and was.

"So there it is," said Higgins. "You had a hunch. Whole family a bunch of wrong ones."

Mendoza studied the information Philadelphia had dug out for them; he was smoking in short drags, nervously.

When Rodney Yorke, which was apparently the legal

name, had been tagged as a juvenile in 1953 he had been living with his mother, Margaret Yorke. She was in domestic employment at the time. She had been charged with theft from an employer in 1949, had a jury trial and been acquitted. She had a previous record of accessory after the fact on a burglary—she had helped her husband, Donald Yorke, sell some loot to a fence; she'd served one year of a one-to-three for that, in 1943-44. She had worked as a practical nurse as well as a maid. The husband had died of a coronary in the state pen in 1960, while serving his third term for burglary. There was another son as well as Rodney; Michael Yorke, born 1946.

"So we looked Mike up, just for fun—he was only eight when they came to California, and he might have built up a record with us," said Higgins. "Since you'd said—we looked, and there he was."

There indeed he was. The wild one smelling of the jungle. Tagged in 1959, at thirteen, for threatening another kid with a knife. 1961, grand theft auto. 1962, assault on another boy. 1963 drunkenness—another attempted assault—1964, mugging— "¡Dios!" said Mendoza. "These judges, the slap on the wrist—thirty days, sixty days—and these are just the times we know about. What's he done that we don't know? How many muggings stashed in Pending? How many—"

"Well, it's interesting anyway," said Higgins dryly.

And an old, frail woman was being taken up to that house today, where the wild one also lived. That curious household, the oddly assorted family of wrong ones. The mark, the victim—gallant old Mrs. Weaver. Maybe most of the other victims had also been proud, self-respecting old people, living out their days as best they could.

"¡Diez million demonios!" said Mendoza violently. "And nothing—nothing to do—"

Chapter 13

FOR no very good reason, after he left the office Mendoza didn't go home. He went out Sunset, driving almost at random, and cut up into the north part of Beverly Hills, up the little winding residential streets, until he hit Coldwater Canyon Road. This sprawling metropolis was a peculiar one: map names running into each other, overlapping. No sign said so, but past Monticiello Drive here he was out of Beverly Hills and back in Los Angeles. This would be the Valley division's beat up here. He came to Royal Drive and turned up it. He went halfway up; no sign of Rodney's tail so Rodney wasn't home. Home? Had Rodney moved in for good?

Mendoza backed down the narrow road. What was he doing here? A quarter of the way up from Coldwater Canyon, another street cut off to the right. He wondered if he could get a look at the house from above: By its sharp right curve, that street—which was Royal Place—might climb above it. He turned up it, and there was a white Corvair sitting half-hidden round the bend. Mendoza stopped doubtfully. Rodney's tail?

The driver leaned out and Mendoza recognized him as one of Callaghan's men, vaguely remembered from some joint job. Mendoza got out and crossed to the Corvair. "Mendoza," he identified himself. "You on Rodney?"

"I haven't got to first names with him yet. I'm Hanson. The Lieutenant said you were on another part of this, some way. These are both dead-end streets—this one curls round and comes back to hit Royal Drive—and I figured I'm a little less conspicuous here. Hell of a place to put a tail. He can hardly help spotting me—I don't suppose there're many neighbors up here."

Mendoza didn't suppose so either. "I thought I might get a look at the house from above."

Hanson nodded. "Expect you can. Try it anyway."

Mendoza went back to the car and on up Royal Place. When it began to curve left he parked on the shoulder and went on foot. He didn't like hillside houses himself; these foothills were all sand and shale, potentially dangerous. The hill went up steeply to his right, steeply down ahead and to his left: no other houses visible anywhere. Isolated all right. The wild hillside was well covered with native brush and a few trees. The street led him around farther left, and he found himself looking down on the rear and side of the house.

It was an old house for this area, and big: half of it two-storeyed, and all of it painted a rather bright pink. There was a pool at the side nearest him, sandwiched in tightly between the house and the side of the undulating hill rising there. Around the pool, house, a partly-paved patio, and a good-sized rear yard, was a low cement wall. The house sat on an artificial level plateau carved and flattened out of the hillside. Below and to the left he could see other such plateaus ready for building on: He was around fifteen hundred feet above the valley here. At the far side of the yard, the low cement wall guarded what must be a sheer drop to the valley floor, quite a way down. Raising his eyes he could see the glittering hazy panorama stretching away miles distant, Hollywood and the overlapping metropolis down to the beach.

Mrs. Weaver had been right on that at least—no smog here today: It was very clear, very still, and some birds were singing loudly somewhere near.

Mendoza eyed the cover down the hill. If he could get into position crouched alongside the wall— A lot of well-grown manzanita, six feet high, and one immense pine right by the wall on this side. And what good would—

A car came up the other road and turned into the drive-way of the pink house: the garage was on the side opposite the pool, with a big cement apron in front of it. The car was an ancient M.G., and it stopped with a squeal of brakes. Mike Yorke got out of it and went into the house the front way, passing out of Mendoza's vision.

Damn it, if Rodney was there, there might be some talk he could overhear, if—

Mendoza sat down on the steep shoulder and began to edge himself downward as quietly as possible, staying behind cover as best he could. He noticed suddenly that there was a cat sitting on the wall near the big pine: a large and plump marmalade-orange cat with a white vest. Evidently some neighbors fairly near: Mendoza refused to believe that Margaret Yorke kept such an obviously pampered cat.

It was steep going, and not at all what Harrington would recommend for his best tailoring, but he persevered. Once or twice he began to slide on the steep slope and had to catch himself on tree or shrub. But ten minutes later he was snugly ensconced, prone, behind the thick trunk of the pine. And just what good he thought it was going to do him, probably ruining a good suit—

The cat turned to look curiously at him once, and then dismissed him. It was staring fixedly down at a small apricot tree the other side of the wall. Probably a nest: in this climate, some birds nested two or three times a year.

He had a fairly good view of the back yard and patio. Quite a place, he thought. Say fifty thousand at going prices. Well, she'd taken some loot in the last dozen years. He'd had another report from the Forsythe operators last night: As far as they had gone, she seemed to average three months with the patients she picked as marks, and she had been choosy about spending time on those who owned houses. The little cheap pieces of real estate. Mrs. Weaver's house—twenty-two thousand: even five, eight years ago, houses like that selling for fifteen and sixteen thousand. And the old people's houses free of the mortgages. If she averaged ten thousand per patient like that, that was very nice loot indeed.

And he thought sardonically, the bureaucracies. Legally, whatever the old people minus relatives had, belonged to the state, barring wills, of course. But in cases like these, the only record of what they had had was the realtors' certified check, and those records—personal incomes, and death records—were in two different bureaucratic offices. Still, he wondered if the canny nurse had protected herself by getting the victims to sign a statement that they were voluntarily turning over—

The back door opened and Mike Yorke came out. He had taken off his shirt and wore only dark pants: his young, powerful torso was naked-white, untanned, and hairless. He had a gun in one hand. Mendoza craned his neck, peering around his tree. He was looking down, about the level of the top of the wall, only forty feet or so away from where Mike sat down on a redwood bench and squinted down the barrel of the gun. It was a light rifle, probably a .22.

Mike raised the gun apparently straight at Mendoza, sighting carefully. Belatedly Mendoza realized he was sighting at the cat, still sitting on the wall, tail coiled tightly around its bottom. The rifle cracked sharply, and the cat landed lightly on its feet beside Mendoza, looking slightly contemptuous, and stalked off with tail held high. Mendoza grinned after it.

"Goddamn! I missed the damn thing again." Mike's voice came quite clearly up the hill.

A door slammed. "What the hell do you think you're doing?" asked Rodney's high voice. "Shooting all over the—you're the one scared about the fuzz, and then—"

"I ain't *scared* of no fuzz," said Mike. "I just don't like 'em around bugging me. Keep your tail on. A lot of people up here got guns—shoot at crows and things. And who the hell was it brought the fuzz down?"

"I'm clean, for God's sake—I made the bail. Why should—"

"Listen, you lost any sense you ever had, you think I'm some innocent kid, think that Rambler sitting down there yesterday had a couple neckers in it maybe? One guy, and fuzz. I can smell. You got a tail, Roddy. And it makes me a little nervous. I'd like for you to go away, Roddy."

"Why should they put a tail on me, for—"

"Man, you sure have lost any sense, that kooky lay—why you guys like to go to such trouble after the loot I'll never know. Because they got an idea maybe you were the supplier, Roddy. The nice stuff. The little kid stuff—the weed. It grows nice, don't it?" He got up and went over to the other side of the wall, overlooking the steep drop. Mendoza craned his neck again; he wasn't a gardener, but the tall-growing dark green plant that Mike was fondling—marijuana? Could very well be. "I can't say I'm exactly crazy about this as a hideout, call it that—but I like it a lot less with you bringin' the fuzz down, Roddy. Suppose you go away."

"Goddamn it, I can't—unless Ma lends me the price, and you know how she is about that." Rodney sounded aggrieved and frustrated. "I told you that last seven hundred we took on the caper, by the time I paid the bondsman all of it but twenty-five bucks I owed that guy I got in the poker game with—and a tough one, I tell you, I didn't pay I'd be dead. He—for God's sake put that gun down, you make me nervous."

"I make you nervous. That is a laugh. Just how do I know the fuzz here hasn't had a love letter from their buddies back there, look out for me? And you with a tail—"

Well, well, thought Mendoza. Very interesting. And still not one bit of legal evidence to get hold of. So Rodney had been taken at poker. It was a very funny thing, but a lot of the con men were gamblers, and often stupid gamblers, too. And Mike was wanted for something, but where and for what? And Mike suspected—well, as Hanson said, it was a hell of a place for a tail to stay inconspicuous.

"*I* don't know there's a tail," said Rodney sullenly.

"You think I'm blind, too? I *told* you. Tuesday, the old lady gets me go over there, the damn— There's this job tails me all the way back up here, that Ferrari—he must be green he thinks I didn't spot—"

"A Ferrari! So now the cops use sports jobs that cost fifteen grand! Try to tell me—"

"He was trailing me. So not the fuzz, who? I don't like it one damn bit, is all." Mike lifted the gun and sighted on a bird.

"Put it *down!* Oh, my God, I feel terrible," said Rodney with a groan. "If I hadn't owed that fellow the damn money, I'd be in Acapulco right now. Right *now*. Whole thing coming apart, just because Dave couldn't leave the women alone.

I wish to God— And Ma so damn stingy with the cash, so all right, the room and board O.K. but no cash, sonny boy— and I— Please put it down, Mike, I don't like guns. That arsenal of yours—" He sat down on the bench and lit a cigarette. "Besides, she'll be here with that old dame in awhile, and she wouldn't like—"

"A lot of people up here keep guns." Mike came back to the middle of the yard. *"That,"* he said resentfully, and his tone was ugly. "You and her, have to go for the real fancy lays. The real subtle thing. My God. Her and her old folk. What a damn drag."

"Look, stupid, it's money. Safe money. Sometimes a lot of it. Which is more than you can say."

"And you, too, Roddy. What the hell, I say a drag. The old mummies she finds. Have to put up the front—while they're here. What the—"

"Listen, Mike." Rodney's voice was suddenly persuasive, pleading. "You she gives the cash, you ask. If you ask all nice and polite. Listen, you want me out of here, and God, don't I want to be out? You get Ma to give me a couple of hundred, I'm out of your hair. I know a fellow in Chi owes me a favor, he'll cut me in on whatever he's—"

"I might. O.K., I'll ask her. Anything to get you off my back. Bringing the fuzz down—" They both fell silent. There was another car coming up the road.

"So there she is now," said Mike. He spat aside. "Her and this damn mummy, the latest one. God, what a way to get it."

"It's good, safe money. Listen, Mike, you ask her—a couple of hundred. I'll—"

"Jump bail. O.K., it don't matter, not to me, but she won't like it. That's a tail down there, and they'll connect us. So then I have to take out, which I wouldn't mind with this setup here now, the old dame and all, but Ma won't—"

"Oh, hell," said Rodney unhappily. The blue Ford appeared on the cement apron before the garage. The fat nurse got out, a white balloon shape in the deceiving respectable uniform, and bustled around the car. She waved at the two men in the yard and beckoned.

"Oh, hell, I suppose one of us better go and— You go, Mike. Look good. Act right, now—polite. She'll get mad if you do anything to upset the old dame."

Mike said, "Damn old bat. I'll ask Ma when I feel like it. Right now I feel like a good shot. Real jolt." He started away toward the back door.

"You damn fool! She'd have a fit if the old lady— Listen, don't you know that stuff's dynamite? I told you before—"

Mike laughed silently, mouth wide. "It's a good kick, Roddy—you gone all preachy bein' a preacher." He walked to the back door and slammed it behind him.

Rodney hesitated for a moment, his hunched shoulders betraying indecision and worry; below, the fat white figure beckoned again. "Oh, hell," said Rodney to himself, and smoothed his hair, straightened his tie and went down the cement path around the side of the house to the garage apron. It was too far for sound to carry, but Mendoza saw him smiling and speaking, the automatic front put on. He helped old Mrs. Weaver out of the car, and she stood leaning on her cane, looking around the yard, at the house, as Rodney and the nurse brought out suitcases from the trunk. Looking at what she supposed would be her last home, Mendoza thought. And unless he could think of something to do about all this, it would be. It would be indeed.

Mrs. Weaver, he thought suddenly, rather unique in that long list of patients: she had arthritis, but that was all. Mairí had said so definitely: old Mrs. Weaver's heart was sound, the doctor had said, and she hadn't been seeing a doctor. So presently the nurse would let a doctor see her—sufficiently doped to look senile? Or, he wondered again, was there to be some convenient and regrettable accident? Rodney was now getting a collapsible wheelchair out of the car. That steep path down the yard, and the low wall with the long drop below—

The nurse disappeared around the front of the house. Rodney, a hand under Mrs. Weaver's arm, helped her along the walk; they vanished. Three minutes later Rodney came back for the suitcases. And that was that: end of scene.

Mendoza began to wriggle backward from his tree. Talk about food for thought. Maybe worth ruining this suit for. Or was it? The upward progress, equally cautious because someone might be looking out a window, was harder than the downward had been. He panted and swore, pulling himself up, but at last heaved over the shoulder of the road and sat for a minute to regain his breath.

A very interesting little scene. So Mike was wanted for something. Something violent, Mendoza would bet. And he was nursie's favorite—he could coax money out of her, but not Rodney. Funny, when Rodney evidently took after her: the inventive con games. And Rodney was broke.

And what did Mike mean by a real jolt? Common variety of such, the whiskey or gin, or something else? And nothing of all that was evidence of any kind. Hearsay. So, tell Pat Callaghan there was a nice stand of marijuana up here, and he'd descend on Rodney: was that any use? Might annoy Mama enough, bringing the fuzz down, that she'd lend him the money to jump bail. Without Rodney here, no excuse for the tail nearby.

But what use was the tail, a man down the road in a car? From Mendoza's viewpoint—or Mrs. Weaver's? Against the little white tablets or the shove off the cliff?

"¡Mil rayos!" said Mendoza, and got up and brushed himself down fastidiously. At best the suit would have to go to the cleaners. He went back to the Ferrari. At least, he seemed to be definitely over the measles. He was tired, but only as tired as all that unaccustomed exercise would usually make him.

He got into the Ferrari and drove down the hill, waving a hand at Hanson as he passed.

Just how to get at the woman—

Higgins called Hackett to relay the information from Philadelphia and their own records. "My God, what a bunch," said Hackett. "Makes you wonder about people."

"I just thought you'd be interested," said Higgins. Hackett had been mowing the lawn, keeping an eye on baby Sheila in her playpen and Mark in his sandbox. When Angel came home from the market he told her about Luis' extra-curricular case. The really offbeat one.

Angel looked horrified. "But it sounds like a—a Hollywood plot, Art. Just incredible. Of all——"

"You're behind the times," said Hackett. "Can't be Hollywood—there's no sex in it. I suppose Matt would say, not Hollywood but hell behind it."

About three o'clock a teletype came in from Baltimore, Maryland, and Lake put it on Higgins' desk pending his return. Everybody was out but Palliser, and he picked it up idly; for the moment he was at a loose end.

Baltimore thought it was possible that an escapee from the state penitentiary was in their territory, one Jeff Gadsworthy—description appended. He had a brother living in Los Angeles, at an address on Valencia Street. Brother James was perfectly clean as far as Baltimore knew, and possibly Gadsworthy had contacted him; information received led them to think— And would L.A. please go and see.

Palliser yawned. It was a little routine job someone had

to do, and he might as well go and do it, clear it out of the way. He picked up his hat and went out; Sergeant Lake was sitting with feet propped up reading a paperback.

Valencia Street was just this side of the Santa Monica freeway, the other side of the Harbor freeway. A run-of-the-mill street, old houses and courts and duplexes, nothing fancy but respectable. Palliser found the address he wanted, parked and walked back to it. It was one side of a duplex, needing paint. He pushed the doorbell. After a minute he pushed it again.

The door opened and he said, "Good afternoon. Mr. Gadsworthy? Mr. James Gadsworthy?"

"Yah," said the man. He was a tall, thin man about forty, in tan work clothes, and he was chewing something.

Palliser brought out his badge. The little routine to be cleared up. "I'm Sergeant Palliser, LAPD, sir. We had a request in from Baltimore to ask whether your brother, J—"

"Goddamn *fuzz!*" said a voice behind the man in the doorway, and a gun went off and Palliser was slammed back hard against the cement pillar at one side of the porch. He felt the most immense astonishment. He didn't feel any pain, but he was falling to the wooden porch floor, he mustn't— that must be the wanted man in there, and he must— The gun went off again, and he staggered up to his feet, reaching for his own gun that he used only once a month at target practice, never any great shakes as a—

A man came running out of the duplex, gun in one hand. He fired again at Palliser, who fired back at him, a random shot. The man flung himself into the car in the drive and started the engine with a roar. Palliser fired at the front tire and missed it; the man leaned over and fired at Palliser and the bullet hit the cement pillar and Palliser ducked. The car bucketed out to the street and raced away wildly, and Palliser fired a last shot at it.

He really ought to get in more target practice. You were supposed to keep up a certain standard.

"What's all the backfirin', Jim?" asked the woman, coming up to the door behind Gadsworthy. "Who's that? What got into Jeff, anyways? We was lookin' at TV, and he jumped up all of a sudden—"

"That was Jeff?" said Palliser.

Gadsworthy looked dazed. The neighbors were starting to come out now, asking excited questions. "You a cop—after Jeff? I didn't know any cops wanted him for anything. Mister, you know you're bleeding? You better—"

Palliser twisted his neck and looked, and he'd been nicked on the right shoulder, he just felt the pain now, must have hit a blood vessel, bleeding like a stuck pig, not an artery because it was just pouring out sluggishly. "For God's sake," he said, surprised. "Have you got a phone?"

"Sure." Gadsworthy held the door open. "What you want with Jeff? He said he was on parole—"

"Whose car was that he took off in?"

"Uh—mine."

"You know the plate number?"

"Huh?"

"The license plate, for—"

"Oh. Gee, I dunno. Why?"

"For God's—" Palliser dialed the office. "Jimmy, John. Relay an APB for me. One Jeff Gadsworthy, thirty-two, five-ten, one-fifty, Caucasian, dark hair, blue eyes. Maryland wants him. He's armed and dangerous. I just lost him. He's in a Ford—what year?" he asked Gadsworthy.

"Huh?"

"Your car—what year is it?"

"Uh—nineteen fifty-four."

"A 1954 Ford, two door, solid tan. Send an urgent request

to the DMV for the plate number, it's registered to James Gadsworthy at this address—" He read it off.

"O.K.," said Lake. "Will do."

"I'll be out for awhile," said Palliser. "I've been shot."

"*What?*" said Lake. "Where you calling from?"

Palliser started to shake with laughter. "Not the great beyond, Jimmy, I do—assure you. I'm O.K. But I think—maybe I better call an ambulance." He was feeling a little light-headed by then. He sat down to call the ambulance, and Mrs. Gadsworthy brought some clean rags to put under his jacket.

"I don't know what got into Jeff," she said.

The interns insisted on taking Palliser to the General. "You've lost some blood, buddy," said one of them. There he was examined and bandaged. That took fifteen minutes; and it took half an hour for a clerk to get all the forms filled out—name, address, nature of injury, LAPD badge number, superior officer, and so on.

They said he could go at five o'clock, and Palliser took a cab back to Valencia Street, collected the Rambler, and cautiously drove home to Tamarind Avenue in Hollywood. He was feeling all right, just a little shaky—all the blood—and they'd said he'd have a stiff arm for a few days.

Roberta was stirring something on the stove, and looked surprised to see him. "You're early."

"I got shot up," said Palliser.

"What?"

"Hey, don't look like that—I'm O.K., you can see I'm O.K. It was only a nick on the shoulder—"

"It's just—" Roberta buried her head in his other shoulder—"it s not funny, John. It could be—for real—any day. Like—that other detective in Homicide."

"That's a while back," said Palliser. "It doesn't really

happen so often, honey. And his wife's got another fine upstanding officer to look after her."

"I'm not interested in another fine upstanding officer," said Roberta. "I've got one. I'd like to keep him. You're sure you're all right? Let's see—"

"Just a little blood lost."

"So I'll fix you a steak to replace some."

And Palliser swore a little—by Friday morning his arm was damned stiff—but Rodolfo Valdez was being arraigned and he had to be there for it. He felt justified in taking the rest of the day off.

It was Grace's regular day off, but Landers was thinking seriously of something Grace had said yesterday. He thought about it even more seriously after Scarne came up at ten o'clock and said, "About those prints on Mrs. Garcia's bag. Exercise in futility. We brought 'em up—four nice prints— but they're not in records. Ours, anyway. We sent 'em to the F.B.I., but I hardly think—"

Nor did Landers. Stella Garcia had, in all likelihood, been the victim of a rather amateur burglar. Possibly even a first-time burglar; possibly even a juvenile, climbing in the window after the handbag and panicking when she woke up. Nobody but an amateur would panic like that and try to shut her up. And that said, of course, somebody fairly big and strong, not realizing how permanently he was shutting her up. But Landers didn't think the Feds would have his prints.

What Grace had said was, "What does the Lieutenant always say, Tom? Simple first principles. Same like the idiot boy and the lost horse. If you were a horse— I say, let's ask around the neighborhood. Ask the priest. He'll know people—and the people, as a rule, mostly law-abiding people.

215

Ask about any wrong ones living around—anybody they might think would snatch a purse. We'll get a few names. And sometimes it's just as simple as that."

Landers thought he might just do that. Because he didn't think the prints would be on record anywhere. And a first-timer, and/or a juvenile, might break down under very little pressure, if they could locate—

He got up, intending to go to Vignes Street and start to ask the simple questions, but he was diverted by Sergeant Lake.

"New one in. Squad car just called. Man found dead in a store over on Grand."

"Oh, hell," said Landers. "Where's everybody else?"

"Hackett and Higgins are still on the routine with the punks. On Moreno and—Palliser went home. There was another wino dead on the Row, Glasser—"

"Skip it, skip it," said Landers. "I'm on my way. What's the address?"

"But, Mairí," said Alison, "you know he said it'd do no good. We mustn't—rock the boat."

Mrs. MacTaggart said stubbornly, "I see the sense in what the man says, yes. About the nurse. But I'm thinking about old Mrs. Weaver. I just say, if somebody was to stand up to that evil woman and tell her her evil was known and the knowledge would follow her—*ach,* what is the lawyer's sense in it? I just say—"

"You know he said we mustn't do anything. Oh, I know how you feel!" Alison absently twisted one shoulder-length strand of red hair round her forefinger. "I—I wonder if it *would* scare her a little? Have any effect? She must feel— rather terribly self-confident, after all this time. If Luis is right about— And he usually is."

216

"I've done a bit of praying over it. And it just seems to me—"

"But, Mairí, he said—"

The jungle in the city has a grapevine. Nothing in the papers about Jeff Gadsworthy and Palliser yesterday, but some people in the jungle would know.

At four-thirty on Friday afternoon Lake answered an anonymous caller. He said, "Homicide, Central, LAPD," and the voice at the other end of the wire said quickly, "You want the guy shot up your boy yesterday, try the Regent Hotel on San Pedro," and rang off quickly.

And of course such tips were not to be ignored. Gadsworthy might be there. Lake relayed that to Piggott and Glasser.

They started down Los Angeles Street in Glasser's Ford. "It's a false alarm probably," said Piggott.

"So optimistic. It mightn't be."

As the light changed at Fifth, an old Chevy convertible roared through the intersection, smashed into a too-eager sedan traveling the other way, the two ricocheted into the right-lane traffic on Fifth and ended up half on the sidewalk, with the pedestrians screaming and the rending crash of metal.

And Piggott said resignedly, "It's just, I feel we're being pursued, Henry. By fate or something."

Chapter 14

FITZPATRICK and the other operative from Forsythe and Mason showed up that evening, looking serious, and Alison took them down to Mendoza's den, where he sat at the desk absently practicing crooked deals. "So what more have you got?" he asked, glancing up as they came in. "And can we offer you a drink?"

"I guess we could stand one," said Garrison gloomily; he was as short and thin as Fitzpatrick was the opposite.

"I'll get them." Alison vanished down the hall.

"Well, we've got a good part of the history for you, Lieutenant," said Fitzpatrick, "and a kind of incredible one it is—in a couple of ways. But as far as I can see, unless you get the authorities to take it up—and maybe not even then—there's just no legal evidence. That *is* evidence, you get me."

"Well, what have you got?"

"We've covered—as well as we can—about three-quarters of that damn list. And that's only up to a few years ago when they stopped keeping such full records. We've got," said Fitzpatrick, "thirty-eight people. And by everything we could get—by all the implications—that—that vampire of a nurse got everything those people had." He looked outraged. "It's incredible. Just—I'm telling you. And when I say thirty-eight, I'm not counting the people she was with a day or so, to find out they weren't possible marks. Thirty-eight, my God. Sure, over a long period, but— Every one of them elderly, without relatives or at least close ones, and twenty-nine of them owned houses. This is strictly a capsule report, you understand—I've got details if you want 'em. Houses all over—Hollywood, the Atwater section, West Hollywood, West L.A., all over. We've seen the houses, except some torn down to let the freeway through or something. All the same kind. Little shabby old houses. But these days— And listen, Lieutenant, how the *hell* did she just stumble on so many of that kind, through the ordinary job? Sure, not everybody she was sent to was—the possible mark—but *thirty-eight,* my good God—"

"I've been thinking about that," said Mendoza. He shuffled the cards absently and laid the deck on the coffee table; he had swiveled around to face them where they sat side by side on the leather couch under the reproduction of Cézanne's Card Players. "You could say there was a high probability factor. Which she also would see."

"Come again?" said Garrison.

"Well, think. Probably southern California—L.A. county —has a higher percentage of elderly retired people in the total population than anywhere else except the state of Florida." He shuffled the cards again. "And among elderly retired people, like the rest of the population, there are a lot more with just a little money than a lot of money. And most of them, the elderly retired people with just a little money, on the small fixed incomes—savings, little investments, pensions. And elderly retired people on small fixed incomes don't generally go to the hospital unless it's absolutely necessary. And the hospitals are always crowded and don't keep them when they're convalescent. And elderly retired people who have families—grown-up married children, grandchildren—get nursed and waited on by the families during convalescence. *¿Como no?*" He cut the deck and turned up the ace of diamonds. "And—thanks, *querida*—" as Alison brought in drinks on a tray, tall highballs for the other two, straight rye for Mendoza. The door shut behind her. "And such elderly retired people generally need just the practical nurse, not a trained one. And so it was always more probable that she'd get sent to the elderly retired people without families living nearby at any rate—" he shuffled the cards—"who were on pension or living on small savings, than any other kind of patient." He cut and turned up the ace of diamonds.

Garrison said, his eyes on the cards, "That's quite a trick. I hadn't thought of it like that."

"So tell me what you've been doing." Mendoza swallowed rye.

"And thinking," said Fitzpatrick. "We've kicked it around. Thirty-eight we've found. Asking the former neighbors still living around, canvassing the neighborhoods. We haven't got details on 'em all—three we couldn't find anybody who remembered them at all. Makes you think, doesn't it? And those we did hear something about—" he shook his head—"it's just by implication. Just suggestive. But there's a pattern showing. The old people had strokes, 'flu, an operation, this that and the other. So they had to have a nurse for awhile. They got Mrs. O'Rourke. In some cases the doctor suggested it, arranged for the nurse from the County Health service—in some cases a neighbor thought of it, or the old people themselves. She came, and sometimes it was one thing, sometimes another—this is piecing together what the neighbors told us with what we got at the Hall of Records, you understand. Among the thirty-eight were five more who made wills. Everything of which I die possessed. Those five people died at home. Other cases, definitely fourteen of the former neighbors remembered that the nurse had arranged to take the patient to her own home to look after permanently. They didn't know the details. Nobody seems to have suspected the nurse of any—nefarious motives. We don't know the details, I should say, except in one case— which also suggests this and that—an old man who told the neighbors he was going to sell his house and then he'd have enough to pay the nurse to take care of him the rest of his life. They'd signed an agreement, he said."

"Oh," said Mendoza. "Yes, I wondered. She's a canny one. In case the state came down later— Yes, go on."

"What did she get out of the ones who didn't own houses?" asked Garrison. "I can't—"

Mendoza shrugged, finished his rye. "Those—I'm guessing—she charged the going rate, and also—mmm, yes—she wouldn't prolong the agony. It's a wild guess, but those nine patients minus any real estate, was she with them as long as the others?" He shuffled the deck.

"I didn't—let me check—" Fitzpatrick studied his notebook. "I've got all the dates here, as well as— By God—by God, no, you're absolutely right—a month, five weeks, three weeks, my God, a month—" He stared at Mendoza. "For the love of—"

"Before they died? The happy release?"

"That's right. Before they—"

Mendoza cut and turned up the ace of spades. "Mmm, yes," he said meditatively. "You've been visiting around in those neighborhoods, the modest little houses, the very middle-class city streets. Did you take a look at the contents of the average house like that? Most of the elderly retired people would once have had better incomes and been able to buy more possessions than they would on the fixed incomes. Almost always a TV, sometimes solid good old furniture—even a few valuable antiques maybe—the plated silver, odds and ends—and quite often some family jewelry. She wasn't losing anything, marking time at the full salary. Who knows what those people had? Some old people secretive. So, a quiet exit of the patient, and she clears away anything of value. I'll just bet you those nine people had something worth her while—bearer bonds, a drawer full of grandmother's diamonds, hoarded cash tucked away behind pictures, under rugs." He cut the deck and smiled at the ace of spades. "Yes, and that's another thing, of course—in some cases they'd have had securities. Stocks and bonds. A few. That she couldn't do anything about, unless— ¡como no! Unless, of course, they signed the pretty will. Yes, I'll bet you something else—that in the cases where there were wills, there was property like that, securities. She'd know how to draw them out, the sympathetic listener, and find out whatever she—"

"But there's absolutely nothing in the way of proof!" said Fitzpatrick. "It's all—implications. We got interested in this damn thing and tried to turn up something concrete. Like the realtors' checks. When the houses were sold. They keep records, and we were persistent. We got confirmation on three—we just started that today—sure enough, the checks paid to the elderly patients. When the real estate cleared escrow. But, for God's sake, banks won't open records to us. They'd have to, to you people."

"Under pressure. . . . And the patients incapacitated in some way, some of them trusting nursie absolutely, some of them generally ignorant about business matters, and all of them apt to be under the influence of the little white tablets to turn them mentally vague, so the check endorsed and paid

222

into her own account. And, as I said, quite possibly the agreement signed to make it legal."

"But thirty-eight—! Well, twenty-nine on the real estate deals— But, my God, anybody can see—"

"Very nice circumstantial evidence," nodded Mendoza. "But not really enough to build a legal charge." He put the cards down and leaned back.

"It makes me think all right," said Garrison. "It sure does. I tried a few of the doctors. Names from the death certificates," he swallowed the last of his drink. "God. And I'm not saying I think they're careless or incompetent. I don't think they are—probably very good doctors. But—all business, as doctors tend to be nowadays. Whatever happened to the old friend-of-the-family G.P.? Anyway, they were all annoyed at a private eye interrupting their schedules. And not one of them—the five I tried—remembered even the patient's name. A lot of patients, you know. They had to look in their records. Then they vaguely recalled. The elderly patient—the chronic troubles, or the operation. And finally the happy release. I don't suppose one of 'em had any hesitation about signing the certificate. Cardiac failure, stroke, whatever. Makes you think. I'm a bachelor myself."

"*Nadie me ama,*" said Mendoza. "You don't tell me. Fancy that."

"But look," said Fitzpatrick, "if you could get at the bank records, show that all that money was endorsed over to the nurse—and there are the wills—and in every single damn case the patient conveniently dying off a month or two later —I should think the D.A. would say it was enough to build a charge—"

"I don't know. I think he'll have to be approached on it. I really do. But I'd take no bets on whether— *¡Que!*" said Mendoza, startled at sudden invasion.

There erupted into the den, Johnny clad in the top half of his pajamas and clutching a large stuffed panda, and Terry clad in nothing at all but one of Alison's few hats, a white turban of satin flowers.

"Say good night nice to Daddy—*Buenos tardes*—and Terry said a *malvado* word and Mairí is mad—Terry—"

"Did not," said Terry staunchly. "*Buenas tardes.* Daddy doesn't have naughty words. Damn duck wouldn't be floating—"

Mrs. MacTaggart came panting after them. "I swear a body needs four hands and legs to keep up with the pair of you! Terry, where did you get that— I'm sorry, Lieutenant, they—"

Mendoza was still laughing. He waved feebly at the twins as Mairí bore them out, her soft voice scolding in Gaelic. "I see I'll have to watch my language," he gasped.

Fitzpatrick and Garrison were grinning. "Well, at least you won't have to worry about being an elderly retired person all alone," Garrison said.

"Oh, no?" Mendoza sobered. "Which of us ever has a guarantee of that? How many of those thirty-eight people once had families around them? . . . Nothing to get hold of on it, damn it. Nothing like sound legal evidence— So, we bully the banks and see the checks endorsed over to her. Ten to one she's covered herself with the little signed statements. And technically, once the check is endorsed, that implies willingness to let her have the money—the patient's own money, nobody's business what he or she does with it. And technically, the wills are— ¡*Un momento! Segura mente que si!*"

"You've thought of something—" They both leaned forward.

"I don't know. It just occurs to me—" Absently Mendoza picked up the cards again. "Legally, if the nurse hadn't come along, all that property would have fallen to the state of California. The old people minus relatives dying intestate. I suppose she found out they were intestate before— And any bureaucratic state will go to some lengths to lay its hot little hands on money it thinks belongs to it. *De veras.* It's an argument to put to the D.A. I will. But—"

"Well, what about us?" asked Fitzpatrick. "This is costing you something. We've turned up this much, but—you want to leave it as is until we know whether—?"

Mendoza lit a cigarette. "I don't think so. Let's ferret out every last detail and fact you can find. Just in the hope that she slipped somewhere, just once. If I'm right and most of these happy releases were in fact homicides—well, there's no statute of limitations on that. And most mass murderers —*caray,* you could say, a mass—are prosecuted in the end on only one or two of the victims. I know it's a damned tedious job to work. I've done my share of the routine. But— let's get all there is to get."

"Well, it's your money. And what we get paid for. And I wouldn't say just so tedious at that," said Fitzpatrick. "The usual dirty little jobs we get nothing like—of all the incredible— I hope to God the D.A. decides they can make a charge on her. *Thirty-eight* people—"

"A very simple M.O.," said Mendoza. "Old people, Fitzpatrick—in run-down physical condition or they wouldn't have needed the nurse. And—" he cocked his head at the two private detectives—"trusting people. A nurse? Who doesn't take it for granted she honestly wants to help people, take good care of her patients? It's a tiresome, dirty job. Like my job. Who'd take it on if he wasn't on the side of the angels, so to speak? Same with a nurse. People are generally—mmm, frighteningly trustful of each other. Trust the newspapers to tell the truth—and all the truth. Trust the market clerk to give them the right change. Trust the realtor that the house for sale isn't riddled with termites. Not that I want to undermine your faith in human nature —any you may retain. But sometimes we'd be safer not trusting quite so much."

Fitzpatrick laughed. "I'll not say you're wrong. There is that aspect of it. And people have a *right,*" he added suddenly. "They have a right to expect—the house isn't riddled with termites. It's the ones like this—vulture—"

"One of the reasons we're here," said Mendoza. "On the thankless job." He had thought it before: by consciously choosing the job, any man made his commitment, to light versus darkness, law against anarchy, good versus evil. And it had to be a whole commitment.

You weren't just committed to the war against evil on your particular assigned front, but everywhere.

"I'm going back to work on Monday," he said, hanging up his jacket.

"Now, Luis, the doctor said—"

"Damn the doctor. I'm fine. I'm O.K. And I can't take sitting around like—"

"Sitting around!" said Alison. She massaged cream into her face, bending to the dressing-table mirror. "Gallivanting around like a private eye. You ought to——"

"I'm fine," repeated Mendoza. He took off his shirt and thrust it into the hamper. Go back to work, he thought, and forget it? This sorry business with no handle to it. Nice kind nursie. Thirty-eight people. *Dios,* thirty-eight—

Even the doctors having trouble remembering them. The old, alone people. But for the grace of God— Well, doctors saw a lot of people. And so many people, in a busy big metropolis, everybody intent on his own affairs, pausing to say hello to old Mrs. Blank on her front porch, but when old Mrs. Blank went to the hospital, had a nurse, died, it was a warm *Too bad, I'm so sorry to hear,* and next day or next week you forgot it. Even the doctors—

Old people died quite often. It didn't surprise anybody. Doctors least of all.

He shuddered suddenly: something walking on his grave.

Go back to the office, his own place, all the idiocy and malice and blood and dirt down on Central's beat. He felt that this incredible fact he'd uncovered, starting idly with Mairí's little problem, held more of real evil than he dealt with in a year down there. Essentially, it was the same kind of evil which was not so much evil as plain stupidity and selfishness—the utter inability to imagine another human being's feelings; but in another sense it was worse, a deliberate denial that another human being had feelings, was worth any consideration at all. *Too much Ego in his cosmos—*

He thought about Mike yesterday.

"Are you coming to bed?"

"I'm coming. You look very delectable," said Mendoza.

"So you're feeling fine. Yourself again."

"You read my mind."

"Those two private eyes—what more did they have? I keep thinking about that awful woman—do you think—"

Mendoza switched off the lamp. "I don't want to think about her any more tonight, *querida*. I'd like to forget her permanently."

Back to work on Monday. The routine, the mess and violence and stupidity, and greed. But meanwhile—

Jason Grace reflected that it was really surprising how good most people were, in a broad sense. How trusting and hesitant to accuse one another— To the law at least, he amended.

He was down on Vignes Street, this Saturday morning,

227

working at the simple first principles. Asking the neighbors about any wrong ones who lived around here. They told him earnestly, "I wouldn't want to accuse anybody, when I don't know for certain" and some of them refused to give him any names at all. But he got this and that from others, a real wild kid over on Avila Street, that poor little wife of the Gonzales fellow, he's a mean one and always out of work and I wouldn't put it past him—a guy down the block, I think he's the one stole my lawn mower—

Grace thought it would do no harm to look at them. The ones the neighbors could suspect of being wrong ones.

He didn't get very much; it was all up in the air. By noon he'd decided the morning had been wasted, and drove up to Federico's to find everybody else there: Hackett and Higgins looking glum, Palliser and Landers; it was Glasser's day off. The waiter pushed two tables together, took orders, and went away.

Palliser winced as he picked up his drink. "Damn it, this arm's so stiff I can hardly drive—"

"Serves you right," said Hackett, "going out alone after a con. Didn't you learn at the Academy why we like to travel in pairs? And you should complain—we've got just damn all on this rapist. About eight out of records who could be, minus any alibis, but nothing says they are. If the lab could give us something definite—"

"Ditto on Garcia," said Grace. "But it's early. Something may break."

"A new case, likely," said Piggott, and everybody told him not to be such a pessimist.

"I tell you what it is," said Palliser seriously, "it's because the boss is off. We need him to wield the whip or something. Ever since he went off, I swear we haven't—oh, the routine, but on the big things—"

"We're supposed to be trained detectives, too, John," said

Hackett. "Don't be— The rough patches come along, time to time. Just because—"

"Well, speak of the devil," said Higgins. Hackett looked up. Mendoza was making for the table, dapper and slim as always—he had filled out a little since Hackett had seen him last, and his color was better. He pulled a chair around from the next table and sat down between Grace and Piggott.

"Hello, boys. . . . Bring me some straight rye, Adam. And I need it. What a session. And I swear to God—"

"What are you doing down here?"

"On my extracurricular case. But I'll be back with you Monday. I'm recovered. And bored to death. That is a lie —this damned thing—"

"Your practical nurse," said Hackett. "It's moving? That is a thing indeed."

"It's not moving, damn it to hell. Nothing— I've just come from the D.A.'s office." Mendoza looked annoyed. "I twisted his arm and got him to listen to me, Saturday or no. He was interested, but negative. Even the state— And I see the point. He said, even with the bank records, nothing that's real evidence—not even a charge of fraud could be built on that. And the money's long gone, it'd cost the state more to try her than it'd ever get back. I *see* that. But this diabolical—"

"Wait a minute, you've lost me," said Hackett. "Bank records?"

Mendoza told them about it, over a steak sandwich. They listened interestedly, the offbeat one, the mass murderer. *"Thirty-eight—"* said Palliser.

"And not one damn thing— I don't mean to tell you the D.A. wasn't horrified. He was. He kept saying *thirty-eight,* too. This vulture. The new twist on the con game. He said his only suggestion was that somebody scare the living

bejasus out of her. Which was helpful. But the state—
of course—" Mendoza stopped with his mouth open, shut it,
lowered his fork and said, "But Pat—a *kind* of excuse—if
he'd go along—and with Mrs. Weaver there—stir up the
animals a little anyway, and see what came of— And I could
see how she— No, damn it, I can't, she knows me, that time
I went through the house—but—"

"Luis, you're maundering," said Hackett.

Mendoza's eyes focused on him. "You she doesn't know."

"The nurse? Listen, I'm busy. We've got that—"

"You can transfer to Narco for the afternoon." Mendoza
finished his coffee. "Come on, I want to go see Pat Callaghan."

"What the hell have you got in your head now?"

"Stir up the animals," said Mendoza. "It just could buy
us some time—we'll see. We'll see."

He was, as usual, persuasive on Callaghan, who regarded
him resignedly.

"We're just here to oblige Homicide, of course."

"It's not even Homicide's business, Pat, but it's a devilish
thing that ought to be stopped cold if we can. This
female——"

"The things you get into," said Callaghan. "So, it is our
business in a very small way, Luis, that Rodney Terhune—"

"Yorke. Listen, *amigo,* I think that's a very fine stand of
marijuana up there. How do you know the nurse isn't supplying a whole fleet of peddlers? Not that I want you to sug-
gest it. Don't even mention the stand of marijuana. That's
an excuse for you to go back again later, one of your men
ostensibly remembering it. And Art's temporarily one of
your men. I want his impressions."

"Don't trust me?" said Callaghan.

"Not on the nuances, *compadre.* Big tough Irish cop."

"This thickheaded Homicide dick—"

"He majored in psychology."

Luis in action, and Hackett was amused. . . . Ostensibly they would be Narco men interested in Rodney because of the possession charge; no curiosity about the nurse or her patient. But the descent on the house would alarm the nurse; the LAPD knowing her address, the house connected with Rodney, the charged man. . . . That had been another double play, Hackett reflected: the house in her legal name, Yorke, as they now knew her car was. If any of the old people had neighbors and friends interested enough to try to follow them up, a dead end. . . . And at the same time this would alert old Mrs. Weaver that perhaps nursie wasn't quite the respectable motherly soul she had seemed, so Mrs. Weaver might (barring the little white tablets) think about signing or this or that—might wonder and doubt.

Hackett thought the animals got stirred up. They left Mendoza fidgeting in Callaghan's car down on Coldwater Canyon, and drove up Royal Drive in state in two black-and-white squad cars. When the door opened to them, to reveal the fat nurse, she looked alarmed—for one second. Then the mouth smiled widely at them, but Hackett saw her eyes—the little black eyes, dead and cold, no expression in them. The vulture.

"Why, certainly," she said in answer to Callaghan's mention of a search warrant. "I always try to be a good citizen, help the police." It was the first time Hackett had seen her; she put up a good front on short notice, he thought. Her tone was limpid and honest. "I know my boy Roddy got into bad company, it's been a grief to me, he was brought up right and I try to set him on the right path again. Anything I can do—but I got to ask you, please, I got a patient here, an old lady not feeling so good, if you won't disturb her—" Hackett looked beyond the nurse here in this big living room with its picture window over the panorama of the city below, to old Mrs. Weaver sitting on the couch. A nice-looking old lady, he thought. The current mark, marked for death as soon as she was no more use. To the nurse.

He said in a deliberately loud voice, "We won't disturb your patient, Mrs. Yorke," and he made that distinct. "The fact that your son has falsely posed as a minister doesn't constitute a police charge, but his possession of drugs—" He saw Mrs. Weaver start and her eyes widen. Evidently she hadn't had any of the nurse's tablets, and was very much in possession of her faculties. She knew the woman as O'Rourke, and the minister son would have been proudly introduced.

Rodney was sullen in the background.

Ostentatiously they went through the house. Play acting. Mendoza's idea: but useful to see what was there, at that. On both cases. It was a big house, five bedrooms, two full baths. The bedroom at the back, overlooking the pool, Hackett judged to have been assigned to Mrs. Weaver: a pair of old-lady oxfords tidily beside the bed, open suitcases not yet put away. In the nearest bathroom, next door to the nurse's bedroom, he found in the medicine cabinet a plastic bottle with a label: *Mrs. M. O'Rourke, one every three hours.* It was half full of white tablets. The label further said, *Dr. Harvey Pfeiffer.* The crooked doctor supplying her? They'd check. Anyway, for the moment no more white tablets for Mrs. Weaver, if that was what these were. He put the bottle in his pocket.

He went into the next bedroom and one of Callaghan's men, Benedettino, said, "He's out." He was looking down at the man sprawled on the bed there, undoubtedly Mike Yorke. He was stark naked, snoring slightly and dead to the world. "Drunk? I don't think so."

"No," said Hackett. No smell of liquor in the room. They

shook him, but he only gargled faintly and rolled over. They went over the room and found nothing suggestive. No heroin, reefers, anything like that: only the arsenal. That was in the closet.

"Is he starting an army?" wondered Benedettino. There were five rifles, two shotguns, and in a professional carrying case six revolvers. There was also ample ammunition for the arsenal.

Hackett raised his brows. "And no permits, of course. He doesn't need one, unless he's carrying these around. We'll be assured he isn't. Not noways."

"Oh, sure."

The second bathroom was evidently shared by the two men. Shaving cream, after-shave lotion, cologne—that would be Rodney—in the medicine cabinet; and Hackett was a little surprised to see another plastic prescription bottle labeled Michael Yorke. Considering Mike, he didn't seem exactly the type—but of course that was specious reasoning— He picked it up. *One drop in each eye once a day. Dr. Wm. Court, 115 Adams St., Phoenix, Ariz.*

So, thought Hackett, maybe Phoenix was where Mike was wanted. They would be checking that, too.

Downstairs, he thought further that the nurse was nervous. Flurried and scared, but she had herself in hand, she was still putting up the front. Rodney was silent and wary. She was caught between two lies here, Mrs. Weaver the current mark within earshot; the police knowing her real name and Rodney's history—she would know they knew that— but she had to put up a front for the police, and trust to luck and her native wit to explain it all to Mrs. Weaver later.

"Who's the other man upstairs?" Callaghan, looming and abrupt.

She wouldn't know they knew about Mike. "Oh, that's my

other boy, sir, that's my boy M-Mark, he works nights and so naturally he sleeps days—and anything I can do, but I can't have my patient upset—"

Hackett thought Mrs. Weaver looked very shocked and upset, sitting upright on the couch taking it all in.

They had, maybe, stirred up the animals. And now what?

"You really find 'em," said Callaghan. "So we played your little comedy just like you wanted. Now what?"

"I wish to God I knew what was happening back there in that house," said Mendoza distractedly. "What have we accomplished? *Nada absolutamente.* I was woolgathering. So now she chases Rodney out because he's brought the fuzz down, and we're back where we started. She— One thing, we'll put tails on all three of them now."

"What?" said Callaghan. "I've only got so many men, damn it, and it's a nothing, Luis, from our standpoint—"

"You don't *know* she's not supplying—it's Narco business, my God, you can't deny that, Pat, and—"

"We'll ask Phoenix if they want Mike," said Hackett.

"And if Rodney does jump bail," said Callaghan—they were standing on the road shoulder beside the Ferrari and Mendoza had just stepped on his second cigarette in ten minutes—"we've got no excuse to waste manpower. My God, Luis, on a two-bit punk con man, Rodney, I can't—"

"Catch up with everybody but her," said Mendoza. "The vulture. The— *Dios,* I wish I knew what was happening back there. Mrs. Weaver—" He lit another cigarette nervously.

Chapter 15

"—And what the hell I thought it would accomplish—" said Mendoza for the sixth time. "So, buy a little time, I said! For what? If we traced her back to first grade, my God, no legal—I'll tell you what it'll do. One of two things. Either she'll kick Rodney out for bringing us down on her, or she'll decide to cut her own losses and get out, too. She'll dump Mrs. Weaver and that'll be that—she might put that house up for sale and begin looking at travel brochures from Miami. Damn it—"

He'd been nervous, pacing the living room and saying that all evening. Alison said patiently, "I see all that, Luis, but anyway she won't do anything to Mrs. Weaver now. Not when she knows the police are apt to—even if Rodney leaves, they might come to quest—"

"No. No. Mrs. Weaver's safe enough for the time being. I think. I wonder if she asked nursie some questions— Art said the old lady looked entirely *compos mentis*."

"She's a sharp old lady," said Mairí, passing through and overhearing Mendoza. "When she's herself. And Mrs.

Weaver is what I am thinking about. It's your business to catch up with such evil as that nurse. Nurse!"

"Which we can't do this time, Mairí. Damn it, stir up the animals, I said—now I'm thinking about that Mike. Hairtrigger. And he doesn't like Mama's inventive con game—the elaborate waste of time. *¡Dios!* If she did start to ask some questions—"

"For what she gets for the house," said Alison thoughtfully, "she could afford a nice rest home—there are some very good ones, good service and—"

"What I was thinking," nodded Mairí. "She can stay with Mrs. Oliver until we can get her settled."

Mendoza hardly heard that. "I wish to God I knew what was happening up there. Anything could— And that arsenal—"

"Don't worry so, Luis. You just agreed she won't dare do anything now she knows the police might be coming back. And Mrs. Weaver's house isn't sold yet anyw—"

"Oddly enough," said Mendoza, lighting another cigarette, "I'm not worried about the nurse doing anything. I'm worried about that Mike. Art said he was dead out, but not drunk. No heroin or anything showed, but there might be a false bottom in a dresser drawer or— Yes, my God, that day Rodney said to him—that stuff dynamite. I wish I knew—"

"Look, you said Narcotics had three men there as potential tails. They'd—"

"And I had to argue like hell with him before he agreed to spare the men. But they're not sitting on the doorstep, *querida*. They're away down the hill waiting for the quarries to start somewhere. We couldn't— I wish to *hell* I knew—"

Alison got him to bed finally, but he lay awake with the problem gnawing at his mind—no way to charge her, and it was morally certain she had accounted for thirty-eight people, my God, so easy of course, the frail old people—the chloroform, too many little white tablets dissolved in a glass of milk, the shot of morphine— Art had said they'd check that doctor's name, but over the weekend difficult to— She might have quite a supply of all sorts of things. And the happy release of the frail senior citizens, the doctor wouldn't come galloping up to examine the corpse. Come when he had time—maybe to the funeral home—sign the certificate without a qualm.

At least that wouldn't happen to old Mrs. Weaver. He hoped. But a situation could build up in that household now. Rodney anxious to jump bail and get away. His mother nervous and angry and a little flurried for once, caught among her many lies, caught between two goals. She'd want Rodney out—but if he jumped bail, well, the fuzz knew where he'd been, that she was his mother; they'd keep an eye on her, in case he contacted her. And caught with her mask down before the current patient, the mask of the nice respectable motherly nurse—now (he hoped Mrs. Weaver had taken it in) the patient knew she had used a false name, and that the minister son was known to the police—

Yes, and maybe he had been a little stupid in chasing Pat up there, Mendoza thought worriedly. Mairí said that was a sharp old lady. She might ask too many questions—and Mike hair-trigger—and the old lady stiff with arthritis—

The last time he looked at the clock it was two-thirty. He slept lightly, and woke at dawn to start worrying again.

Hackett called him at nine o'clock. "I thought you'd be interested to know—the lab just reported on those tablets, and I asked Bainbridge about them. It was Empirin Number Three."

"What's in it?"

"Codeine. Not too big a dose, but the average directions

237

are not more than one every three or four hours. If you took one every hour or so, Bainbridge said, it'd keep you dopey, mentally dull. Enough would kill you, especially if you had a weak heart."

"How much?"

"I didn't ask him. Should I?"

"No. It's not that imp— Have you heard from Pat?"

"Not a thing. Look, sorry, we're busy—I'll see you." Hackett was gone.

"¡Mil rayos!" muttered Mendoza to himself. "I wish I knew—"

"Well, I suppose we'd better do something about this," said Hackett to Higgins, who agreed unenthusiastically.

"I think it could just be this Rooney. He's wanted for the same exact type of M.O. And—"

In which case they were wasting time on all the sex-violent ones out of their own records. But at the moment they had something on Rooney, who was on the Ten Most Wanted list. It had been spread among the pigeons that he might be here, and one had called in just now with a tip: a flophouse over on the Row.

It was the kind of beautiful sunny bright Sunday that January in southern California can produce; it seemed a pity to spend any part of it over on the Row, but the job was there to be done, so they went out on it.

The flophouse was over a bar and a pawnshop. The sign on the street door said simply, *Beds 50¢ a night men only.* The proprietor, a scrawny old man who smelled of perspiration and sour wine and needed a shave, looked at the official photograph of Rooney and said, "Yeah, it looks like a guy was here last night. Noticed him account of all them tattoos. You want him?"

"We do," said Hackett. "Do you know anything else about him? Where he was going? When did he leave?"

"Couldn't say. I dunno. But," said the proprietor brightly, "he'll prob'ly be back because he paid for two nights. Listen. Listen, you want him—all right—but please don't make no disturbance when you take him, I gotta a lot o' nervous guys in here—no disturbance, hah?"

"I hope not," said Hackett. They'd have to stake out the place. Damnation. But if it was Rooney, and if he was X on Moreno and Romano—

They went back to the office and told Glasser he could sit on it. Glasser asked why he'd ever joined the force.

"You tell me, Henry."

"Over on the *Row*—all those stinking bars and smelly bums. And he might not show until midnight."

"Then Bob or Nick Galeano can take over," said Hackett.

"All right, all right, I'm on my way," said Glasser, and went out.

Thoms said from the desk in the anteroom, "By the way, that car turned up. While you were out just now. The Santa Monica boys called. Jim Gadsworthy's car. Abandoned down near the Venice pier."

"Helpful," said Hackett. The APB hadn't yet turned up Jeff Gadsworthy. He might be out of the state by now.

"The lab's bringing it in, but—"

"No, nothing there, probably. . . . One thing I've been thinking, George, is about that Charles Starke. You know. He— *George!*"

"What?" said Higgins, turning from the window.

Hackett reflected that after all he'd been married to the girl for less than three months. "Charles Starke," he said. "The one out of our records. We thought he looked good on Moreno, but nothing showed positive on it, and no knife.

239

We got a search warrant then, but N.G. Then he turned up without an alibi for Romano, and he looked better, but still no real evidence. Now he can't tell us where he was when Jeannette Anderson was attacked. And maybe it is Rooney, George, but if it isn't it could very well be Starke, and we can't just sit here daydreaming until Glasser—or maybe Nick tonight—drops on Rooney—if it is Rooney at the flophouse on the Row—can we? I mean, the city likes us to do a little work, protecting the citizenry and catching up with the bad guys, for the pittance they pay us, George."

"I get the point, I get the point. You think we ought to lean on Starke some more. I guess I do, too. Let's go find him."

"Not," said Hackett, "that I'm given to the hunches, George, but I've got a random feeling that somehow Rooney is too pat an answer. I've got the feeling that the X we want is homegrown."

"If Rooney is here—" Higgins pushed the elevator button—"why look further for a wild one like that? Quite a coincidence, two at once even in a place this size—"

"I don't know. Rooney may have just hit town. And the fact that they've all been in that one area—a rather tight little area, George, which does not include Skid Row—whispers to me, somebody very familiar with those streets."

"I'm not saying you're wrong, I just say if Rooney is here—"

"If it is Rooney—"

The elevator came and they crowded in, two big men going out on the tiresome routine that so often paid off in the end.

Grace at the moment was having heretical doubts about the simple first principles. Proceeding on his list of names of possible wrong ones gleaned from Stella Garcia's neighbors, he and Landers were getting precisely nowhere. It was all very vague, nothing even suggestive. When they finally headed back for the office, he said to Landers, "You know something, Tom? I think Palliser's right, we need the boss back. We haven't been getting anywhere on the important ones since he's been off."

"You could be right," said Landers thoughtfully. "Psychological factor maybe. I mean, he's always there, to get a hunch or see a little further through a thing, and when he's not—"

Stefan Benedettino, sitting in his Rambler up from the first curve on Royal Place round the corner from Royal Drive, was bored. Tailing work could be interesting, if something was going on, like trailing somebody in traffic where you needed all your wits—but just sitting on somebody like this, God, it was a drag.

From force of habit he looked at his watch. Eleven-fifteen. The guy might not stir all day. God. He yawned and reached for the Sunday paper on the seat beside him. Then he raised his head sharply.

What was that? Sounded like—very faint from up the hill —a woman's scream. Cut off kind of short.

He got out of the car in one quick motion, and listened, facing up the hill. Only one house up there. He listened, holding his breath.

Nothing. It was very still up here, in the clear air, except for all the birds singing. Presently he heard a mockingbird utter a high sharp shriek, and he shrugged. That was probably what it had been. A cat, and the mocker warning it off. That was all.

He got back in the car.

At one o'clock Mendoza said he was going down to Wilcox

street to see Garden and Collins. "If they're there. Bring them up to date on this damn thing. God, I wish—"

"All right, anything but watching you pace the floor," said Alison. "I forgot to get coffee, I'll be going out to the market in awhile. Anything you want? Cigarettes—"

"Nothing," said Mendoza, and went out. The Ferrari came down the drive carefully and then took off in a hurry down Laurel Canyon.

He found both Garden and Collins in the Wilcox Street precinct house, and worked up more worry talking to them about it.

At two-thirty the phone rang down the hall and Mrs. MacTaggart went to answer it.

"Oh, *Mairí*—thank God I've got hold of you!" Janet, it was. Mairí had made an excuse not to stay with her today, after they'd been to mass together; with Janet doubtless talking about it, she'd never have been able to hold her tongue about what the Lieutenant had found out about that— "Oh, *Mairí!* We didn't know what to do— Edna Fogarty's here, old Mrs. Weaver just called her on the telephone and she said she was afraid and didn't like the place and would Edna please—and then Edna said she just said, *'Oh,'* all startled like, and the phone banged down— And it sounded *queer*, Mairí, and we thought— And if you'd tell the Lieutenant, he'll know what we should do—that awful woman, if she—"

But they didn't know how awful, thought Mairí. She said calmly, "Yes, Janet, I'll tell the Lieutenant. Very queer indeed it sounds. Don't you worry, we'll see to it." But all the while her mind was moving briskly and she knew what she must do. There really wasn't time—if anything was going on, anything queer, in that house—to do anything else. Alison was out, the twins playing in the backyard. The cats would be fine until Alison came, which would be soon. Mairí put down the phone and went into action. She wrote a note for Alison; she knew Mrs. Spencer was home, weeding her rose garden. Mairí took up her handbag and went out to the backyard.

"Come along, you two. You can play across the street for a bit while Mairí's away."

"Want to go with Mairí!"

"Johnny, too! Want to go with—"

"Not this time, my dearies." She shepherded them down the drive.

Her silver curls were all in place and her firm jaw a little firmer than usual. As a born MacDonald, of upright Highland stock, Mairí knew her duty when she saw it and no MacDonald in the memory of the clan had ever turned a back on duty or responsibility.

She got behind the wheel of her ancient little car and drove away.

"Well, so it's up in the air," said Hackett, annoyed. "He's just as much a possible as Rooney, all I say. If the damn lab could give us something definite—"

"They gave us the knife," said Higgins. "The wide-bladed knife, Art. And the rape-killer who uses a knife is sufficiently unusual, and that's in Rooney's history. A knife. And——"

"Starke belongs in that area. Grew up there. All I say—"

Sergeant Thoms came in with a teletype. "Just in. From Phoenix," he said laconically.

"Oh, thanks." Hackett picked it up. "Well, well. It seems Phoenix does indeed want Mike Yorke. Very happy to hear where he is, and hope we can put the arm on him and send him over. They want him, George, for violent assault inflicting grievous bodily harm to a bartender, in the process of holding up the place. And a suspected similar occurrence previously. Mike is not nearly so subtle as the rest of his

243

family, is he? Let's see, that place is on Valley's beat, isn't it? I'll—"

"Oh, why don't we go pick him up?" said Higgins. "I'm tired of arguing with you—there's no proof either way and may never be. Save Valley a little work. Besides, I'd like to see that nurse of Luis'."

Hackett shrugged and got up. "O.K. If he's home. Nice day for a little ride. Narco's keeping the eye on him, we'll pick him up sometime, anyway."

Alison came in the back door and set down the big market bag. The house was quiet—no sign of Mairí. Then she spotted the note on the kitchen table, held down by a bud vase with a single dark-red rose in it.

"Janet called and said Mrs. W. called Edna F. and sounded frightened. Someone must go and bring the old lady away, I have said it whatever the man tells us. It's an evil place for her and I am going to fetch her away. Twins with Mrs. Spencer. Will be back when I have Mrs. W. in safe place with Janet or Mrs. O."

"Oh, dear," said Alison inadequately. "Oh, *dear*." She ran down the hall, scrabbled through the phone book, after an endless time was put through to Captain Garden. "This is— If you'd— He's not *there*? On his way h— Oh, *dear*." She put the phone down. She found a pen, scrawled an addition to the note, and ran out to the Facel-Vega in the drive.

Mendoza came in five minutes later. He read the note, said violently, "*¡Valgame Dios!* Females—and that God-damned—" He ran out, tripped over all four cats sitting in a row waiting to be let in and fed at the usual hour, swore again, and ran for the Ferrari.

What—? All out in the open—? How come? Mrs. Weaver —The tails there, but down the hill—

No siren on the Ferrari. Get through town faster, but approaching, sirens only maybe make things worse— What would they run into up there, what—

He turned on Sunset on the amber. Thank God not much traffic this time of day, Sunday, but—six, seven miles direct, but the way he would have to go, surface streets, nearer ten—

Alison wasn't three minutes behind Mairí MacTaggart; neither of them had been there before, and made about the same time. Alison turned up Coldwater Canyon, peering to the left at each street sign, anxious and tense. And she thought, silly—being melodramatic. What did she expect? She'd find Mairí there, and what could anyone do, if Mrs. Weaver said she wanted to come away with them? The nurse couldn't—

Royal Drive. There were two cars parked down there on the shoulder; the tails from Narco? Should she— No need. She drove on, up the curving road, and came to the dead end at the plateau where the big pink house sat. Mairí's car stood behind the blue Ford, another car, and a red M.G. And Mairí was on the front porch of the big house.

Alison flung herself out of the Facel-Vega and ran. "Mairí, you shouldn't—you know he—"

Mairí pushed the doorbell again. "I know my duty, *achara*. I havena liked all this not rocking the boat. If Mrs. Weaver—" The door opened suddenly and the fat nurse faced them.

It hardly seemed the first time they had seen her; they knew so much about her. She was just what Luis had said— fat, the little dead black eyes, starched white uniform—but she didn't look—*formidable*. She looked, Alison thought, frightened. The nurse. *Thirty-eight* people—

"I have come for Mrs. Weaver," said Mairí calmly, and

pushed past her into the house. The nurse fell back, one hand going to her mouth. Alison went in behind Mairí. She thought, looking around, but the loot: all these expensive things. The men wouldn't have noticed, yesterday, but— Oriental rugs, the antique furniture wildly mixed as to period, and she couldn't be sure but that looked like a genuine Van Gogh— "Where is Mrs. Weaver?" asked Mairí sternly.

The nurse shook her head dumbly. What was wrong with her? What—

"Who the hell are you?"

Alison swung around. Mike Yorke, she thought. Luis hadn't said he was so big. He stood at the foot of the stairs, swaying a little, and he had a gun in each hand. "Don't matter," he said. "You jus' go over there beside Ma an' keep quiet, see. The Goddamn safe game—*her*—gotta be *subtle!* I told 'em—waste o' time. Roddy bringin' the fuzz down—" He raised one gun. "You jus' stay quiet—till I get out. Tail on Roddy—but they don't know—"

He was drunk or— But not so drunk he couldn't fire the guns. Another man coming down the stairs, carrying two suitcases. He looked cowed and frightened. "All right, Roddy —li'l gennelman Roddy—put inna car, that's right. I'm gettin' shut—whole mess. Goddamn—"

"Put the gun down, Mike," said the other man nervously, placatingly. "All right, I'm taking them out to the car just like you say. Please, Mike—"

Rodney. The con man. Luis always said, con men so averse to violence. But he was as big as Mike, thought one part of Alison's mind contemptuously, if he jumped him—

The guns looked very big, and they wavered here and there, but for all his slurred speech the guns were firmly held.

246

"All right!" he said. His eyes narrowed, flicking over all of them. "Ma, you cunning ol' bitch, I know you! You *try* 'n' stop me—ol' bitch, I found your little hidey-hole for the pretty cash, di'nt I knew you had one, 'n' I hunted till— Ol' miser, turn your fav'rite boy into the cops, get your nice cash back, wouldn' you? I know you, Ma—"

"No, Mike. I wouldn't do that." The nurse's voice firmed. "You take it, Mike, but like a good boy you put down that——"

"Be a good boy? I know *you*, ol' bitch. Minute my back's turned." The gun gestured savagely. "You get out there with Roddy—all o' you, *move!* Keep an eye on *all* o' you till I—call the damn cops if I—"

They all moved out onto the porch ahead of him, down to the cement apron of the garage. Rodney lifted the suitcases into the M.G. "Mike, please—"

"You don' like my pretty guns, Roddy? Lot o' bastards, whole bunch of—call down the f—" He fired deliberately and Rodney dropped like a shot bird, with a whimpering womanish scream.

"Mike!" screamed the fat woman. "Don't—" And he turned on her. They all saw his eyes, wild and unhuman, and Alison thought, this wasn't a thing that happened, their ordinary quiet life, she and Mairí and—this wasn't—

"You ol' miserly *bitch!*" he said, and fired at her. The nurse turned and ran.

She ran grotesquely, the soft flesh wobbling, legs spraddled, the ungainly fat woman in the billowing white uniform—he fired again and missed—and she was running blindly, straight for the low wall with the panorama of the city beyond and below—

Sound of cars coming up the road. "Bring the fuzz down," he was mumbling, and he lifted his arm and fired again, and

247

the grotesque figure in white staggered, turned half around, to show them the mouth open widely, and then fell. It toppled in slow motion over the wall and out of sight.

And he turned, laughing crazily, raising the gun. *"All* of you—bring the fuzz down—I show you—"

Alison heard, incredibly, Art Hackett's voice somewhere behind her. "Get out of the way, Alison. To the right." She took two steps to the right and a gun roared behind her, and she turned. Art was standing beside his Barracuda twenty feet behind her, with Higgins beside him, gun also out.

And the Ferrari came roaring up and braked with a scream of tires and Luis plunged out of it. "What the hell are you doing—Alison, you're all right? Alison—"

"Everything under control, Luis," said Hackett. "You can stop worrying about your extracurricular case there's no evidence on. It's been—disposed of. Suitably, I would say. And did I kill Mike?" He holstered his gun and walked over to see.

"Luis—such an awful— And there's no sign of Mrs. Weaver! I know you'll say I was a fool, but when Mairí—"

He hugged her. "I'll say it twice over. Females! And the hell with——"

"It is Mrs. Weaver we came to bring away," said Mairí firmly. She was pale but the jaw was still in evidence.

"My God—females!" he said.

They looked, and found Mrs. Weaver tied to her bed upstairs. *"Och,* the poor dear—it's all safe now, you mustn't be worrying—"

"Well, I must say," said old Mrs. Weaver in her reedy voice, helped to sit upright, "such terrible people I never expected to be mixed up with—and me such a ninny, taken in by that woman—the police coming and all, I didn't like it, and I asked this and that, and that son of hers—" she shivered—"turned nasty. I got away from him once, and managed to get to the phone, but he caught me—and, well, *such* an experience I never—" She sat up a little straighter and patted her white halo of curls. "But after all," she said brightly, "it's not every old woman turned eighty can boast of being rescued from a murderer! It'll be a story to tell, all right."

And Mendoza hugged Alison again, laughing. "Females! It's no wonder you outlive us!"

"—And Mike was full of LSD," said Mendoza. He had just come back from the phone. "The acid. He had a supply in that eye-drops bottle. Speaking of dope, of course it was Rodney who came to the Weaver house that day, with his supply of the—instant uplift—in the briefcase. For Ma to store for him while the fuzz were snooping around. . . . They had to rout out the Fire Department to get the nurse's body. He got her through the lung, but they thought the fall finished her. And good riddance. One for the books. Thirty-eight—"

"But not Mrs. Weaver," said Alison, sipping. They were both, unprecedentedly, having preprandial cocktails. "We'll find a nice comfortable rest home—" Mrs. Weaver was staying with Mrs. Oliver until they did.

"All's well that ends well? Rodney's expected to recover. To invent more imaginative con games. The instant uplift, *Dios.* You don't imagine you're a heroine, do you? Chasing off up there—some day you'll give me a heart attack."

"Merely an innocent bystander," said Alison meekly. *"No,* Sheba—I can comb my own hair—" El Señor stood on his hind legs, pawing at Mendoza's glass. "He thinks it's rye. We should have—"

"Develop a taste for martinis next," said Mendoza, and finished his cocktail and let El Señor sniff the glass.

He got to the office at eight-twenty on Monday morning, dapper in silver-gray herringbone; the moustache was looking more satisfactory with judicious care and trimming. "I'm late," he said. "Traffic. So what have we got on hand?"

"Reports on your desk. It's good to have you back, Luis. You're really O.K.? The doctor said—?"

"Damn the doctor," said Mendoza. He was scanning the reports rapidly. "For the love of God, this Moreno thing still open—and another one, the same M.O.—"

"That Rooney is very possible. He didn't show last night but—"

"And what's this John's on— And Garcia, I'll hear about that. My good God," said Mendoza, "what have you been doing, all this piling up—"

"Whole office gone to pot," said Hackett, "obviously. You not here to wield the whip."

"*¡Porvida!* You're all supposed to be trained detectives! Who's Rooney? Bring me up to date so I can—"

"Solve everything at once. *Bueno.*"

"Don't be silly, Arturo. I am not a miracle worker."

"But we're damn glad to have you back," said Hackett affectionately.